OUR LAND

2021

To Clay
love your

Aunt Dena!

from my
Dad Manuel

OUR

LAND

Manuel Januário

ARCHWAY
PUBLISHING

Archway Publishing books may be ordered
through booksellers or by contacting:

Archway Publishing
1663 Liberty Drive
Bloomington, IN 47403
www.archwaypublishing.com
1 (888) 242-5904

ISBN: 978-1-4808-9124-1 (sc)
ISBN: 978-1-4808-9125-8 (hc)
ISBN: 978-1-4808-9126-5 (e)

Library of Congress Control Number: 2020914150

Print information available on the last page.

Archway Publishing rev. date: 9/11/2020

Since consumption is merely a means to human well-being, the aim should be to obtain the maximum well-being with a minimum of consumption.

~E. F. Schumacher, *Small Is Beautiful*

If you really want to help the poor, you must first go to the rich and the superrich. They are the ones that own and control nearly everything on this earth, including the small portions of material resources and the economic means essential to overcome poverty.

~Padre José, San Lucas community leader

Contents

Acknowledgments

This book, though fictional, was written to tell a story that can contribute to the currently urgent conversation about critical economic justice issues and the preservation of our planet. It is also a tribute to my community development fellow workers and my friends of several decades who shared their ideals, their knowledge, and their hands-on experiences with me. Without them, this story would have lost much of its authenticity, and without some of them, this book would never have seen the light of the day in its current form. I am particularly grateful to:

Paula Pincho Quadrado, my wife, for the love, the intelligence, and the generosity of spirit with which she has supported me all through the years.

Maria de Lourdes B. Serpa, who has contributed with her unwavering friendship and support and her vast academic talent and dedication through countless hours of tedious editing and preparation of the final manuscript.

Manuela da Costa, who generously offered the wisdom, knowledge, and experience of a genuine book doctor during the final stages of manuscript editing and publication.

Lucia Q. Tucker, my sister, who, through her original paintings, masterfully helps the reader focus the attention on the core message of each chapter and savor its meaning.

To all, I am eternally grateful, and it is in their names also that I am proud to put this book in your hands.

Enjoy!

1 THE LAND OF DREAMS

Flying

had fascinated Mário Garcia since childhood. Even then, he knew intuitively that the higher he went, the better he would be able to see the beauty of the earth below and the better he would understand how all its parts came together.

We were fifteen years old back in 1952 when we met at San Luis College on the island of Atlantica, halfway between Europe and North America. I still remember how he used long strings of vivid words and widely gesticulating hands to show me how he had started imagining himself flying above his native town of San Lucas.

There was such excitement in his voice as he spoke.

One of the things I enjoyed most was standing on the seashore and watching the seagulls fly off the black lava ridges at the top of Ponta Negra, which stood a few hundred feet above me. Stretching my arms out like wings, I imagined myself jumping free into the wind, which grew stronger as I climbed the steep cliffs.

I imagined how wonderful it would be to feel weightless in the air and to spiral up with the seagulls as high as Pico Alto (the tallest peak in the center of Atlantica). From up there, I knew I would see every-thing. As I climbed higher and higher, I knew I would be able to peek over Burnt Ridge and see the villages and the city of San Luis, cuddled in the green of Atlantica, on the other side.

Then I would turn around and see the vastness of the sea to the west and the roundness of the earth beyond it. I would also be able to fly over and look down on the big ships under those tiny masts that, from shore, I could barely see above the horizon. And if I went up even higher, perhaps I could see Europe and America, where Grandma said those ships were going to and coming from.

Seeing things at great distances wasn't all I wanted to fly for. I also craved looking straight down and seeing how all the things below me came together. I craved seeing the whole town of San Lucas in a single glance, with all its streets flowing into the church square and its fields full of people and animals casting their tiny shadows on the ground, under the bright sun.

And after all that, I still wanted more. I wanted to glide down swiftly, feeling the wind racing past my skin, and then skim effortlessly over the ocean, spying on the colorful fish as they pastured on the vast seaweed forests.

Oh yes! It was while listening to Mário Garcia explaining to me in such detail his childhood dreams of flying that I first realized that the mind ticking inside his brain was also designed to fly high and reach amazing views.

So, twenty years later, in 1973, it didn't surprise me at all to receive from him a detailed and exciting handwritten letter about what he called "a dream of a flight over America." It came right on time because I had recently decided to tell you about Mário's long immigrant story, and his letter gives me an ideal way to introduce him to you.

~

My unusual flight adventure is taking place aboard one of the Human Wings modern transporters in its regular voyage around the world in the year 2050.

As I begin to fly, I am sitting at a large, clear window, and the sun is rising in the sky in front of me. You can certainly begin to observe the growing excitement on my brightly lit-up face, and you can guess what a volcano of activity the circuitry of my brain is turning into.

My brain is overwhelmed by all the synchronized impressions being made upon it as the outside environment pushes itself in through my wide-open senses and as the sun warms my skin.

The magical panorama of the earth below me appears so brightly colored that I feel as if I am seeing it for the first time, through a set of new eyes open wider than ever before.

A tangle of inner sensations wells up inside me. These feelings also feed into the deeper-than-emotional regions of my being, where my mind is overwhelmed by a sentiment of awe. Clear thoughts print out on the screens of my mind, followed by strings of clear insights that hang together like tasty grapes to be savored one by one.

Surprisingly, among all the marvels I am observing, the one that fascinates me the most is this Human Wings transporter itself. And an overpowering thought floods my mind. When driven by noble dreams, we humans can indeed accomplish amazing marvels! This transporter is a hymn to human ingenuity and the power of dreams.

And instantaneously, the most relevant episodes of the history of the Human Wings transporters flash through my mind with extraordinary clarity and logic. I see the exceptional scientists that seventy-five years before 2050 began to study methodically damaged human lungs and forests killed by acid rains.

I see their fingers courageously pointing at the culprit: the pollution caused by the zillions of internal combustion engines used excessively to satisfy the selfish whims and the culturally induced needs of overconsuming humans on a grossly overpopulated earth.

When ignored by the political and economic decision makers of the world, I see and hear the scientists' crescendo of red-alert warnings to one and all—vis-à-vis the limits of our small planet. "Our overconsumption habits are incongruent and unsustainable! They are threatening our own survival!"

And later, when enough humans began to understand their message, the same scientists rolled up their sleeves and with computer-interconnected minds developed the earth-saving technologies that were so urgently needed. Voilà! These Human Wings transporters were born.

Super excited, I observe and savor the privilege of my first flight in one of these miracles of practical and clean American technology.

In front of me, twenty blimp-like modules are lined up like a flock of migrating geese cooperating with each other in synchronized flight from continent to continent.

Each module is made to be filled separately with a lighter-than-air gas and can land and rise individually from an open field anywhere. Its huge skin is built to gather and store the solar energy necessary to help guide, propel, and synchronize it until it joins the other modules in flight. When together, all the modules share the solar, jet stream, magnetic, and other natural forms of energy they produce and collect.

And with it, they move slowly but steadily, as if connected to a conveyer belt, in a continuous and stable flight around the earth.

Indeed, these Human Wings transporters are astonishing!

They transport from continent
to continent the lesser amounts
of international cargo needed
today along with countless human
travelers. They substitute entirely
the industrial age jets propelled
through the air at supersonic speeds
mounted on tons of metal. And
they allow humans to gain wings
and glide in the air naturally
like the birds always did.

They have forced multinational
corporations to give up their
unsustainable economic "growth for
profit only" paradigm based on the
irrational transportation of goods
and persons from place to place.
And they induced the creation
of "business for benefit" practices
closer to the soil of our regional
homelands, strengthening the
natural characteristics already
embedded in our local native
"cultures."

Yes! This is how human evolution
works!

What a privilege to live as a
member of this happier and wiser
human family on this flowering
and environmentally sustainable

earth that I can observe from up here now in 2050.

It is not only the earth I can observe so much better from up here. Indeed, thanks to the scientific advances, I can also see the universe and me in it more clearly.

The sun is much bigger than I ever imagined. It is the sun that reaches down and enlivens me and this beautiful earth, making me one with it.

Truly I live "inside" the sun!

And through the earth and me, the sun is also alive. Wow!

At that moment, I understand the sun—the total sun—better than ever before. And I see it as much more than the daytime lantern in the sky.

The sun is the rising power that is uplifting and propelling this Human Wings transporter.

The sun is also the magnificent source of all the patterns of life that dress the earth below me with those dark green forests and the lighter grasslands inhabited by countless animals and diverse peoples.

And I feel myself almost bursting inside with delight as I look down on this fantastic America under the sun, beautiful "from sea to shining sea." Wow!

Now my mind takes yet another cosmic leap. I comprehend clearly how the sun itself is not alone—how it is a child of the universe.

Like other stars, the sun is born of and exists only because of the accumulated layers of supercharged particles of celestial dust. Dust that is made up of atomic and molecular particles intelligently designed to become the earth, the moon, the sun, and the constellations always emerging through the vortex of time as a new universe at each moment, as if it were the seamless outer skin of a super intelligent and powerfully sustaining inner soul.

And I am a tiny part of this astounding universe! Indeed, from up here, I can see myself much better. Now I feel complete. Like the rest of the universe, I am one with my inner soul. Without it, I could never be.

What a privilege to have this unique experience while flying over this beautiful America. And what a joy to realize that I am not the only one.

How wonderful it is to see these American hinterlands restored to their original matrix, to times immemorial when Native Americans roamed the land with similar visions of the Great Spirit and with their hearts in tune with the rhythms of the earth, which they believed the Great Spirit was generously sharing with them.

How wonderful to see Americans living today according to this original vision, after less enlightened newcomers renamed these ancestral lands and mercilessly deforested, burnt, and emptied them of most of their native peoples and animals.

What a privilege for me to have lived in this "flowering new country" that has finally made peace with itself in the mutual "pursuit of happiness," sharing their lands and resources with equity in "One Nation under God!" as their Constitution

proclaimed from the beginning.
And how lucky I am to be now
flying over this America on my
way back to Atlantica, equipped with
the know-how to help rebuild my
homeland to the image of this New
World.

Suddenly the thought of
returning to Atlantica and
Monica woke me up. And
I opened my eyes inside
this oppressing darkness that
surrounded me. I had just been
dreaming again.

As you see, André, even asleep
and in jail, we are driven by our
dreams. And there is no reason
for us to be capable of having such
dreams if it weren't to make them
real, as we humans surely can.

~

There was indeed a sharp contrast between Mário's vision of a future better world and his waking up in the very bowels of the earth in a Latin American jail in 1973. Yet he did not lose his optimism and his sense of unwavering commitment to his dreams of social justice to his fellow men and fellow women … and this is why I want to tell you his story.

But, before I do, allow me to introduce myself briefly.

I am André Castro, a Latin-American man from the Brazilian state of Santa Cruz. I was born to a traditional rich family, totally unlike Mário's country family in San Lucas, a small town in the island of Atlantica, in the North Atlantica Sea.

On my father's side, my oligarchic roots go back to the earliest Portuguese colonizers of Brazil in the early sixteenth century, but not without a half measure of native blood, which came from an indigenous woman-servant given to my Portuguese noble ancestor by the king of Portugal along with the huge piece of land she and her family lived on.

The noble lady, who came from Portugal with her aristocratic husband, had proved to be totally impermeable to the nobleman's sperm, and as a practical necessity, she felt compelled to depend on her native servant girl to provide her husband with a son, whom she brought up as her own. Her "adopted son" became my mestizo ancestor from long ago, and it explains my tanned, round face, long nose, and a taller-than-average stature for a Brazilian.

On my mother's side, I have also Portuguese roots, equally noble and ancient, but they came to Santa Cruz, Brazil, much more recently and, as it happens, from Atlantica Island. In 1934, my grandfather was looking for a noble, pedigree-enhancing wife for his only son. He met a very distant relative, Atlantica's Count Barbosa, and his two daughters at a social function in Lisbon, and he knew right away that he had found a suitable match for his son.

After that predestined encounter, Count Barbosa allowed his second daughter to marry my father, who for different but equally strong reasons shared my grandfather's enthusiasm for this union. This is how I inherited my recent share of Portuguese nobility.

My Portuguese-Atlantean roots would have been totally irrelevant to Mário Garcia's story had it not been for the most unfortunate tragedy of my life. My mother died when I was just a toddler, and I was raised by my father who never remarried.

My father did all he could for years, including sending me to the best religious schools in Santa Cruz, Brazil. When I became a teenager, much to his dismay, I began to show a lack of interest in my studies and a growing interest in my father's frequent young female companions. It was then that he turned to my mother's sister, my aunt, Countess Beatriz Barbosa, in Atlantica, who had always felt called by God to ensure my proper education—away from my frivolous father's way of life.

In the early 1950s, even though Portugal had for long been a republic, the Portuguese island of Atlantica continued to be a remnant of the old monarchic order in the hands of oligarchs and land barons. My aunt, Countess Barbosa, was their generally recognized economic and moral leader.

She was only a bit taller than the average woman, but she stood head and shoulders above all the men of the island. Indeed, she picked her socially minded younger brother to be the administrator of the Mercy Hospital and other government-funded social services. She also found ways to pick the San Luis College president she wanted, and she even informed (informally, of course) the pope that Don Miguel Carvalhal was the best qualified man to become the new bishop at Atlantica. With her self-assured long face, her authoritarian demeanor, and her always deliberately chosen strong words, she showed forth that she knew she was truly "the man of the house" in Atlantica.

But my father, who hated her with a passion, understood that she offered the best solution to the problem he was having with me. He would send me to the prestigious San Luis College of Atlantica, under my aunt's strict tutelage, in order to prepare me for an American university where I would get the business administration degree that was considered essential for my future as a trader in Latin American natural resources.

The San Luis College, established by elitist Jesuits in the seventeenth century in Atlantica, was the premier institution for the building and maintenance of the Iberian-Christian culture on the island. The sons of Atlantica's nobility and the wealthy young men were sent there to prepare for higher education and the reins of leadership. This college also educated a few select boys from the low socioeconomic families who were expected to enter the church's seminary, where they were educated to become the future parish priests, a pivotal function in the maintenance of the Iberian-Christian culture of the island.

Having been identified as a gifted country boy from the isolated San Lucas town, Mário was sent to the San Luis College to test his potential for this kind of future leadership. Mário and I met in 1953 at this college. We studied there together for four years and became the best of friends despite our diametrically opposite socioeconomic backgrounds. In 1957, after graduation, we took separate paths that made it unlikely that we would ever meet again in this lifetime.

In accordance with my father's plan, I went to the Stratford University of Santiago in California. Mário remained in Atlantica, approved to continue his studies in the San Luis College's Philosophy School, but uncertain as to whether he would ever want to become a priest. The only thing he knew for sure was that he wanted to dedicate his life to the eradication of poverty in Atlantica. He perceived poverty as an intolerable violation of social justice mostly due to his main mentor, Padre José, of his native San Lucas.

As it turned out, our separation was short-lived.

A few months after I had settled in at Stratford University, I received a letter from Mário:

Dear André,

I want you to sit down and brace yourself because I am about to tell you something that might make you faint.

André, with your help, I must soon join you in the "land of freedom and opportunity," the laboratory where I will learn about the mechanisms of social justice and democracy, which my Atlantica Island needs to achieve the eradication of the poverty that is so pervasive through this fertile land.

One day, I will return here with that knowledge, and I will be able to help my fellow Atlanteans achieve economic and social justice, making Atlantica socioeconomically more like America, so that it will not only be the most beautiful place on the face of the earth, but also a most just society.

André! No, I am not mad. The circumstances propelling me in the direction of the United States have been brought about by none other than your honorable Aunt Countess Barbosa!

First, let me tell you what I did this summer that contributed to this situation. And then, my friend, I need to ask for your help in cushioning my arrival in the United States.

True to his commitment to dedicate himself to solving the problems of poverty in Atlantica Island, during the summer before he was to start his philosophy studies, Mário volunteered to work in the Vila Miséria slum with Padre Elias, an urban activist known as the Tea Pickers' Priest, and most intensely disliked by my aunt.

He was so moved by what he saw in the slum that he decided to dedicate his future to eradicating poverty in Atlantica—and to start doing something right then and there.

Mário had come to know the famous Countess Barbosa well during his frequent visits with me in her palace. Though aware of her patronizing attitudes toward countryfolk like him and her quick-tempered reactions when she felt confronted with certain societal issues, Mário felt he had the moral obligation to bring to her attention the needs of the poor of Vila Miséria. According to Padre José (Mário's San Lucas community leader and his mentor), "Only the rich can solve the problems of poverty. In this world of economic unfairness, you need to change the hearts and minds of the rich, who have monopolized the earth, so that they will release some of the resources they legally control to meet the basic needs of the disenfranchised poor."

My aunt, Countess Beatriz Barbosa, was the largest landowner in Atlantica. Mário knew that at the heart of the Vila Miséria, there was an old tea plantation she had abandoned—with all its workers—when it ceased to be economically viable. She also controlled many of the cultural and economic institutions of the island, which were at the basis of the chronic and systemic problems of poverty affecting the twenty thousand slum dwellers.

On a Sunday afternoon after his work, Countess Barbosa received Mário with some surprise due to his worn-out clothes and unkempt appearance. After all, he was just a country boy who happened to be my friend and who had accompanied me to her palace on my week-end visits. She invited him to her study and asked him to sit down across from her.

"Well, Mário, I did not expect to see you here so untidily dressed. After all, you will be in the San Luis College's School of Philosophy next month. So, what is your problem?"

"I apologize for my appearance, madam, but I have been spending some time with Padre Elias in Vila Miséria, and I haven't—"

"You were where? What gave you such an idea? Couldn't you find something more inspiring to do? Or at least with someone more inspiring to do it with than Padre Elias?"

"I don't think I could have, madam. I have wanted for a long time to gain firsthand experience working with the poor in the slum by living with them, so—"

"So, you forgot the very purpose for which you were charitably picked out of the poverty of your country life—and you threw yourself right back into it! What you did, young man, was very foolish."

"I am sorry I have to displease you, but the time has come for me to be honest and straightforward in the name of what I saw in Vila Miséria."

"If you must! But your presence here in such inappropriate attire is an insult to good manners and contrary to the regulations at San Luis College."

"The misery, the pain, and the suffering I have seen in Vila Miséria are the reasons why I am here, but that is not the worst of it—"

"I should say not!" interrupted Countess Barbosa angrily. "You missed mentioning the stealing, the prostitution, and the drunkenness you find in Vila Miséria. You name the crimes, and they are all there, and it is for those crimes that the pain and suffering you talk about are just punishment."

"The worst of it," said Mário, as if he had not been interrupted, "is the lack of social and economic justice that is at the root of all the conditions that deny those twenty thousand human beings the very basics for a decent existence."

"What lack of justice are you talking about? Who ever heard of a thing like that? What better justice is there to mete out to criminals than punishment brought about by their own crimes?"

"Who are the criminals, Madam Countess?"

"What do you call thieves, drunks, prostitutes, swindlers, and occasional murderers?"

"Crimes exist in society, and there are many in Vila Miséria. Yet, the situation that perpetuates our unjust system is equally of a criminal nature because it gives rise to the desperate conditions where some criminals prey on the vast majority of innocent residents. These people struggle for food and basic survival, without protection from the law, and with the vicious hatred and false incriminations from the upper society. Madam Countess, isn't it your crime, and that of your fellow landowners, to have unjustly appropriated for yourselves all the goodness of this land while your fellow human beings suffer misery and starvation?"

"Young man, don't you think you have said enough?" Countess Barbosa bellowed, and her face was red with fury. She got up threateningly and stared down at Mário.

He remained calm.

"How dare you, a good-for-nothing country boy, whom I have often fed at my table, come here to my house to tell me that the burden of providing food and housing to the scum of the earth is my duty as a matter of social justice? Would you mind telling me the appropriate rewards of justice for you and that skunk Padre Elias, who put you up to this confrontation?"

"I do not think there is any special prize or punishment for telling the truth, Madam Countess, and that's all I have done." Mário stood up and walked away without another word. He had the courage to look the countess in the eye and calmly tried to make her face the unjust facts.

This was perhaps the most important thing I have done in my entire life, Mário thought. He felt a special kind of elation in his new sense of self-worth, not realizing that he was walking into the shadow of hopelessness.

My aunt's response was so negative that, later that afternoon, she swore to her niece, Monica, that he would never set a foot in the San Luis College's School of Philosophy.

However, my aunt was unaware that my cousin Monica was Mário's secret girlfriend and his soul mate—all wrapped up in one. Monica was Dr. Carlos Barbosa's younger daughter, and they both lived in the countess's palace where she had come to know my friend Mário in our frequent weekend visits. She was a very beautiful young woman with a profound sense of generosity, equity, and caring for other fellow human beings, and she highly admired Mário's courage and commitment to bettering the lives of others.

Monica became extremely concerned about Mário's fate at the hands of her aunt, and she rushed immediately to San Lucas to persuade Mário to get in touch with me. Why? Because she felt there was no time to lose in exploring the possibility of Mário going to the United States as an international student. By so doing, Mário would be away from my aunt's rage and vengeance—and he would avoid becoming a nonstudent and being immediately recruited into the Portuguese armed forces, which was sending soldiers to fight unfair wars in the African territories of the Portuguese colonial empire.

Mário's last encounter with my aunt gave origin to a cascade of life-changing events, including his journey to the United States, which, as you will see, proved to be even more noteworthy in his life than leaving his rural San Lucas to come to the city of San Luis, but that is another story.

Before I tell you about Mário's arrival in America, let me start with the conditions under which I am writing his story. This is 1974, and I am no longer in the United States.

Indeed, I am in a tiny, poorly lit, and extremely uncomfortable prison cell in my native Brazilian state of Santa Cruz. In the same jail, Mário is just a few iron doors down the hall from me.

We both are dependent on a jail guard, Toro, for the brown paper bags that we both use as writing paper. Toro can be the most uncooperative and temperamental creature one could possibly imagine. Each day, he seems increasingly more irritated and with the apparent intent on making both Mário and me suffer for what he considers our unforgivable "airs of moral superiority," which obviously offer no clear target for all the hatred stored up in his heart. I only hope that he doesn't interrupt the brown paper bag supply as he has done before.

A month ago, as I finished writing my story of Mário's "growing up" years in Atlantica, Toro decided to cut off my paper supplies. He also threatened to throw all I had already written into the "shithole" if I begged him again for paper. Fortunately, I was able to ship my writings out through the jail chaplain, with the intent to recover them later.

I hope these harsh conditions will not diminish the clear message of optimism and hope that I have experienced with Mário ever since I have known him, and which is the heart of what I want to share with you now. Optimism and hope are what keeps us alive here, waiting for our day in the sun again and our opportunity to work more closely with you, my reader, and all people of good will who want to build a better and environmentally safer future home for humankind on the way to become one human family someday. Absurdly as it might seem, this is what we were trying to do when we were arrested, put out of sight in this dungeon, inactive and quiet. Unfortunately, it seems as though they have thrown away the key. This is our tenth month in this stinking hole.

A bit later, I promise to tell you how and why Mário and I got to a prison in my own state in Brazil after our prior experiences in America.

Come along. Let me share with you more about Mário's journey from his lost-in-time island of Atlantica to the land of dreams, the "land of freedom and opportunity for all!"

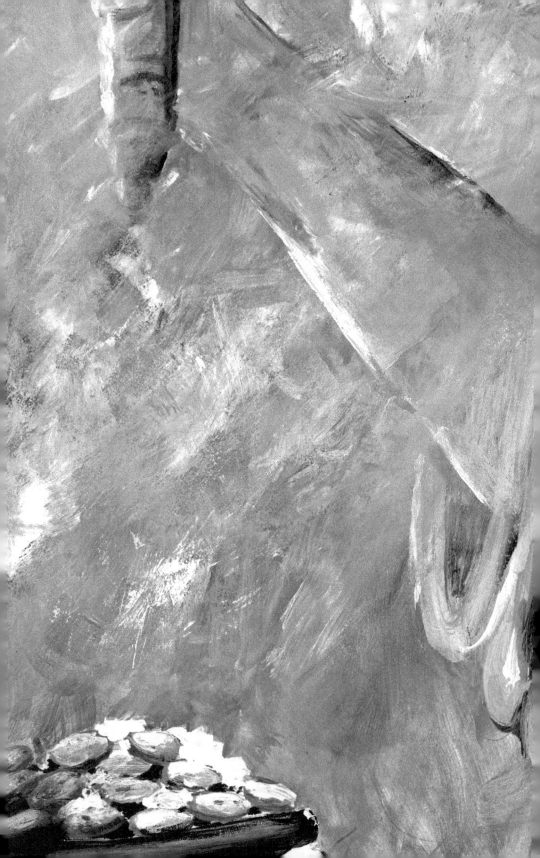

2 COMING TO
AMERICA

Entering

the United States back in the 1950s, as an international student from Atlantica, wasn't easy, but for a young man who was a potential soldier for the colonial wars, leaving Portugal under António Salazar's dictatorship, it was even harder.

Being aware of this challenge, along with the account of his conversation with my aunt, Countess Barbosa, Mário also sent me a copy of a letter he had sent to his uncle, Toni, an Atlantean emigrant living in California not far from Stratford University. He pleaded with me to explain his predicament to his uncle and to anyone who I thought might be in a position to help him enter the United States with a student visa as well as to ensure financial support until he could find adequate employment and pay everything back.

Even before I went to visit his uncle, I talked to my father's American business partner. Gilmore was a practicing Catholic, a graduate from an American Catholic university, and a golfing companion of the San Antonio Catholic College president. This connection eased things most for Mário right from the start.

Gilmore immediately called his university friend, and the wheels started turning. This goodhearted and well-intentioned call to his ecclesiastical friend was one that Gilmore would come to regret years later.

It took three months for Mário to submit all the required documents and obtain admission to San Antonio College. Finally, in

January 1958, Mário walked up to the giant Pan Am Constellation aircraft parked on the runway of Atlantica's airport. He sat in a metallic monster, being pushed through the air by the unimaginable power of four roaring propellers, which would take him nearly halfway across the earth and drop him into another world, and into an environment comprised of entirely different human and cultural dimensions.

Shortly after takeoff, Mário could see the tiny tip of Pico Alto piercing the clouds before it disappeared like the masts of distant ships he had watched as a child sailing away from San Lucas. On that small piece of land, now out of sight in the middle of the Atlantic, were nearly all the persons and things that had meant everything to him so far in life.

It was there that he had learned to dream about a better world for those less fortunate.

It was there that he had experienced the love of his caring family.

It was there in Atlantica that he had met my lovely cousin Monica, the woman of his dreams, on whom all his thoughts converged now. She had enthusiasm, brightness in her eyes, and a sense of deep commitment to her less fortunate fellow Atlanteans. She had inherited these qualities from her father, Dr. Barbosa, the countess's younger brother. A woman like her would normally have never been available to him, but she fell in love with him. And when no one else was in sight, she pledged her love and support to him. Without it, he would have felt totally lost, just like another ship adrift in the big ocean of life, battered by waves that might just swallow it up.

Mário sank deep into the pools of his emotions and reminisced about their long and intimate goodbyes and the words they repeated countless times in each other's arms: "Someday the physical distance between us will disappear. Someday we will be together again in a new Atlantica. It's only then that our time will really come, but it will last forever!"

Eventually, a feeling of absolute quietness settled in his heart. He felt as if he were floating gently with the wind—and there was nothing around him as he peered down upon the distant face of the earth. What was once a dream had become real.

He was actually flying, effortlessly, speedily, so high that the very same waves that blasted thunderously against Atlantica's island shores now appeared to be no more than little ripples and wrinkles on the surface of the unending blue ocean below. *How wonderful it is to be flying in an airplane!*

Mário had a feeling of awe, such as he had often felt before when confronted face-to-face with the unfamiliar and unknown wonders and miracles of life. Instinctively, he wrapped his emotional arms around these new wonders in an integrating embrace that made him feel one with it all.

He blocked out the engine noise, the other bodies and faces around him, and he glued himself to the airplane's window as he marveled at the hugeness of the universe. No, he would never have too much of this soul-stretching feeling of wonder.

These thoughts in Mário's mind—and the emotional wrappings that enveloped his heart and his mind at that moment—were signs of his limitless potential for growth, the exhilaration that he often felt and caused others to feel, and the abundance of actual accomplishments that he was capable of achieving.

Let me try to help you understand Mário's hopeful mind-set at this time of transition in his life. He was not so much an immigrant looking for opportunity as a dreamer seeking to prepare himself for his life's mission, which he envisioned as working for social justice on behalf of the poor who were still denied access to their rightful share of the earth by the legal and illegal concentration of wealth and power among a few.

Mário was a very handsome young man of above average height and sensibility. He had an open, well-proportioned face and curly black hair that waved gently down his forehead and gave it an appearance of uncombed, natural orderliness. At twenty, his full lips and bright eyes often gave way to intense expressions of joy, excitement, pain, and other emotions; it was not hard to see what he was feeling. To put it another way, Mário was the kind of young man who would easily demand a second look; perhaps this is why the young flight attendant noticed him looking repeatedly at his watch and out of the window with a somewhat puzzled look on his face. She told him they had just crossed another time zone and that their racing after the sun was now prolonging the dusk by almost an hour.

Mário responded quickly with an amused grin. *As much as I appreciate your help, I do not understand a word you are saying. But here is my watch. Maybe you can make it understand what I would very much like to know.*

The flight attendant took his watch, changed the time back four hours to Boston time, and slipped it back on his wrist, holding his hand momentarily while their eyes met.

He thanked her for her kindness and smiled gratefully for the gift of some more time. The flight attendant went looking for a large map of the United States, and upon her return, she unfolded it and inquired about Mário's destination.

He responded with his airline ticket in his hand: "Santiago, California."[1]

The flight attendant pulled out a red pencil from her pocket and drew a line along the Newfoundland coast into Boston, then on to New York, Chicago, Denver, over the Rockies, into the California Central Valley, and on to Santiago on the Pacific coast.

---

[1] Santiago is a fictionalized location in California.

After she left him with the forest green map, all the curiosity pent up inside his islander's psyche bubbled up to the surface of his consciousness, where his imagination was beginning to paint this vast land in living color. After spending hours flying over a seemingly endless ocean, he had a much clearer idea of what hugeness really was. He could more easily imagine America's unending green pastures irrigated by wide rivers and, here and there, studded with Pico Alto-like mountains.

His curiosity was palpable. Yes! He wanted to see, but even more deeply, he wanted to comprehend, assimilate, and fit it all into the magnificent framework of his mind, which was still full of unused compartments.

As the flight continued, the plane lost the race with the sun, and nightfall engulfed it. Below, there was no visible blue ocean, nothing but darkness inside the cabin after the pilot lowered the lights.

Suddenly, Mário saw a flame coming out of the engine in the dark, right outside his window. He saw it and sunk into his seat. His palms quickly got sweaty, and his skin tightened up on his body until he felt strangled inside. Surely, he was going to die! It was a feeling of great fear, total lonesomeness inside a shrinking bag of skin that was soon to vanish into the outer emptiness. His fear made him feel as if God's sky, God's earth and, therefore, God Himself had all vanished into that scary, empty space surrounding the flame—and him.

I am still here! The flame is still there! Should I pray to God?

When he felt alone, Mário had often tried to imagine how he could relate to God in a personal relationship. But thinking about Him as a person, that is a God who thinks, listens, and sees things as we do, always ended up making him uncomfortable. It was like making God to his own image, and that was not very fair to God, he thought. Even if God were out there inside a separate, gigantic, invisible, supernatural skin of His own, it still didn't seem right and reasonable to go running to Him in prayer, seeking to interrupt His ongoing creative work to modify His plan and open a capricious exception on behalf of such an insignificant little person.

Besides, praying for a miracle seemed to imply criticizing God for lack of love or sensibility to us, whom He had cared enough about to create and sustain. Yet what was one to think about the intermittent flame behind the engine outside?

It's God who is ultimately causing that flame. How else could there be a flame—any flame?

No! He would not pray to God for a miracle. He did not need to tell God what to do. He would always try to feel safe in His hands and accept Him on His own terms. What he needed was to be conscious that God had everything to do with that flame and that He was also his own one-and-only living soul.

Mário thought, *The roots of my existence are sunk into Him here and now. Indeed, His hand is on me, as much here in the air as it is on the ground. It is He who fills me from within. He sustains both me and that flame. Still out there … yet nothing has blown. No one is in a panic around me. Maybe it belongs there. I sure hope it does! It would be a shame to die when I am in such a mood to live.*

Many minutes later, palms still sweaty, still sunk into his seat, almost in the womb position, into which his instincts made him fold to feel more secure, his heart still racing quite uncontrollably, Mário felt that something more soothing was beginning to percolate from deep inside onto the surface of his consciousness.

Padre José[2] is right! I am like a glove on God's hand, and right now, I feel His fingers tickling me into all these emotions and feelings. I have to thank you, Padre José. You are again the lens on front of my dim eyes.

---

[2] Padre José was Mário's mentor back in San Lucas where he grew up.

Mário sat up straight and observed curiously and attentively the flame sticking out intermittently, like a tongue of fire licking oxygen out of the air. Then he pushed his seat back and closed his eyes more calmly, assuming that the flame was a natural phenomenon of flight, or perhaps just hot exhaust coming out of the engine.

Hours later, the plane shook and squeaked through the thin veil of a rain cloud. A voice came over the loudspeaker, and Mário woke up and looked out of the window. Below him there was an island of lights, perhaps bigger than Atlantica, extending almost as far as the eye could see. That was America, rivaling with the spotty, starry sky above.

He had arrived!

After the layover in Boston spent rushing through unending corridors and showing immigration papers to people he did not understand, another plane took off. When it gained altitude, Mário could not believe his eyes. America was not green like Atlantica; it was mostly white under a fresh mantle of early snow, still with a few hints of reds, bright yellows, and oranges of New England trees. And then came New York, with its skyscrapers in the distance, countless other airplanes in the air, and the patterns of suburban housing designed like tree leaves along branches of roads, connecting to unending highways. He was literally dizzy from the bombardment of new colors and sights and the immeasurable sizes of the ever-changing panoramas. He had to strain to see the ant-sized cars moving along highways, drawn like black lines on the surface of a panoramic painting.

Mário looked at the map he had unfolded on his knees, as if to reimagine America based on his current observations. What would he find all the way on the Pacific coast?

His amazement grew over the unending Midwest plains, the barren-looking prairies, the snowcapped mountains, the empty and dry deserts, and, at the end, the green valleys of California.

Finally, when he got off the plane in Santiago and met his uncle Toni for the first time, he was speechless. He could not utter a word, such was his emotion. They just fell into each other's arms driven by the feelings that attract every villager to their kin and endure through generations and distances. When he finally turned to me, I couldn't help but see how happy and excited he was. I could only imagine then how so very fulfilling and sometimes painful life would always be for him because of his great and keen ability to feel.

On the way to his uncle's home, while answering his many questions, Mário could not ignore his own sense of awe. When peeking out of the window of his uncle's car, it was obvious for instance, that looking at Santiago's famous bridges across the bay, he didn't just see tons of iron across a long span. He was also thinking about the thousands of people who planned each of them, built its giant foundations from the bottom of the sea, wrapped countless wires into huge cables strong enough to hold up tons of iron and concrete, which allow thousands of people to cross it every day to work in the solidarity of city life, like bees building their life together in the beehive.

Mário was obviously seeing America at its best, sharing a common intelligence and its creative capabilities, each person contributing their utmost toward the common good until what seemed impossible happened: a miracle of technology and goodwill, capable of building this "land of dreams" and showing its potential to build a human paradise on earth.

"I want to learn how all this was accomplished in America," Mário said as he looked at the magnificent golden arches overhead. "And then I can bring some of this know-how back to Atlantica Island. That is partly why I am here, Uncle Toni," he said to his astonished *tio*. "Someday I hope to be able to go back and help make our Atlantica more like this America."

Looking at me, Mário asked, "Don't you think, André, that the marriage between this American technology with our best cultural values can bring our *better world* to my Portuguese Atlantica and your Brazilian Santa Cruz?"

This is how my friend Mário completed his journey from Atlantica to his "land of dreams," from sea to shining sea, seeing nothing but its glory.

However, Mário's imagined America was quite different from the real one, though that he would discover only little by little.

To start with, San Antonio College looked much more like an isolated oasis with a life of its own. It was surrounded by tall palm trees and visually fenced in by ancient oaks, standing along thick brick walls. It was built in a small community not far from the city of Santiago. And though San Antonio had become one of the numerous suburbs around the big city, its core college campus was built of century-old brick buildings, and it had not lost the isolated and parochial aspect of a locked-in community, somewhat disconnected from the world around it. In other words, San Antonio College seemed to provide effective isolation from America rather than exposure to it. At first sight, it didn't look much like a vital part of the nation-building laboratory of social justice, freedom, and democracy Mário was searching for in America.

Yet, this isolation wasn't necessarily all negative. In fact, the college provided an ideal environment in which to tackle some of Mário's most pressing initial problems. Like me, Mário had to learn to speak English quickly to be able to carry out the required classroom assignments. The discipline and isolation of the college worked to his advantage, and he wasted no time getting to work.

Beyond Mário's new language-learning challenges were the more difficult ones related to adapting to all kinds of everyday lifestyle and cultural differences. Every aspect of daily life was new and unfamiliar. For instance, imagine living in America in the late 1950s and not knowing how to drive a car, operate a laundry machine, or use a pay phone!

Take a person, like Mário, coming from a basically rural, self-sufficient culture that is concerned primarily with making life understandable and simple from the cradle to the grave. Imagine that person unable to communicate in a new language (spoken English) with the people around him.

For instance, imagine Mário coming to grips with the way one is born in the United States. You take the woman in labor, from her own home and a familiar midwife, to a hospital room, where she knows no one, in order to give birth to her baby and be helped by people she has never met before. After birth, she will observe these medical strangers holding, cutting the umbilical cord, cleaning up, weighing her baby … before she has a chance to hug her dearest child and start building the bonding connection between mother and baby that will last a lifetime!

Now imagine Mário trying to figure out why, at the other end of life, a person's body shouldn't be buried in the ground immediately but kept in cold storage for several days after death, while a number of appearance-enhancing procedures are performed before burial.

Indeed, for Mário, there was a whole lifetime of cultural practices to be learned between the cradle and the grave.

As he began to learn more about the new culture and the environment surrounding him, he began to feel that the deep values holding America together were wrapped in utilitarian, materialistic priorities. And he slowly discovered that his imagined America was quite different from the real one.

In Atlantica, Mário was raised to believe that the world, though sometimes strange and hard to understand, was comprised of more than the physical conditions humans experience. It was unquestionably here and now God related. One was easily persuaded that the world in its totality had a deep, built-in fountain of being with an intelligent inner core sustaining things pretty much the way they were intended to be. So, one lived in this mysterious world as a part of it, with respect for its Source. There was a natural belief in something greater, more enduring than the finite limits of one's own existence, and that humanity was ultimately driven and sustained by intelligent reason.

In America, however, Mário found a world that was focused on short-term material superficiality almost to the exclusion of anything else. He couldn't identify with anything that could be described as an enduring inner core in this new culture. There was simply a relentless effort to achieve gratification without any concern for consequences or sustainability.

Mário's deep-seated sense of universal harmony and his ability to feel the contiguity between material reality and his inner core were being challenged by this utilitarian culture surrounding him everywhere. For instance, in America, any feature of the natural landscape that made travel from one point to another longer or more difficult was eliminated, with no concern for the consequences to the people and the destruction caused to the environment. The priority was to make the journey easy, direct, and fast, regardless of the waste and damage in its wake.

These specifically American attitudes toward the physical world, detectable even within a religious college's walls, were at first puzzling to Mário. But, eventually, after months of intense language study, an enormous amount of reading, and many hours with his friends,

Mário finally began to understand better and function well in his new college environment in America.

He also did well in his studies. He focused on social work, picking courses that emphasized community development and administration of social services, always thinking of building the skills needed to help the working poor of Atlantica Island.

Mário's first two summers in America provided him with opportunities to supplement his income as well as learn about America and its economic practices. During the first summer, he washed cars for one dollar each—of which the employer kept ninety cents and gave him the remaining ten cents to take home in his pocket along with his detergent-swollen hands and a lot to think about.

The following summer, Mário picked pears in the San Joaquin Valley—and he learned even more. From the Mexican braceros, he learned Spanish and developed an appreciation for the hardships and insecurities those agricultural workers had to endure around the country in order to stay economically afloat for another season.

For three years, Mário tackled his studies as a priority, but it became obvious to him that what he had come to America looking for couldn't be found in the college's classrooms or in the well-researched cross-referenced textbooks written by great scholars in their ivory towers.

Apart from ongoing conversations with socially aware classmates, Mário had not yet learned much more than the general objectives of the *movement* now afoot to bring social justice to American society or about the tools to develop such a movement from its grassroots.

Instead of acquiring practical skills to resolve social problems, Mário felt he had ended up discovering more social problems in the heart of this paradoxical country, which, from afar, was perceived as the land of promise for everyone.

As America entered the 1960s, she appeared terribly unhappy with herself. This country was not the laboratory Mário had imagined, where one would find ready-made answers to the problems of his native Atlantica.

Although discouraging, his situation wasn't entirely hopeless. A while back, Mário had found his way to the basement of one of the old college buildings where the Young Christian Students (YCS) met regularly in a dedicated effort to "observe, judge, and act in our world today like Jesus would have done were He here with us."

This group of restless classmates spent some of their free time in frank conversations about the implications of being a Christian in the United States in the 1960s. The new civil rights movement was also coming alive and beginning to shake up many American institutions, including traditional churches.

Accompanied by friends, Mário started visiting the Santiago Flatlands, home to predominantly poor and unemployed blacks, who had first come to build navy warships during the Second World War, and Chicanos, who had moved from their bracero farmwork into entry-level positions in the city's garbage collection and maintenance services.

The discussions in these meetings shocked Mário as he and everyone began to understand the extent of the social problems in America at that time. It was also surprising to all of them to discover that in the American South, even the Catholic churches commonly practiced school segregation. It was equally jarring to learn about the inhumane conditions in the bracero camps of the San Joachim Valley and elsewhere, where, among others, Cesar Chavez had begun his work in community service organizations.

This growing awareness in the hearts and idealistic minds of young college students made them realize what it meant to be a Christian in this broken society. For starters, it seemed to most of them that there was a need to roll up their sleeves and join the civil rights movement. Crusaders, inspired by Dr. Martin Luther King Jr., began to support and participate in targeted nonviolent actions and demonstrations in the South. These events reminded Mário of the many activities of his mentor Padre Elias in the Vila Miséria slum of Atlantica and his fateful summer work there, prior to coming to America, when he made the decision to dedicate his life to the service of the poor and voiceless.

In the midst of this awakening, and right before his summer break from school, Mário heard from the YCS chaplain that Monsignor Cogan, pastor of St. Martin's Parish in the Santiago Flatlands, was seeking someone "qualified to update the parish census, preferably someone who spoke Spanish and could substitute the sacristan for the month of June." The compensation was minimal, but the position came with free room and board at the parish house.

St. Martin's Parish was situated in the oldest part of town, which was the repository for the most serious problems of poverty in the region. For Mário, Monsignor Cogan's announcement seemed to be made to order. He immediately sought an interview.

Having my own car, I was the one who visited Mário on his

college campus, whenever I had a chance. This time, however, he took the initiative. He asked if I was free to take him to a job interview immediately.

On the way to the interview, I detected some uneasiness in Mário's usually positive attitude. During the ride to St. Martin's Parish, Mário confidentially shared with me the following thoughts:

"André, I am aching inside. Life is so full of irony and contradiction. In this land of abundance, all the advances created by people to serve the people have now enslaved them instead of freeing them. All these patented and monopolized advanced technologies in the hands of American capitalists have become instrumental in creating innumerable artificial needs, which the same clever capitalists claim to fulfill. This has led Americans to become addicted to a lifestyle dependent on material satisfaction that ends up being harmful. Much like cattle pinned in a feedlot they crave for their ration of comfort, unaware of the reason for the special care they receive. The problem is that this has created consumer habits and totally money-dependent lifestyles, while effectively denying to large segments of the population access to the means of making money. The result is that moneyless persons in this money-dependent society are relentlessly pushed away from their 'fair and sufficient' share of the earth, even more than are the poor self-sufficient farmers of rural Atlantica. What can I really learn in this America, André, that can help me back in Atlantica Island?"

I replied, "Cheer up, my friend! At least you still have a love for learning and for books, and you apparently have found a lot of utopian-minded friends with whom you can continue to dream about your better world. I am not so fortunate. I hate books, and my friends have proven to be worse than useless. In other words, I am pretty stuck with what is—and have no illusions about changing it. In fact, I am painfully aware that in America, I am being taught each day more businesslike and efficient ways for me to participate in and prolong the unjust exploitation of my country and my people, so that Americans can continue to enjoy the superior way of life you criticize so strongly. More specifically, Mário, I am being trained to get richer selling what is left of my poor country to our business partners, the Gilmores of America, who build with it the ultimate consumer society, which you and your idealist friends want to do away with, to make room for the poor! Good luck, my friend!"

"We seem to be quite upset with ourselves today, André. Look! Let's stop complaining! Unless we come up with some answers to the problems we face in this world, we are going to be more part of the problem than of the solution. Don't you agree?"

"You are right, but there are times when I'd give anything for some personal peace of mind and an escape from what seems like an inevitable future being part of this unfair system."

"You stop that, old cynic! I don't believe your sad prognostications for a second. I don't think you will ever accept such schemes! Look, André, both you and I, at our better moments, have understood well what we are here on earth for. We wanted to discover and be able to help build and live within the confines of a better society based on principles of socioeconomic justice and offering fair opportunities to everyone. The Santiago Flatlands is proof that the right socio-economic justice formula hasn't yet been discovered and applied in America. This means that we have still got a bit more searching to do."

"Show me the way to it, San Antonio scholar! Where do we go from here?"

"Don't give up too soon! I believe that the needed revolution is around the corner, and it is up to us to speed it up today! Can't you hear the drums? There is a call in the air for us to start breaking barriers and building bridges. We must learn to destroy prejudice and injustice in practical ways—until there can be a flowering human fraternity in Atlantica, in America, and everywhere in this world."

"That won't be easy, my friend! The real world out there is the Cold War world acting like one car with two drunk drivers, one Russian the other American, both competing for the same steering wheel."

"You are right there, but there is one thing I am not confused about: no matter how deep and invisible God chooses to bury Himself inside His world, He is still there sustaining it. So, somehow this world must be okay with Him, at least until we understand that we are here to change it. Right now, He is putting it in our heads that we should roll up our sleeves and start improving things everywhere, don't you see? And since your aunt, Countess Barbosa, won't allow me back in Atlantica Island to change anything there yet, I am beginning to think that I should get to work right here where I am. I hope Monsignor Cogan will help me get started. Wish me luck!"

3 THE SANTIAGO FLATLANDS

lucia RT

We

parked in front of the old rectory and rang the bell. A short, overweight lady in her fifties came to the door.

"Good afternoon! I am Mário Garcia, a student at St. Antonio College, and I have an interview with Monsignor Cogan."

"You are a bit early! The monsignor is still resting, but at two o'clock, I will let him know you are waiting. Please sit down and make yourself comfortable." She wobbled away through a swinging door.

We sat on two overstuffed chairs facing the wall, and I became aware of that stagnant odor common to old churches and convents, county archives, old library basements, and perhaps mortuaries. In all these places, the past seems more real than the present, and there is nothing indicative of the future.

Mário anchored himself to the oversized armchair and buried himself in his mind, maybe organizing his thoughts for the monsignor.

I sat quietly and very uneasily on mine. The loud ticktock of the old wall clock in the adjacent office finally turned into two sonorous rings, and one minute later, Monsignor Cogan walked in, dressed in his kimono-like cassock, with a small purple cape solemnly hanging over his shoulders.

"I am Mário Garcia, Monsignor! I have a scheduled appointment," said Mário while extending his hand.

"Oh yes, you are from San Antonio College. You speak English pretty well. I was told you were Puerto Rican and could help me with the Mexicans."

"No, Monsignor. I am Portuguese, from Atlantica, but I do speak Spanish pretty well."

"It's all the same, then, as long as you understand Mexicans. They are coming here in large numbers, and we don't understand them. Some want to send their kids to my school, but before I register them, I need to know something more about their background, and that's why I need somebody like you. The black persons who now live in most of the houses left behind by the Irish and the Italians will not support the parish, so we must give the Mexicans a try. Come on in and let's talk."

The two of them disappeared through the swinging doors, which closed behind the monsignor, but in those few minutes, his commanding image was stamped in my mind. He was nothing like the grandfatherly type of an older parish priest I had expected. Nor did he resemble the lean-faced, keen-eyed, insightful, and ascetic "padre." He wasn't anything like the stereotypical gregarious and humble Irish priest (as his name might suggest), always ready to crack a joke and laugh the loudest at it.

Monsignor Cogan, regardless of his name and heritage was a tall Anglo-Saxon, and he must have been athletic and fiercely good-looking in his prime. He did not have the poise and slickness of the typical business executive, which he could easily have been, but he still cast the image of a man of unswerving puritanical uprightness.

As a monsignor of the Roman Catholic Church, he had the same blind commitment as a zealous military leader ("My country, right or wrong!"), plus the advantage of knowing that he was always right because he was in the service of the one and only true and infallible church of God.

As we came to learn later, the monsignor had been born fifty years ago to a family of strict, practicing Catholics. He attended Catholic schools and colleges, where along with being taught about God, he was taught about the world of law and order, understood to be sanctioned here in America by the same God.

After he became a priest, he lived among a group of well-to-do, rich, and influential people. In their midst, he learned to wield a strange kind of multifaceted power over a large and diversified group of powerful people. It fulfilled him more than if he had been an attorney or a businessman like his older brothers.

He was recognized among fellow Catholics as the spiritual architect of the ideological dome that should cover a well-ordered American society, "one Nation under God," as was written on all the dollar bills circulating in the land. It was the role that he successfully carried out since he came to St. Martin's Parish nearly thirty years ago, as Mário would find out in the following months. The monsignor did everything he could to maintain the comfortable status quo during that time, but in the past few years, everything around his parish was being altered by the social upheavals in Santiago's inner city.

Finally, a good hour later, the monsignor and Mário returned through the swinging door, apparently with some kind of agreement.

"Monsignor, this is André, my friend. I volunteered him to be my driver today. He is also an international student at Stratford University. He is a Latin American with some powerful friends here."

Monsignor turned to André and said, "Is that so! Like who?"

"Mário exaggerates, Monsignor. It's true, however, that I am quite familiar with Mr. Gilmore … of Gilmore and Associates."

"Gilmore! There are no strings Gilmore cannot pull! Ever since I've known him!"

"How do you know him, Monsignor?"

"We went to school together. He decided to get rich, and I decided to become a priest."

And the conversation gained new life, so much so that the monsignor decided to invite Mário and me to see the just finished new wing of the rectory where Mário would live that summer.

"It cost me sixty thousand dollars to build this upper floor, but it was necessary. There was no housing for the missionaries who occasionally come to St. Martin's. Mário, this will be all yours for the summer."

Another miracle of immigration to America! Here, I will surely be one of the best housed Atlanteans in the world, thought Mário.

From the terrace, we could see the old houses and apartments (worth between six thousand and ten thousand dollars each) where the St. Martin's parishioners lived, the same ones who contributed the sixty thousand dollars for Mário's summer penthouse.

When the conversation ended, and we left, Mário told me the conditions that Monsignor Cogan had laid out regarding his stay in St. Martin's: he would earn room and board plus some pocket money, and he would be expected to visit and collect information from new parishioners, particularly Mexicans with school-age children, and some other grown-ups "who always try to forget their obligations to God," as it was explained to Mário by the monsignor.

The Hillside was the most desirable area of Santiago, extending for many miles around the steep hilly sides of the half bowl surrounding the city. There, the more selective suburbs of the metropolitan area had been built over the years, served by a six-lane suspended freeway that curled around the flat bottom of the bowl, designed like a centipede with a hundred peduncles on the ground, through which thousands of people entered every morning for a ride into the moneymaking zones of the city, and through which they returned home each night to enjoy the comforts that money could buy.

On the day I had agreed to drive Mário to his summer penthouse, I invited him for a late breakfast at a small Hillside restaurant that we knew had good food and a great view. From there, we could see some of the new Hillside suburbs and some famous landmarks. On our right was the huge Mormon Temple, which had been built to replicate the famous temple in Salt Lake City, and right below us was the architecturally famous Orthodox church, which was located in an area crisscrossed by small pine-shaded roads where the houses and mansions of the well-to-do nestled in well-landscaped yards. From the lookout point near the restaurant, way down beyond the freeway, we could see Mário's future "battlefield," Santiago's inner-city ghetto, and there in the middle of that distant mass of gray buildings, stood St. Martin's newer white buildings huddled around a tall steeple, all of it looking too perfect to fit in.

As we gazed at it, I commented to Mário, "It does look as if I am just moving you from one oasis into another."

Mário responded, "Before we go there, as we are a bit early, do you mind making a quick stop at the Orthodox church? The other day, the YCS chaplain said that walking into that church is like stepping into a postcard sent directly from early Christianity."

"If the Orthodox Church is aiming at simplifying the complexities of our traditionally gloomy church buildings centered on the crucified Jesus, I am all for taking a good look. Let's go for it!"

We walked in through a small, dark vestibule, which led into a flood of light inside focused on the wall-sized mural of Jesus of Nazareth telling his apostles to go out into the world and build his proposed community of love and peace among peoples. In reality, the whole place had a quality of quiet relaxation, brought about by the dominance of a meek, humble, and lovable image of Jesus, much like He was portrayed in the early centuries of Eastern Christianity.

We sat there quietly for a while, but soon I sensed that Mário was lost in another world. I wanted to leave him there for as long as he wanted. Therefore, I excused myself, and went for a walk outside. After quite a long while, Mário too came out, but he didn't say much then.

Some days later, though, when we were discussing our futures, Mário told me that the visit to the Orthodox church was one of the best experiences he had recently. "At first, I wanted to sit there a while to clear my mind because I had been feeling intellectually and emotionally conflicted after meeting the monsignor, but then I felt myself returning to the way I used to be in my native San Lucas beside Padre José. That helped me focus on what I was going to St. Martin's Parish for. Like Padre José when he came to San Lucas, I wanted to live a life of total dedication to humanity, particularly to those in the greatest need." He paused for a while before adding, "I felt I was going into the ghetto in the spirit of the Man of Nazareth joining His right-minded followers of the past twenty centuries of Christianity, represented by those painted on the church's walls all the way back to where I was sitting until their images mixed with my own, at the last pew of Jesus's ageless congregation. This was the human community Padre José introduced me to, which included all those who down the centuries aspired to be united to each other in a true human family, connected by the common mystic ground of the God-soul Jesus personalized and called his Father, the One he recognized as the Intelligent and Powerful Fountain, both of his life and the universe's own existence."

When Mário left that Hillside Orthodox church, he felt his best self again, the curious and enthusiastic young man from San Lucas who once itched to climb Pico Alto in Atlantica, so that he could explore the territory beyond the horizon, on the other side of the mountain.

His new territory to explore now included a patch of America, defined by many as a hopeless ghetto. However, as Mário understood it, the civil rights movement was now challenging the status quo and leading to the creation of economic opportunities for all, as proposed by the thirty-fifth president of the United States, John F. Kennedy, a Catholic Christian, who made so much sense to America that it elected him.

When I delivered Mário to St. Martin's Parish on that Saturday morning, Monsignor Cogan invited me to accompany him and Mário on a tour of the vast, pearly white parish facilities, beginning with the school.

"I built this school in 1948. It took a lot of determination to do it because money did not come easy in those postwar years. However, I paid it all in half a decade, and nine hundred children have been educated here every year since then and have been taught by our nuns," the monsignor said. "In 1953, I began planning the new church, and I finished building it in 1957 while incurring a one million-dollar debt of which I still owe three hundred thousand. This is also why you are here. I need to know who all my parishioners are so that I can find ways to persuade them to fulfill their obligations to God; otherwise, they get lax and my debt doesn't get paid. As our new bishop insists, Catholics must be taught to tithe. And I need to expand the numbers of parishioners who contribute 10 percent of what they earn."

Mário responded, "Monsignor, food costs are always getting higher, and I assume that work must be scarce for some of the poor people around here. Rents and car payments are a constant demand on their meager incomes. Low-income parishioners must find it hard to make ends meet with 10 percent less to spend!"

"People have money!" replied the monsignor sternly. "The problem is to make them realize that, as in everything else, God must be their first priority. Even the Jews in the old days considered the first 10 percent of all they had God's property, no questions asked. We must teach people to thank God every day for the 90 percent of their earnings and to generously deposit God's own 10 percent in the hands of His church!"

Mário was surprised and overwhelmed by the monsignor's clear explanation about what was expected from him. He realized now why the initial interview with the monsignor had been so vague. Mário didn't quite know how to deal with this new information, so he decided to remain silent.

Continuing with the tour of the parish facilities, we arrived at the church. The monsignor's face appeared to light up. There was no doubt this man was proud of this monument he had built to his God and himself, through the generous gifts he had persuaded the faithful to make. There it was: Roman Basilica style, thirty-foot ceilings over rectangular walls slit with many stained glass windows, depicting the preferred saints of the donors who paid for them. Their names were immortalized into the very artistry of the glass designs below each saint's feet.

The length of the building was such that the people in the back couldn't possibly hear the service, but in St. Martin's Parish, it did not matter much because the priest still reenacted the Lord's Last Supper at an elaborate altar not a table, quietly and mysteriously, in Latin, with his back to the people, as it had been done for centuries now. The installed loudspeakers all around the church were only connected to the pulpit for the homily, which was preached in English.

"This is the only new church in Santiago built in the true traditional church style. I understand there are some Catholics these days who favor new architectural designs. If we give in to these new trends, pretty soon we will be building churches like the Orthodox tent up on the Hillside."

"Oh! But have you seen it, Monsignor?" Mário asked.

"No, I haven't! I wouldn't be caught in anybody else's church. All this ecumenical mixing among religions, which many of our rebellious youngsters are favoring these days, is giving Catholics the wrong message that other denominations are also God's churches. These attitudes are going to hurt us. There is only one true church, and there can be no compromise with others to suit their likes." The monsignor was now obviously lecturing Mário, whose silence he interpreted as discordance. He decided to warn him and said, "Young man, you need to be more cautious about this in the future. What do you think of my church?"

"You have certainly come a long way from the biblical Upper Room of the Lord's Last Supper, Monsignor," answered Mário with a smile that belied the sincerity of his "compliment."

With that, the monsignor ended the tour of the parish, somewhat abruptly and began heading back to the rectory. "Lunch is at twelve thirty every day," he stated. "And we are very punctual here."

Mário and I stayed behind for a short while, to exchange some opinions, sitting on one of the pews where parishioners sat every Sunday thirty across, forty rows deep, all facing Jesus nailed to the huge cross over the main altar. Indeed, nothing there resembled the Upper Room of the Last Supper. Nothing there inspired the joining of hands to build a better world in the heart of this American ghetto.

Back in the rectory, Ms. Jordan had cooked up a feast. She put on her white apron and at exactly 12:30 p.m., she rang the bell and served the soup.

Mário entered the overdecorated dining room for the first time.

The long table, which could seat twelve, stretched out before them. The monsignor said grace and asked Mário to sit to his left. Father Mahoney, the monsignor's assistant, sat to his right.

"I hope you will like the food here," said the monsignor to Mário. "Those who work for the good of the church generously deserve to live with some comfort."

"Please don't worry about my comfort, Monsignor. I went barefoot as a kid. I have experienced occasional hunger in my life, and neither the San Luis College I went to in Atlantica or the San Antonio College's cafeteria have developed sophisticated habits in me. It is unfortunate that the other ten disciples didn't show up for supper, Monsignor. From what I see here, Ms. Jordan has prepared enough food to feed them all," said Mário while hiding again behind his customary amused grin.

When lunch was over, the monsignor left for his other midday ritual: the afternoon siesta. Father Mahoney and Mário used this time to get acquainted. They had barely talked to each other before then. Father Mahoney was one of those churchmen who believed firmly in a clear hierarchy within the church: God, through Christ, had given his authority to the pope, who passed some of it on to the bishops and other religious "superiors," who then delegated it down to the parish pastors, in clearly hierarchical and well-measured fashion.

He further believed that those vested with that authority bore a heavier burden than those who obeyed it. Consistent with this point of view, Father Mahoney did not object to the monsignor's authoritarianism. Obedience and conformity to all the monsignor's rules made life simple for him, and it shaped an unusually peaceful and lasting relationship.

"The monsignor has been here for thirty years," said Father Mahoney. "He has rebuilt the whole place and probably thinks of it as his own. Psychologically, he must feel that he is irreplaceable because he has built it all, and now he has to ensure that all the expenses for sustaining it are met."

"I assume he also takes the whole Sunday collection to cover those expenses," interjected Mário with a smile.

"Look, Mário, I am not trying to sell the monsignor to you. I am only saying that he is the church here. Things have always been done his way, and he is not open-minded or inclined to change."

Father Mahoney and Mário continued to talk until the monsignor came back from his nap to explain to Mário his duties as the substitute sacristan. After he had completed clarifying his expectations, he left Mário at the back of the church and entered his confessional.

Mário sat on the last pew, observing how the sacrament of confession was performed in the monsignor's church. There were two separate cubicles against each sidewall of the church, each with three doors to the front. Those were the confessionals. Mário noticed that on the one bearing Monsignor Cogan's name, the light over the center door turned green at the precise moment that the monsignor entered and sat on the automatic switch that activated it. Over both side doors, the lights were red, indicating that penitents were already kneeling on automatic switches in front of each side screen, ready to confess their sins and obtain forgiveness.

On the opposite side of the church, Father Mahoney was already at work forgiving sins in his confessional. The penitents scattered through the church looked like the most innocent and the least sinful men and women in any crowd of average people.

Mário thought, *Why should these good persons be so guilt-ridden and guilt-driven? Why are they apparently much more concerned with the evil they must avoid than with the good they can practice? Why can't genuinely good people find reasons to rejoice in the sunshine of ordinary friendships and, instead, isolate themselves into apparently unending loneliness and guilt?*

He slept uneasily that night, but the next day, he began to find some answers.

It was Sunday morning. Mário got up in time to open the church at eight o'clock, and he prepared the sacristy and the sanctuary for Mass on his first workday as St. Martin's Parish as the temporary sacristan. Every Sunday, at least six thousand faithful Catholics, about half of the Catholics of the area, came to St. Martin's Church supposedly to celebrate the Last Supper of Jesus with His disciples and be reminded that all men and women were meant to be and live as one family, feeling alive in God, whom Jesus lovingly called the ever-present Father of their lives, ready to respond to all their needs.

At nine o'clock, the church was full. Monsignor Cogan put on his own special golden garments for the celebration of the first of five Sunday Masses, to be repeated on the hour, to accommodate all the faithful. He looked magnificent, dressed like a monarch from the Middle Ages.

Mário stood quietly in the sacristy to the right of the altar. Through the open door, he could see the huge elaborately sculptured block of white marble attached to the frontispiece wall. That is what the table of the Lord's Last Supper had become in the monsignor's church and in many others throughout the world. In addition, there was the traditional huge image of a crucified Christ frozen at the moment of His greatest agony, fresh-looking blood painted all over His body, with a huge crown of thorns piercing His head and a fresh sword wound on His right side.

In front of this altar, the monsignor stood with his back to the congregation, which was now kneeling thirty feet away behind him separated by a closed sanctuary rail over which they would later receive the bread of Communion directly placed on their tongue.

"In nomine Patris,et Filii et Spiritui Sancti," began the monsignor.

"Ad Deum qui letificat juventutem meam." The two young altar boys were still considered innocent enough to represent the worshipers inside the holy sanctuary and to give mysterious Latin expression to their silent vernacular prayers.

Listening to the beginning of the Mass in Latin, Mário wondered how the Christian Church had come such a long way from the simplicity of the Last Supper of Jesus and the religious rituals of the early Christian communities gathered around a table in their own homes or in the catacombs of Rome in times of trouble and persecution.

After a lengthy and soft-spoken Latin prayer dialogue between the altar boys and the monsignor, he finally turned to the congregation, separated his praying hands slightly with his eyes looking at the floor, and said softly, "Dominus vobiscum."

The altar boys responded, "Et cum spiritu tuo."

When the monsignor turned around to the altar, the boys became obviously restless as they waited for their next intervention. The congregation continued kneeling quietly, focused on their private prayers or compulsively reciting Hail Marys, while passing the now polished rosary beads through their fingers.

The monsignor continued by reading Latin excerpts from a letter of St. Paul to the Corinthians and the Gospel of St. Mathew, in his usual quiet tone still facing the crucifix. Only when he was finished did he walk to the pulpit, turn on the microphone, and ask the congregation to listen to his homily.

"My dear parishioners," the monsignor began in an authoritative voice. "Just a few weeks ago, on Good Friday, the Son of God died on the cross once more. This time, He died, not at the hands of the

Romans and the Jews, but at the hands of the sinners of today. And right at this Mass, once again, He will spill His blood in reparation for today's sinners and for the salvation of their souls.

"In the meantime, what are the sinners of today doing for Him in return? They go on sinning every day. They go on risking their salvation and the salvation of others through their bad behavior. So, it is fitting that all sinners should feel guilty and repent!

"If you have been sluggish in the things that pertain to God and His church, and most of you have from time to time, you should pay attention to John the Baptist's warning to the sinners of his day: 'The axe already lies at the root of the tree, and the tree that produces no fruit will be cut down and thrown into the fire.' As your divinely appointed shepherd, I would be remiss if I did not clearly warn you, like John the Baptist, that if you continue in your ways and do not repent you are risking burning forever in the fires of hell.

"My dear parishioners, you must renounce the pleasures of this world and live in the world knowing that you are not of it. You must despise riches. The Lord said, 'It is harder for a rich man to enter the kingdom of heaven, than for a camel to pass through the eye of a needle.'

"But how many of you are willing to part even with a tithe of what you have, a mere tenth of all that God gives you, for the support and upkeep of His church, where you come to pray and obtain forgiveness for your sins every week?

"It is legitimate for you to want to have things for yourselves and your families, but you are not entitled to reduce God's share of all that He gives you. Even the Jews gave a tithe, one-tenth of all they received, to God, whom they knew less well than you do.

"Don't, therefore, become overly attached to your money. Do not frequent sinful places and do not indulge in the desires of the flesh.

Remember that you have been mercifully warned before the image of the Lord crucified by those who sin. Listen to the warnings of *The Imitation of Christ*: 'Oh, senseless people and infidels of heart who lie buried so deep in earthly things and relish nothing but the things of the flesh. Miserable wretches: Oh, how great is human frailty, which is always prone to vice!' Before you go on sinning, take another look at the crucified Jesus hanging on that cross! When you sin, you are cruelly telling Him, "This is how little I care for you!"

In the sacristy, Mário could not hold back his tears and feelings of bitter disappointment. No wonder the people were guilt-ridden! The gentle, lovable Jesus of Nazareth he got to know as a child had just been used and abused by the monsignor. To his parishioners, he had created an image of Jesus akin to that of a heartless dictator berating his scared followers. How could he? In all the years that Mário had spent learning about Christianity in church and at Catholic schools, he had never been exposed so crudely to this ugly reality. What could he do now? What would his Padre José of San Lucas say and do if he were faced with the likes of the monsignor misusing the power of God in such a terrible way?

This terrible day of awakening had finally passed.

When Mário went down to lock the church in the evening, he was already telling himself: There is a new pope in Rome speaking of *"agiornamento"* in the church (bringing the church up to date). Maybe this pope will find a way yet to convince the monsignor to put hinges on his church windows so they can be opened to the world outside. Maybe one day soon, we might be able to see the full-ness of the daylight that shines on the world instead of this distorted stained glass-colored light designed to create a separate world of fear for those who come in here. Maybe one day perhaps another monsi-gnor—instead of trying to recruit children to grow up in this isolated community—will try to convince parents to send them to the schools of their world and to work there to make them better, while releasing the sixteen pairs of hands of the now teacher-nuns to go into their neighborhood in the spirit of Jesus binding the wounds of those hit by poverty and exclusion. Maybe. Maybe.

Later that night, mentally and emotionally exhausted, Mário slept like a rock in the penthouse overlooking the ghetto. It was as if his body went into overload and decided to turn off his hypersensitive, idealistic, and usually superpositive mind.

Mário spent his first two days in the rectory preparing himself to begin his visits to the parishioners in order to conduct the monsignor's "census" with the help of Father Mahoney and occasionally the monsignor himself. The list of names to be visited started with those living in the City Housing Project, which provided the perfect excuse for Mário to become involved in the lives of the real people whom he had come here to meet.

The City Housing Project, in the heart of the Flatlands ghetto, was a catch basin for the vast majority of the city's social problems. It was also the cause of many more problems and, therefore, drew the attention of all the private organizations and public institutions that wanted to address those challenges. Though no community leaders would openly admit to deliberately developing policies or projects that generated more problems, the perhaps unintended consequences of their actions are not hard to identify. Here is how community leaders, politicians and businessmen collaborated to address needs in a way that resulted in the creation of more needs: First, well-intentioned community leaders, supported by advocacy groups, took a firm position: "We need affordable housing for the poor residents of the Flatlands!"

Next, a consortium of politicians and business leaders responded, "No problem. We can build eight hundred cost-effective units for two-parent and single-parent families on welfare, senior citizens, and the disabled. We can subsidize the rent by raising property taxes. All the needy will be together, and the organizations that provide services to these constituents can do so more efficiently!"

The offer was too good for the local decision makers to pass up.

The negative consequences of similar housing projects across the country were not fully visible yet in the early 1960s. Therefore, Santiago built the Greenwood Gardens City Housing Project in the Flatlands, which eventually became the most treeless jungle in the metropolis of Santiago and the nursery where new social and economic problems generated by the concentration of poverty and inequality could grow. This pattern was repeated in metropolitan centers throughout the United States.

As Mário walked into the Greenwood Gardens Project for the first time in search of the Perry family, he noticed that all of nearly one thousand residential apartments looked almost exactly the same. Each four-story, faded yellow-green building had twenty units. Blacktop parking areas surrounded them, and sterile concrete sidewalks led to rows of garbage cans.

Mário came to 1113D Ross Place, where the largest family he had to visit was living. He knocked, and Mrs. Perry came to the door. Behind her, in a small living room with two beds doubling as sofas, Mr. Perry sat in a wheelchair.

"I am Mário Garcia from St. Martin's Parish."

"Oh yes, come on in. I am Pearl, and this is George. What brings you to see us today? It's the first time anyone from the parish has come to see us in the four years we've lived here."

"I have been assigned to visit parishioners this summer, and since I had a chance to meet nine of them all at once if I came to your house, you were an ideal first choice, so here I am!

"You forgot that the kids are in school at this time of the day though."

"No, I didn't forget, Mrs. Perry. I just wanted to work my way to the kids through the parents," Mário joked. "The truth of the matter is that I was told that your children are not attending Sunday school or Catholic school, and—"

"I think I know what you are going to say next. Well, George, why don't you tell Mário what happened?"

"Come now, Pearl! We don't want to go into that. It's all water under the bridge. God blesses us daily in many ways, but it is not usually through Monsignor Cogan. Yet I don't want to condemn the man."

"I will if you won't," said Pearl. "It's good for Mário to know the truth, and it's good for me to let it all out."

"You are right, Mrs. Perry. I'd like to know what happened. After all, I have been assigned to help ... if I can."

"Well, it's like this, Mário. My husband was a very successful construction manager, with a Catholic education all the way through. I am a Catholic college graduate myself. We were well off and lived up on the Hillside with all the good folks, whom God has blessed with high incomes. We were pillars of the church up there, ideal Catholics, you know. We had a kid every year to prove that, and all of them were going to Catholic school. Then George fell off a scaffold and was in the hospital for months. We spent everything we had on doctors. George ended up in a wheelchair and had to go on social disability. We proceeded, in quick succession, to lose our home and move to this rathole. Well, to make a long story short, I wheeled George over to St. Martin's Parish to talk to Monsignor Cogan about transferring the children into his school ..."

Pearl was obviously getting very tense.

George told her to take it easy, because it wasn't that important anymore, but she continued.

"The monsignor was very happy we came in," she said with some sarcasm in her voice. "He found out where we lived and how many children we had. He congratulated us for having such a large family. Then he explained to us how happy he was that we were so enthusiastic about a Catholic education for our wonderful Catholic family, making that judgment on the basis of size alone, I guess, because he had not met any of our children yet. Then he explained to us that fortunately the Sunday school program in St. Martin's was very good and the public schools in the area were good enough. When it came to our children attending his school, he said it was full, so it wouldn't be possible! Yet I knew he was trying to get some of my well-to-do friends from the Hillside, who could pay full tuition, to send their kids there even though they lived in a different parish."

"The monsignor needs tuition payments to run the school, and people living here, like us, cannot afford it," said George.

"In the meantime," continued Pearl, "he takes in more than five thousand dollars a week in Mass collections alone, mostly from his poor parishioners, supposedly to run the parish school, and then he builds himself a church monument for a million bucks. A couple of years later, he enlarges the house—where only two priests live—to about four times the size of this place the nine of us have to crowd into!"

Mário did not volunteer that the new floor of the rectory he lived in alone had the equivalent of six rooms and three separate bathrooms. He tried to say he was sorry, but he sat there very embarrassed and quite shaken up by what he had just heard.

George said, "As you see, Mário, we have lost some of our

innocence—and some of our ideals along with it. That is why we don't send our kids to Sunday school at all and stay clear of the monsignor. We decided that the monsignor and the good people whom he chooses to teach Sunday school do it to soothe their consciences, but they are no better equipped to teach Christian values to our children than we are. So, we do it at home, the best way we can. It is not that we want to do without our fellow Christians; in fact, we go to church every Sunday. It's not that we don't need help here; as you easily see, we do. But we feel that our chances of survival here as a family are better if we work together at evolving our own rules and values, right at home.

"The good intentions and instructions of the Sunday school teachers would be enough to satisfy the monsignor, but they would not satisfy us. Besides, we encourage our kids to get involved as much as they can in their public schools and in the extracurricular activities there; we ourselves do all we can to help the public school make our children the best of citizens. In fact, our recent experience has convinced us that Catholics would do better for their children and the world if they joined other Christians and all others in the public schools in order to make them better for everyone instead of isolating themselves in their own parochial school ghettos."

Pearl said, "You know, Mário, even though I am still mad at the monsignor for not allowing our children in his school, I am sure glad they aren't going there. Some of his thoughts and words simply don't seem to have anything to do with the Christianity I believe in."

Mário glanced at his watch. "I have to make it to the rectory for lunch, but I would like very much to come back and meet your children and chat with you again when I get over the shock of what you have just told me. I am beginning to think there is much about working here in the Flatlands that I could learn from you ... if you are willing to teach me. For now, I really have to go. The monsignor is very punctual!"

"Do come back! We will be here!"

Mário walked out of the Perry's door and headed for lunch at the rectory to sit alone beside the monsignor, at the gigantic table loaded with more food than either of them could eat. As he walked up the front steps, his stomach was churning, his palms were sweaty, and his fists were clenched tight. He momentarily thought of quitting, but then thought, *No! I cannot quit because of my dislike of the monsignor's attitude and behavior. This is my first opportunity to learn about the real problems of America. I have to make the most of it.* Besides, Mário realized, the monsignor's dedication to maintain St. Martin's Parish in comfortable isolation from the world around it was not unique to this congregation or other religious or civic organizations throughout America.

The entire system needed as much to change now as it did when the republic was formed. Modern-day America seemed to Mário to have abandoned some foundational truths, enshrined in its Constitution: "All men are created equal, that they are endowed by their Creator with certain unalienable Rights, that among these are Life, Liberty and the pursuit of Happiness." It seemed to him that America apparently was no longer pledged to form a more perfect union, establish justice, ensure domestic tranquility, and promote the general welfare.

The America that Mário found himself in was far from the perfect union that he had hoped to learn from. What he found was pervasive and institutionalized racial segregation, especially in the South, the widespread lack of economic opportunities for the poor (deemed losers by many members of the economic and political elite), woefully inadequate social welfare systems that were unable to support the elderly and disabled, who were often forced to give up all they owned before being placed in miserable assisted-living facilities or nursing homes, a widespread and intense feeling of disenfranchisement because of the barriers to participation in a democratic process capable of bringing about effective change.

It was true that America had just elected John F. Kennedy with his promise that things were going to change. Indeed, the new president offered moral support to Martin Luther King Jr. and to the sit-ins being staged throughout the South. As president, he had even issued new directives to abolish segregation in public transport systems. However, America still had a long way to go to fully implement the high moral principles of equality, freedom, and personal rights for all immigrants to the country since the British first crossed the ocean in the *Mayflower*!

Indeed, instead of one nation under God, America was now more than ever divided into the haves and the have-nots, and the Santiago Flatlands provided a clear example of such a divide. Even though this disparity went clearly against the fundamental principles of the Constitution, the politicians had legislated economic and social policies that perpetuated this disparity. Furthermore, the various churches did not seriously object to them. More often than not, the institutions of American Christianity flourished by serving the upper echelons of society, and unlike Jesus, they did not reach out to serve the less fortunate in their midst. They were unable or unwilling to stand up to the monopolistic and greedy capitalist owners of America or to demand a more equitable education or a distribution of means and resources to resolve the growing problems of social and economic injustice.

Apparently, the Catholic bishop of Santiago suffered from this kind of schizophrenia. On the one hand, he wanted to maintain and strengthen the influence of the church on the population of his diocese almost exclusively through Catholic schools for those who could afford the tuition; on the other hand, he realized that the teachings of Jesus, which rested on the principles of equality and inclusion of all people, did not tolerate the exclusion of those without money and/ or those who were not members of his church.

In his episcopal conscience, the bishop knew that, at least in theory, all Christians in Santiago should, as Jesus taught, treat everyone as part of the human family. He had probably been goaded into a new attitude by Pope John XXIII's call for ecumenical (interchurch) cooperation toward a united front for social justice among all Christian institutions in Santiago, despite the resistance of people such as Monsignor Cogan, who believed that the church should not meddle in social justice causes. Indeed, Monsignor Cogan would not go into anyone else's church organization and put his one and only true Catholic church at risk.

When the regular sacristan returned from his vacation, the monsignor decided to cooperate with the bishop's new spirit and send Mário to the first meeting of the new ecumenical parish announced for the Flatlands.

Mário had been already taking the pulse of the Flatlands for more than a month, and there was nothing that he welcomed more than the monsignor's new assignment.

The day after the first meeting at the Flatlands Ecumenical Parish, Mário gave a verbal follow-up report to the monsignor. He was relieved to know that the few people in attendance did nothing but select a name for the interchurch group and schedule future meetings to be hosted by the Protestant ministers who were present.

"In general, it was a positive meeting," said Mário. "By far, the most interesting and practical thing that happened to me yesterday, Monsignor, was a conversation I had late last night after the meeting with a member of the Flatlands Workers' Collective."

The monsignor immediately interjected, "In fact, I noticed you were out very late last night. I don't think you should continue to do that for various reasons, including your own safety."

"Monsignor, the streets are well lit, I don't look like someone worth mugging, and I have good legs to run. I think it's actually pretty safe out in the streets at night, in spite of what they say on the news!"

The monsignor chomped harder on his food and decided to concentrate on what he was doing instead of getting upset.

Mário said, "What I was starting to tell you, Monsignor, is that I had a good conversation with a member of the Workers' Collective who showed me how committed and motivated they are. They actually do Christian work at its best, right here in our community. I wondered if it would be possible to offer them some of our unused space in the parish's vast facilities. Right now, they are lacking a place for meetings and for the storage of food and other donations that they distribute to an ever-growing number of poor people."

"You call their involvement Christian work! Why did they change their name then?

"I didn't know they had changed their name, but what does a name change mean anyway?"

"Sometimes it means everything!" said the monsignor. "Two years ago, most of these young communists who you are so impressed with were unwilling to obey His Excellency, the bishop, when he told them to stop being involved in the Housing Tenants Union—and a lot of other rebellious causes they sponsored—without the church's support or approval. Until then, they called themselves Young Christian Workers, and they conducted all their activities in our parish facilities, free of charge! They even insisted on being allowed to have dances in our social hall, and when we gave in to that, they started inviting 'Negroes' who were not even Catholic."

"But, Monsignor, is it not the church's role to encourage, give strength to, and nurture social justice movements, born in our own neighborhood and aimed at addressing its deepest needs and concerns, be they Catholic or not? St. Martin's Parish could, in fact, become an oasis in the midst of this definitely graying neighborhood. Isn't such a course of action Christianity at its best, Monsignor?"

"Young man, that sounds to me like disloyalty at its best. What you want is to open my parish to waves of uncivilized vandals, who are mostly from the South, where they have already caused all kinds of problems, led by their so-called civil rights organizers. I will never let that happen here again! Besides disloyalty to me, what you propose is also disobedience to the bishop's specific orders. His Excellency does not want the church mixed up in these movements by extremists and troublemakers who have recently found their way into our heretofore decent neighborhoods. I will never tolerate disobedience to the bishop in my parish!"

The monsignor threw his napkin on the table, blessed himself quickly, got up, and left Mário to finish his lunch alone.

"In that case, Monsignor, I am informing you I'll be working out late at night more frequently—on my own time!" Mário had a temper as well-developed as anybody's, and whereas he had been trying to keep himself under control up to that point, he thought the time had come to start pushing the boundaries set up by the monsignor. Besides, the monsignor did not hold all the cards in their relationship.

Mário knew that the monsignor needed him, with some urgency, to update the list of future Mexican parish donors and to recruit Mexican students who could afford the tuition to fill his school vacancies.

Despite the conversation he had just had with the monsignor about the Flatlands Workers' Collective, Mário wasted no time calling Joe Young, the collective's member he had been talking with the night before.

"Joe, as you know, I am a relative newcomer to this country, and I would love to understand better the conditions faced by people in the inner cities of America. After our conversation last night, I thought you might be the right person to learn from. How about dinner tonight?"

"I can do better than that, Mário. I can offer you dinner tonight with the most capable team of experts on inner-city living I know, my house partners, who are also members of the collective. We are trying our best to study and understand our social realities before trying to improve them, which is the main reason we are living together. You might not know this, but we got our start as Young Christian Workers with the help of Father John Delaney, before His Excellency the bishop, exiled him up to the hills, and your monsignor kicked us out of the shelter we enjoyed in St. Martin's Parish. We usually sit down to a meal together at eight o'clock but come anytime. Our door is open!"

The next day, Mário told the monsignor that he had accepted a dinner invitation for that evening—and that Ms. Jordan had agreed to answer the phone at the rectory in his stead.

When he arrived at Joe's home, which doubled as the collectivists' headquarters, all six house partners/members were already there. A couple were busy fixing dinner, and the others were stretched out on the furniture-less living room floor poring over books or over each other, while listening to an oriental sound played into a room slightly scented with burning incense, a trend among hip young adults.

A young woman in the collective greeted Mário at the door. "We are glad to have you among us, Mário, and coming from St. Martin's

Parish, of all places! Are you bringing us news that our excommunication has been lifted?"

Mário said that unfortunately that wasn't the case and went on to explain. "I am so low in the hierarchical pyramid in St. Martin's Parish that it wouldn't even be appropriate for me to deliver such an important message. I can assure you, however, that young as you all are, with patience, humility, and all the papers properly presented to the Holy Office, your situation has a good chance of being rectified in time for you to receive a proper church's funeral and a plenary indulgence—full pardon—which will provide you with an entrance pass into heaven ... perhaps after a short stopover in purgatory!"

All six members of the collective had a good laugh, and Joe Young introduced Mário. They immediately treated him like an old friend. Joe had told his companions about Mário and his quest for answers to the social and economic problems of the inner cities in America. After Lucy Eagle Feather and John Gray had served Italian pasta with an unidentifiable soul food, which was enjoyed by all, a real serious conversation started in response to Mário's questions.

"I come here at Joe's invitation, with great hopes," Mário declared. "When I came to this country three and half years ago, my dream was to learn in America, as one learns in a laboratory, the techniques of modern democracy and social justice, so that one day, as soon as the conditions were right, I could go back home and help build my small Atlantean world to the image of yours. Chalk that up to my naivete! I have already learned that America as a whole, is no laboratory of social justice and perhaps even of democracy. Yet I am now convinced we are all living in a country where the fight against poverty, inequality, and social injustice is slowly being taken seriously, and where I need to catch up and learn from those like you who are already in the forefront of the fight. Will you be willing to help me take the first steps?"

"Certainly, Mário!" said Joe. "You are smart to come to us before going to someone who may fill your mind with pompous theories created in their ivory towers. Ask us pointed questions to keep us on track. We have talked among ourselves about how we could help you. But, for the sake of efficiency and because we are not here just to hear each other talk, we are proposing an organized approach to the issues ... a sort of minilecture approach where we talk one at a time and concentrate on the things we really know about. Agreed?"

They all said yes, and Mário Garcia's education to the realities of inner-city living began. "Why don't you start with this," Mário suggested. "It's about the feeling of community you have here, about belonging together. As soon as I walked into your door, I noticed you have something that seems somewhat rare in your country: the total acceptance and friendship among diverse persons in spite of all the obvious differences of race, ethnicity, and appearance. Why is it that so many Americans out there seem so unapproachable, so distant from each other? They frequently sit next to one other in church, travel on the same buses, live across each other without so much as a nod or a word of greeting to one another. For a country boy like me, this is hard to grasp. Please help me understand this apparent cultural feature."

"Here is the standard answer," started Joe, the sociologist in the group. "The industrial revolution uprooted people from their rural communities into different urban areas, and their prior friendships and kinships were broken. Additionally, thanks to Ford and General Motors, every American became mobile. Everyone now has access to a car big enough to drag a twelve-foot U-Haul trailer, with all he owns inside, to any part of the country, in a matter of days. Statistically speaking, everyone moves, on average, once every five years, and, while they are in one place, others move in and out around them. So, unless people are gregarious by nature and prize friendships, they remain anonymous and friendless in a crowd of uprooted people. At best, they find others who share very similar roots and form a clique, which make the people they meet at work or elsewhere unnecessary and perhaps undesirable, and if one isn't an extrovert, one builds protective barriers against all these strangers."

As he paused, everyone applauded.

Undaunted by his friends' intentional overreaction, Joe said, "But this preference for isolation in the crowd is also a result of the social and economic engineering of our capitalist system, where people are, like capital or raw materials, nothing more than a necessary factor of production. Industries and businesses, therefore, are interested only in the productivity of their people according to their job descriptions as accountants, managers, secretaries, assembly line workers, harvest pickers, etcetera … and the people who fit those 'job descriptions' will naturally want to make sure that the impersonal corporate gods or bureaucratic overlords they work for don't take from them any more than what they pay for. These attitudes, you will agree, are not conducive to promoting friendly relations in the workplace or among those you meet in other public settings. And so, Mário, these are the Americans you see on the streets, offices, churches, and other public places, standing or sitting next to each other as strangers."

Mário sighed and asked, "Why don't people run right back into your beautiful rural America to live a happier, healthier life in communities where people know each other and are naturally friendly?"

John Gray, the economist in the group, said, "By the time they realize what they have given up, it is too late to turn back. They have become thoroughly urbanized, and they are addicted to the consumerism that their paycheck and their urban location give them easier access to." Earlier, John had explained jokingly that he was John Gray because his black mother and his white father believed in full integration. "Like any addict, they can't think of living anywhere far from easy consumerist fixes. Others, like my mother's parents, remember only too well the problems of living in some rural areas, especially in the South. Many blacks had to move out of their rural areas to avoid life-threatening exploitation by corrupt and unscrupulous loan peddlers and property owners who made it impossible to survive on 'shared' farmland. In the rest of the countryside, the only way to make a living is to enter the bracero streams, which relentlessly flow in and out of farmlands at harvest time. In this moving stream, many farmworkers risk drowning; only those who are desperate and who do not have any alternative means of survival tolerate these extreme conditions! The truth is that, if you are poor, no matter where you are, there is simply no opportunity for you to survive economically unless you work for someone else. In this country, everything a poor person needs to survive already belongs, legally, to someone else. In these circumstances, for many millions of Americans, their 'inalienable rights' to 'life, liberty, and the pursuit of happiness' are rendered meaningless by the laws that legitimize the ownership and control of everything by just a few while others have nothing."

Mário said, "Don't the fundamental principles of your famous American Constitution and Declaration of Rights guarantee everyone economic opportunity and equal access to the resources of this infinitely rich land?"

John wryly concluded, "The Constitution and the Declaration certainly imply equality of access, but the laws designed to implement those principles effectively restrict that access exclusively to those who have money. Those who don't have it continue to struggle for survival."

Mário asked, "And their numbers continue to grow! How does

any urban area become a slum or ghetto? How did the Santiago's Flatlands come to be?"

Tony Santos had just finished the dishes and joined the circle in the living room. He had been born and raised in the Flatlands, and in his short lifetime, he had observed firsthand the ghetto being born and attaining its current state of full maturity. Of those present, he was certainly the best qualified to tackle Mário's question, and he took center stage quickly. "Before you go on planting seeds of error in the virgin mind of Mário here, give me a chance to tell him the real truth about ghetto building in America. Believe me, I know! I lived through the process right here in the Flatlands. Hell, I even observed my own father working hard at building it! Twenty years ago, after the war, a new suburban housing project was born on a worthless swamp owned in part by my father's family, next to the shipyards. When it was completed, the whole area became known as Bay Heaven. The new houses were nice-looking units suited to the tastes and pocketbooks of successful young Irish, Polish, Italian, and other European-descent families. So, Bay Heaven became, almost exclusively, a white suburb for second- and third-generation immigrant families, hungry for the good life after the strains of the Second World War. What they didn't appreciate, however, was that some blacks, whom they didn't want to live next to, had also made some money in the local shipyards. Realtors, my father included, considered a black buyer's money just as green and as enriching as anybody else. So, a few years later, cautiously at first, the Realtors sneaked one black family here, another there, into Bay Heaven, violating the then-current practice of segregated neigh-borhoods. Not long after these few sales of homes to blacks occurred, large numbers of white owners began to seek the services of the same Realtors to sell their homes. Smart Realtors quickly realized that their new clients were the neighbors of the Blacks or Latinos they had just sneaked in next door to them. And that is how the term 'blockbusting' came about: if you wanted to increase sales in a white area, just move in a Black family or two and wait.

"To avoid the chaos that indiscriminate blockbusting would create, the Realtors organized weekly lunches that continue to this day, with the purpose of 'sharing current information' and 'keeping up with the trends' in property values in the area. What they were really doing was strategizing on how to be selective and discreet with blockbusting so that they could all maximize on the profits to be made.

"If blockbusting was done hastily and without careful consideration, it would result in general panic, with whites selling cheaply in the rush to leave. Realtors didn't want uncontrolled white flight because when blacks were moved into a predominantly white neighborhood, they would be willing to pay more. After a few years, when the houses got older, you could block-bust well-to-do blacks by moving in a few poorer blacks. The process went on until one day, you woke up, and there was an impoverished ghetto where there was once a nice, clean, and safe residential neighborhood.

"If you don't believe me, Mário, my father and the monsignor can scrupulously confirm all that I have told you. I think there is a genuine 'spiritual' kinship between those two men. That is why I disrespect them just about equally, while I reserve the right to still love my father."

Joe Young said, "Tell Mário, but with less detail this time, the story of the other half of the ghetto, the 'asphalt gardens' on the other side of the tracks, and then Lucy and I desperately need to listen to some good music and make love while the rest of you have to go about your scheduled activities and earn your future night off—like we did!"

Tony Santos continued to tell Mário the story of how the ghetto grew and ignored Joe's directions by providing details that only someone who saw all this firsthand would know. "The City Housing Project story will go faster, I promise. Once Bay Heaven and its surroundings lost value to the real estate professionals, enterprising individuals realized that there was another kind of business opportunity for them among inner-city residents. All they needed to do was persuade Congress to pass 'poverty-eradicating' programs so that large amounts of taxpayer money would be spent on providing 'services' to the poor. Those who succeeded in securing the government contracts to provide these services would be paid handsomely through these public funds.

"So the chamber of commerce, supported by the city, HUD, the schools of engineering and architecture at the university, the Building Contractors Association, the trade unions, the churches, and the charitable organizations all formed a committee to address the housing needs of the poor and advocated for the creation of the federally funded Santiago Housing Authority, which was nothing more than a vast business consortium that made a fortune building the Greenwood Gardens Housing Project, and continued to follow the federal money trail to the more recent 'New Cities' project downtown. There you have it: ghettos filled with the poor continue to be a bottomless economic resource for these 'poverty concessionaires.'"

"What you say is true, Tony," said Rosa Reyes, a social worker in the making, who had remained quiet until this point. "When the Greenwood Gardens Housing Project became operational, it attracted the overflow of the poor from the city and confined most of the problems of urban poverty into this one concentrated area. The project required a host of personnel from public bureaucracies—such as law enforcement—as well as 'do-gooder' organizations to keep things in check.

"No one was there to resolve definitely the problems of poverty.

They were there rather like guards and feeders at a zoo, to maintain the peace and prevent mayhem, while the service providers profited from afar." Rosa spoke in a conversational, clear, and methodical way. "With all the single parents—many of whom were unwed mothers—living in the housing project, the number of school-age children in the neighborhood grew dramatically. The local public school, built for eight hundred kids twenty years earlier, now had to accommodate 2,500, many in temporary structures set up where the schoolyard used to be.

"The developers of this area had not included any open spaces or playgrounds, so now many of those kids, who lived in tight quarters at home, made the street theirs. When the curfew cops came, the kids hid around the corner, many times because Mom was entertaining her boyfriend at home and needed privacy. To show their work, the police often caught a few kids and booked them for vagrancy—or any other charge a judge might find plausible. For many, this becomes a standard ritual: they get caught and sent off for a refresher course in 'street smartness' in juvenile prison, and, as soon they get released, they start their life on the street all over again, only this time with more survival skills.

"By now, they are caught in the 'cycle of poverty,' and the authorities and social science 'experts' all agree that they will be inclined to remain within that 'culture of poverty' no matter what is done to help them. As such, they will live by values that are totally different from other Americans. They are prone, the experts say, to trouble-seeking behaviors and excel in dodging trouble, skills essential for survival in an urban jungle. Eventually, persons living in this culture of poverty no longer have any respect for or desire to obey the rules and laws that the rest of society follow. They know that the law enforcement and the judicial systems use those rules to control them. And so, slum dwellers dodge establishment and government influence at every turn.

"So, when the conscience-cleansing, poverty-irradiating, publicly funded programs are introduced promising opportunity to slum dwellers to lift themselves out of poverty, many of the poor look the other way and rely only on the tangible services they are familiar with such as food stamps and Medicare.

"As a result, the handful of people who agree to be selected to participate in job-training programs and other such opportunities to break out of the poverty cycle are used by the institutions as examples to justify the continuation of these programs that benefit first the service providers, while the numbers of slum dwellers remain unchanged. In reality, the majority of Americans below the poverty line—always a double-digit percentage of the American population, varying only marginally with the ups and downs of the country's economy—continue to survive left to their own devices."

The intense group action intended to introduce Mário to inner-city living in the Flatlands had to end abruptly. One went to a night job at the post office, and a couple went to a prescheduled meeting. Others went to work in their separate ways.

Only Joe Young and Lucy Eagle Feather stayed behind with Mário and continued their conversation.

Mário said, "I still find it hard to accept that, despite the noble words written in the Constitution and the Bill of Rights, and after all the preaching the United States has done to the world, an individual's most basic economic right to a life-sustaining share of the earth is still denied to so many Americans in such callous ways."

With a wry smile, Joe said, "I understand how disillusioned you must be to find out that American democracy and social justice have failed so much to so many. Imagine how much more disappointing it is for those of us who were born right in the heart of America!"

"If you are not totally saturated yet, let me try to throw some light on this—from my perspective," chimed in Lucy. She was a Native American, a student of both political science and economics, and a part-time employee at Stratford University, as required by the terms of her scholarship.

"Go on, Lucy. I am still waiting for your input."

"From my point of view, Mário, the disregard of fundamental economic rights in America began when the first European immigrants arrived and began to take control of the natural resources of this continent by establishing laissez-faire capitalism as the underlying principle for the civic institutions and the rules by which everyone had to live and work.

"The founding fathers articulated the laws and established a system of government that worshiped 'free enterprise,' whereby certain individuals and companies acquired control over vast areas of land and virtually unlimited financial resources, which were used for further accumulation of wealth in favorable conditions, thus barring effective access to these same lands and financial resources by others.

"Predictably, those who became the legal 'owners' of most of the land and controlled the financial capital, removed any obstacles interfering with the exponential economic growth of their enterprises. First, they pushed the Native American populations into 'reservations,' which were among the most undesirable and unproductive parts of the country. Other ethnic groups who arrived from Europe and other parts of the world, who were often fleeing desperate poverty and exploitation in their homelands, found themselves being pushed to the margins of the economy in the New World as well. This was obviously an unjust distribution system in a nation which proclaimed that everyone was 'created equal.'"

"And where does that leave us, Lucy?"

"John Kenneth Galbraith explained it in *The Affluent Society*. The entrepreneurs eventually discovered how to associate themselves with middle-class Americans in ways that benefitted them also. Together, they have created the unstoppable American growth machine."

"Producing what?"

"Comfort and consumerist bliss to everyone inside the system! It builds highways, roads, and power grids throughout the country. Entrepreneurs now go onto every corner of the nation where there are natural resources to be exploited and set up businesses that fuel the insatiable consumer demands of the growing middle class. All the vehicles and machinery deployed to serve consumers, often in futile and wasteful ways, use up boundless energy, resulting in pollution at such levels that Paul Ehrlich, one of my favorite professors, predicts that one day, not only this country but the whole planet will overheat and no longer be habitable.

"Often, I get steaming mad with this bloated, consumption-obsessed society for what it has done to the lands of my ancestors, yet, what gets me even madder these days is the institutionalized economic order that denies today's poor the insignificant portions of the earth's resources that they need to satisfy their basic survival needs. That, I assure you, sometimes makes me weep!

"If you, Mário, still want to find people in America living in solidarity with Mother Earth and each other, you will have to come with me and visit my own people up in the reservation."

"That I would very much like to do, Lucy," replied Mário.

As he walked back to his rectory penthouse, Mário felt the unnatural man-made hardness of the concrete under his feet. He also felt the discomfort of an undigestible steel ball in the pit of his stomach. His muscles automatically tensed up. His fists unintentionally tightened as he felt pressed in the pincher of Monsignor Cogan's platitudes and the hateful despair he sensed was building up in the Flatlands of Santiago.

Who will I become if I stay in this country much longer? Will I give in to hatred? How can I live here and not fight this economic monster? And, if I do stay and fight, what happens to love ... to my love for Monica? And the thought of Monica added one more nuance to the cauldron of emotions boiling up inside. Frustrated, mad, sad, and lonely, his soul ached within. He, too, like Lucy Eagle Feather, wanted to cry.

When Mário walked into the living room of his rectory penthouse, he found me sitting there alone on the fluffy sofa. I had a yellow Western Union telegram in my hand, and I was about to remove the last weak dam holding back his shallow tears. He read the telegram, gathered me in his arms, and without a word, mixed his tears with mine, and truly made me feel that my burden was a little lighter. His embrace was certainly not just that of a friend. It was the embrace of Mário Garcia, my brother, allowing my sorrow to flow into him freely and allowing what was left of his courage to flow back and strengthen me once more.

The telegram informed me that my father had just been assassinated in Santa Cruz, Brazil, by a guerrilla's bullet.

I had been terribly distant from my father during the last four years attending university in Santiago. In my earlier years, my father's image and ambition were so overpowering to me that I had not minded being away from him. More recently, however, he had mellowed, and I realized how much the unfair trade partnership with Fred Gilmore's company had affected him. Gilmore Industries was, as you remember, the provider of the abundant machinery and capital investment that was digging up the iron ore from the land my father inherited from our ancestors in Brazil. It hurt me to see how my father's once proud and independent spirit had been weakened, in exchange for the money he needed in always-larger quantities. For a long time, my father had worried about what would happen when the ore ran out, and he also feared the ticking time bomb of rage and frustration of the exploited mine workers.

Well, the time bomb had, in fact, exploded, and my father was left dead in the debris.

The man who had given me life and was my only real link with the past was gone. Suddenly, I found myself alone before a dark and empty tunnel. The moment my father died, I became what I simultaneously wanted and feared the most: a young, socially aware, but totally inexperienced, Latin American tycoon.

I had no one to turn to but Mário Garcia, the country boy from Atlantica, the man next to whom my strength always seemed to double. It was Mário who accompanied me to the airport, and I went home to bury my father, feeling like I had turned the sharpest corner of my life.

4 COOPERATIVE CAPITALISM

After

his experiences in St. Martin's, it became crystal clear to Mário that he wasn't going to learn much of what he needed to know in Monsignor Cogan's penthouse or inside the white walls of his parish compound.

Toward the end of the summer, feeling at a crossroads, Mário began to think back, almost compulsively, to what Padre José, back in San Lucas, had told him many years before, when he encouraged him to leave town and think of himself as a world citizen: "The human family we seek will be built of a million communities like San Lucas built by people like you, everywhere."

The Santiago Flatlands looked like a community where Mário could begin practicing more seriously his world citizenship. Luckily, his commitment to improve life in the area was shared by the members of the workers' collective who helped him see his surroundings with new eyes. Indeed, with the collectivists, Mário was able to immerse himself in the political and social activism of the early 1960s that could be found everywhere in America. It felt like the country was waking up from the false sense of comfort that was created by the postwar economic boom in the 1950s and finally confronting some painful realities that were not easy to resolve or reconcile.

The contradictions were stark, and the resistance to change was very strong and sometimes virulent. On one side, there was the free speech movement led by Mário Savio at the Berkeley University

Campus; the march on Washington led by Dr. Martin Luther King Jr. for racial equality; the new US president trying to integrate the public schools, and the public transportation systems and restaurants in the South. Also, large numbers of American Peace Corps volunteers and missionaries were traveling to faraway places to lend a hand to their development.

Paradoxically, at the same time, America was threatening to send its military forces to Vietnam to secure its geopolitical and economic interests in Asia, and it was also encouraging American businesses to harness and exploit the vast natural resources of Latin America, supposedly to prevent the spread of communism.

Mário realized there were many similarities between the inner-city ghettos of America in the sixties and the Vila Miséria slum of Atlantica Island. In both places, people were becoming increasingly aware of their basic economic rights and discovering new ways to defend them, such as the use of nonviolent resistance to oppression and discrimination in the American South.

And, though still confused by the contradictions of America, Mário's deep-seated optimism caused him to dedicate himself, without reservation, to becoming an active world citizen right where he was, in spite of his deepest yearnings to return to Atlantica and to Monica. And he did this with Monica's full support. In fact, it was Monica who helped him realize there was no other alternative at that time. Here is what she wrote to him:

> Dearest Mário,
> Before you go on reading this letter, close your eyes and savor my kiss full of saudade ... the kind of saudade you once told me you felt:

the tender recollection of our most
intense moments of love, the sweet
and sour taste of our intimately
shared dreams and hopes, the
nostalgia born of our absence from
each other prolonged much beyond
the reasonable, the longing for
touching and feeling each other
again, the craving to have this
empty place inside us filled again,
the gnawing need to have the other
half of us restored.

But, in spite of my saudade, I
must tell you that right now things
do not look very bright for you and
me in Atlantica. In fact, things
here are getting worse every day,
if you can imagine it!

Your friend, Antunes, has been
drafted into the army and is at
this moment being forced to fight
Salazar's immoral war against the
native peoples of his colonial empire.

In the meantime, our country
is sinking into the deepest misery,
and young men are leaving the
country illegally to avoid military
service. As you see, things are really
gloomy over here for idealists like
you, Mário!

So, please, my love: do not think of coming back! Not yet; not now. If you do, you will be forced to fight in Africa!

Fortunately, from what I read, the forces of change seem to be rising in America. Please stay there, my love. Work and learn for now. Become a world citizen if you must. That won't make you any less an Atlantean.

There are a few more worries I want to talk to you about. As you know, my aunt's death changed many things in my life.

To my father, whom she never wanted as a business partner in life, she left all her urban properties, including her palace, which he is now at a loss to keep from deteriorating. I must help him!

And, although I successfully avoided inheriting her title as countess, she left me all the rural lands she owned, but in the hands of a legal "administrator" she appointed for ten years "in order to allow me time to complete my studies," as she explained in her will.

So, as you see, Mário, for the next few years, I will be helping my father and will be busy with university studies, trying to figure out what I shall do with my vast inheritance, including an old tea plantation and the people therein, whom no one knows what to do with.

But I have many years to resolve these problems.

What worries me most now is our separation, my love! Though I know and understand that you can't come back yet, I want you to know that I miss you profoundly! My whole body and soul crave for you, and, though I know our day will come, I fear it will take too long. I anxiously wish you were here right now!

Etc.

~

Before Mário's commitment to the Santiago Flatlands took shape, he accepted an invitation from Joe Young and Lucy Eagle Feathers to visit her Native American tribe during a short August vacation at the Olympic Peninsula of Washington, where the Quileute, the Quinault, the Chehalis, and other peoples had lived for uncountable generations.

Driving up the coasts of Oregon and Washington, through the remaining fragments of these ancestral redwood forests, Mário experienced stunning views of nature, but nothing had prepared him for his encounter with Lucy's grandfather. Chief Eagle Feather was one of the most fascinating man he had ever met. Indeed, Chief Eagle Feather reminded him of Padre José in his magical ability to see the working hands of the living God behind the green mantle of the earth, whom he called the Great Spirit. Chief Eagle Feather was a worthy descendant of Seattle, the renowned chief of a neighboring tribe—after whom the city of Seattle is named—whose famous pleas for respecting the environment and Native American rights in the mid-1800s are still echoed nowadays.

Chief Eagle Feather had sensed something different about Mário and invited him to come along to a special place in his fishing grounds up the river, where he had put his net in the water all his life, as had his ancestors.

When they arrived, Chief Eagle Feather sat down in the traditional pose of a tribal elder and started to speak—as he had heard many times his wise ancestors before him—passing on by word of mouth the history of the tribe and the wisdom of the ages for future generations. This was, in fact, the most sacred duty of a Native American chief.

It was his profound cultural belief that the only way to preserve the tribe's history and wisdom was via actual rituals, word of mouth, and their daily living practice.

Chief Eagle Feather was moved by this remarkable, idealistic young man. Consequently, he chose to pass on to him some of his inherited wisdom. In the spirit of his ancestors, he began a monologue of his tribal history:

"There was a time when the Great Spirit allowed us to live on

Mother Earth as if we were one. There was a time when the trees around the river were old and holy and only came down to make space for new ones after their lives had spanned over and united many generations of our people. In those days, the Great Spirit made all the trees and all the creatures of land and sea our brothers. We all lived in harmony, and we all belonged to each other as one—until the treaties with the American government were forced upon us by war.

"The white men usurped the land with its trees and other valuable natural resources. With the creation of the federal government's Bureau of Indian Affairs, boundaries were imposed, fencing us inside these tiny reservations. But even then, the few of my people who survived the slaughter brought about by wars and the white man's diseases still lived within these small borders according to the Great Spirit.

"Later, roads were built across the reservation, and the white lumbermen, who had already cut down most of the trees outside our borders, once again tricked us out of what was left in our small forest. They cut all the trees and did not even save some for the eagles to nest. The cedar branches were left in piles by the river, and it will take many generations for them to rot. Now they form dams that hold back the water coming down the unprotected, treeless mountainsides. They have destroyed the salmon spawning grounds, changed the river flow, and stopped the upriver salmon runs. Consequently, the white man has destroyed our links to the earth, the river, and the sea—and our lives have been weakened!

"Under these circumstances, the Bureau of Indian Affairs came to help us again. They supported the building of fish hatcheries, so that we would be able to restore our old salmon runs and again catch the fish we needed to live on. So, we cooperated once more in good faith; we hatched the eggs and then let the salmon out of our hatcheries into the sea, which was also a gift from the Great Spirit as was the land.

But when our salmon were about to finish their journey of many years and miles through the ocean and began the last leg of their trip back to our river to spawn, they met up first with the Japanese nets still in international waters—and later with the white man's trawlers close to our shores.

"In the meantime, we sat here on our fishing grounds waiting for the few fish that survived the Japanese catches and the white men's trawlers, but we still needed to share those with the hungry seals at the mouth of the river. At times, we nearly starved!

"Some were sent to big cities, including to the tribal schools, or even to American universities, which tried to make 'white people' out of them. When they realized what they had lost, some felt so bad that they drank themselves into oblivion in the big-city ghettos or gutters. Others came back to the reservation, hungry for the earth, and tried to eke out a living like me and others here. But we live now on land that was destroyed by trespassers and can no longer sustain us. And yet, some of us still survive, close to our ancestors' burial places and true to the Great Spirit!"

The nostalgic Chief Eagle Feather's words stopped flowing, and a depressing gloom saddened Mário. Both men sat there quietly for a long time, listening to the crackling of the fire as if they were being soothed by its song. Eventually the chief also sang under the unchanging stars. He hummed a soothingly rhythmic melody, reaching pitches of angry intensity, only to return to the sound of a muffled child's cry. Chief Eagle Feather was indeed a child of the universe, consciously curled up in the symbolic hands of the Great Spirit, though at times with an aching heart.

Mário had picked up a piece of cedar lying at his feet. It appeared old and weather-beaten. When he split it down the middle, he made two wings rotating around the knot that held them together.

If suspended by a string, the old piece of cedar would look like an eagle, gliding in the wind. Mário asked the chief if he could have it as a reminder of this special night.

"Good choice, Mário. This piece of cedar resembling an eagle is an excellent symbol of our culture. It has probably lived in Mother Earth for a thousand years, and it might last another several hundred years, as I hope my people will. For you, it may also symbolize the eagle that sees the world from great heights—like the Great Spirit who alone knows everything and sometimes shares with us some of the secrets of our lives."

In Chief Eagle Feather's company, Mário felt special, much like a follower of the real Jesus of Nazareth, the man of the earth, and not the centerpiece of religious institutions and nations that appropriated His name as an excuse to conquer the world and destroy native cultures.

With these renewed insights regarding humanity's relationship to the earth firmly engraved in his mind, Mário came to clearly see the glaring truth about the conditions in the ghetto that he had been in touch with every day that summer. And he kept telling himself, at this stage of human evolution, it is no longer acceptable that a powerful few should own and control all this land and its resources, and lease and sell them "for profit only." It's even less acceptable that the poor are permanently excluded from sharing any of the earth's bounties and are left dependent on the mercy and charity of those powerful few.

As Mário's understanding of the harsh reality of life in the Santiago Flatlands' ghetto was deepening, his personal feelings got stronger. His patience was growing thinner. *We, the people who live here, must*

become agents of change and tell this powerful minority, the establish-
ment, that this situation is no longer acceptable.

Every time he came in close contact with the despair of welfare-supported elderly persons in county hospitals and rest homes, waiting to die in miserable conditions, he realized that his kind words and his passing presence were empty gestures if he did not try harder to do something to improve those conditions.

At other times, Mário shared painfully the confusion of countless teenagers who were put through an educational system that simply perpetuated the status quo and provided very little opportunity for them to realize their potential or break out the cycle of poverty they were unlucky enough to be born into.

In addition to the miserable way the elderly were treated in the Santiago Flatlands, and the alienation of its youth, Mário saw the despair of capable, productive adults unable to earn an adequate salary to sustain their families in this land of opportunity. All these persons lived in the tiny gaps among the excessive abundance of things owned by others. These unemployed and underemployed individuals remained disenfranchised, demoralized, and left with no choice but to seek unemployment benefits, food stamps, and other charity, all dispensed dutifully by the government and private entities inside an economic system that sometimes profited from this misery.

After coming to this realization, Mário would never be the same. He became determined to do more than just be an armchair liberal; he decided he had to act on his convictions.

It was the end of the summer of 1962, a little more than four years since Mário had come to California. He was twenty-five years old and still in college. Mário had assumed that the current well-intentioned leaders at all levels of government and civic institutions in America were persons of goodwill and keen intelligence who would respond to the calls for change articulated by various social, political, and economic justice movements all over the country.

By the end of that summer, Mário realized this wasn't going to happen. It was just wishful thinking on his part, and his verbal expressions of empathy and solidarity toward the poor weren't enough. He had to take a stand and act as one of them, starting with the firm declaration to himself as a Flatlander:

- We, the "needy" residents of the Santiago Flatlands, have rights!
- We are worthy of basic respect and human dignity.
- We refuse to accept the conditions that perpetuate our poverty.
- We demand an immediate end to these unjust conditions!
- We require access to resources that ensure our basic and rightful sustenance.

Finally, Mário was very sure about where he stood and what he had to do. And he would start immediately with a conversation with the monsignor.

Summertime was over. Mário was exhausted and alone. His brain was swelling inside his skull with the pressure of his thoughts. Sunset was approaching, and the more the sun sank into the smog-saturated horizon, the more impressive and soothing its orange hues became. The distant smoke-spewing stacks of the heavy industrial park became indistinguishable from the shadows of the new downtown skyscrapers.

Mário tried to adjust to the soft cushions of top-quality outdoor furniture the monsignor had provided for his upstairs penthouse patio. He should have felt content. Most people in his situation would have appreciated the opportunity to view a stunning orange sunset from the comfort of this vantage point while sipping a nice cold drink, which was easily obtainable from Monsignor Cogan's well-supplied bar.

But Mário Garcia was not like most people.

Instead of looking at the gorgeous sunset, he focused on the freeway below the Hillside to the west, now filled with the shiny new cars driven by businesspeople and public servants who operated this economic system that allowed a select portion of humanity to own, control, and profit preferentially from the earth's resources.

Next to St. Martin's, he saw the Brink's money truck carting away the poor people's money and cash-equivalent food stamps from the large chain supermarket. He saw the public school principal walk away, briefcase in hand, toward the rapid train station that would quickly whisk him away to his suburb, beyond the hills.

Mário was genuinely upset, and a feeling of indignation was rising within. *Thieves! They are plunderers and absentee landlords of the worst kind! It isn't fair! If they don't realize how wrong and unjust their actions are, we need to make them recognize how unreasonable our socioeconomic situation is and demand an immediate change. Anyway, if there is a chance for me to help create in the Santiago Flatlands the better world that Padre José inspired me to pursue when I was a kid, I must believe that I am not powerless!*

He knocked at the monsignor's door, feeling a bit tense but also very excited and determined "Monsignor, I must talk to you. Do you have a few minutes to spare?"

"Sure! Have a seat! Care for a drink?"

"Yes, please! I'd appreciate if you poured me your most relaxing beverage because I need to be very calm to tell you what I must."

"There is no need to be nervous," said the monsignor condescendingly. "I am all ears!"

"First of all, I want to thank you for the opportunity you have given me this summer."

"Don't mention it! You have done a good job, though you have a tendency to go beyond the scope of your assignments and get too involved with causes that are not relevant to this parish."

"Respectfully, I could not disagree more, Monsignor! Those are the very causes that the Man from Nazareth, who you and I both believe in, would urge us to pursue."

"The Man from Nazareth you talk about is the Son of God, and when you try to reduce Him to a mere man who would sponsor your communist causes, you are challenging His own divine teachings as interpreted by His church, including the following: 'Leave to Caesar what is Caesar's and to God what is God's.' Your meddling with social causes is something I will not tolerate!"

"I find it impossible to believe that God put the whole earth in the hands of Caesar for his exclusive use and profit—while many of His other children are dying of starvation for lack of access to that same earth, which is as necessary for human survival as a mother's placenta is to the child that is connected to her by an umbilical cord. Indeed, I am inclined to believe that someone put those words in Jesus's mouth because they don't sound like most of his other meaningful words!"

"I have noticed your tendency to be selective about what Jesus, His church, and the pope teach—as if words have no meaning."

"Words do have meaning, Monsignor," said Mário. "But how can we presume that any one of us understands the true meaning of God's words. I think the best anyone can say about God and His words must be kept simple and leave some room for interpretation. This is what Jesus did when he said things that to me sound like, 'God is a Super Father and Loving Mother in one, and S/He is forever giving birth to everything that is, though never separating Herself from anything S/He is giving birth to. The simple reality Jesus was talking about is that S/He is the Living Soul of the universe, which S/He always carries as Her own 'outer body.'"

"That makes the devil—and all the world's evils and evildoers—part of God also!"

"Yes, Monsignor! Who else do you think is capable of giving someone, including the Devil, existence, and life, and sustaining him continuously, if he in fact exists? As far as I am concerned, evil is the good you, I, and others haven't yet succeeded in accomplishing here in the Flatlands, with our own hands ... hands guided by the tiny share of God's own intelligence, which He has put in our brains to guide us in our work ... work, which ends up being God's own!

"I think, Monsignor, that something as simple as this is what the Man from Nazareth taught the people of his time. But, unfortunately, latter Christians—including many of those who built Christian churches all over this country—misconstrued his original simple teachings to suit their own convenience and comfort. They chose their interests instead of carrying out the easily understandable mission that the real Jesus of Nazareth lived and proposed, namely: to help alleviate the suffering of those in need as if they were our brothers and sisters, born of the same God."

After listening to Mário's tense words, the monsignor said, "You should show some fear when you misuse God's words and blaspheme! God in heaven will know how to punish you!"

"Monsignor, when I heard your first homily in St. Martin's, I cried bitter tears behind the sacristy's door while you used God's words to whip your parishioners into fear—and to give a generous tithe to pay for your monumental church. But I hope I will never fear the God who is here and now my life—a life that I want to use to serve the people of the Santiago Flatlands!"

"You show a lot of bravado, but I fear for you because of that air of superiority you give to your words and beliefs. That will get you into a lot of trouble with those in established positions of authority in our city."

"I thank you for your concern, and I don't wish to make you feel uncomfortable, Monsignor. That's not why I came here. But it did me good to have this conversation with you. I thank you again for your time and for the unique opportunity you gave me to get to know this part of real America, these Flatlands where I want to live. Here, I have already learned where I truly belong!"

Not many minutes later, with the calm that had resulted from his final confrontation with the monsignor, Mário put all his things in an old suitcase. He swung it over his shoulder, said goodbye to the monsignor, and walked down the street toward the collective's headquarters.

When he arrived there, his friends were engaged in the usual friendly arguments for that time of day: who was going to open the chili con carne for dinner, take out the garbage, etc.

Mário had become a regular visitor to the collective, and his presence didn't change any of the other residents' patterns of behavior; he had become a part of them. However, that night, when Mário walked in with a somewhat out-of-focus look on his face and sat down, everyone in the room realized something was wrong despite his outward calmness.

"Speak, man. What gives?" said Tony Santos, expressing everyone's awareness of the importance of the moment.

"I finally had it out with the monsignor, and I am out on the street. Can you good people put me up for a few days while I try to find my way forward?"

Tony stepped up and he embraced Mário. "You are welcome, my friend!"

All the others welcomed him warmly and without hesitation.

"Let's make this a joyful celebration! Let's break out the champagne," said Lucy Eagle Feather.

It was obvious that Mário had made a serious personal commitment to their movement and was now ready to participate in their collective awakening.

Mário became a member of this community, and it took only a few days for everything to fall into place.

With a small loan from the collective, he bought a small motorcycle for transportation. He also reregistered immediately as a part-time student at San Antonio's College, so that he could maintain his international student visa. This time, he was going to take some courses on economics for underdeveloped countries.

The rest of the plan was to obtain a worker's permit as soon as possible from the immigration department and find a job with a steady income. Later on, he would be able to apply for a green card and become a permanent resident of the United States.

It wasn't long before he became a construction worker with a flexible work schedule and good pay in a company that did small home repairs of all kinds. He quickly learned new skills involving physical labor in addition to digging up the ground, which he had learned to do while growing up in Atlantica. The work gave him a level of satisfaction that had eluded him in school. He finally felt a sense of mastery over his own life, part of which he could now dedicate exclusively to the Santiago Flatlands along with his fellow collectivists.

Mário's timing could not have been better. If anything, the collectivists were busier than ever before because the problems at the Santiago Flatlands were multiplying at an alarming rate.

The next two years passed by rapidly, but despite all their efforts, the Collectivists saw little progress being made toward solving the problems they encountered daily.

John Gray, Mário Garcia, and Joe Young all worked with groups of unemployed Flatlanders and had placed many of them successfully in gainful employment, but the Baptist church's basement they used—ceded through the ecumenical parish—was just as full of unemployed persons now as it had been two years earlier.

Susie Capella and Rebecca Williams worked with the Santiago Flatlands Neighborhood Council to provide legal assistance to Flatlands' residents whose basic rights had been seriously violated. However, they found the number of persons needing their services always growing, and no class action suits won on their behalf managed to shorten the lists of the aggrieved. Despite their selfless and earnest efforts, nothing had changed except the faces of their clients.

Moreover, the collectivists needed to think of their own economic and personal futures as they got older. None of them wanted to leave the Santiago Flatlands and give up on their sincere desire to help poor and unemployed residents, but they also had dreams of raising their own families in a stable and safe environment, which the Santiago Flatlands was not!

A new sense of urgency began to permeate their more serious

brainstorming sessions. They all knew they had to address the root cause of all this misery. John Gray and Mário Garcia expressed the most frustration with the practical irrelevance of the economics courses they were taking in college. They began to doubt that a school of economics was the place to find viable economic development solutions to the problems of poverty, as much in the United States as abroad.

Mário began to audit a course on environmental science so he could understand better how the environment sustains humanity.

At long last, Mário became a permanent resident of the United States. As a holder of a work permit and a stable job for nearly three years, Mário was now able to apply for a green card. After all the required documentation was completed, he crossed the border into Mexico and reentered the United States with the new green card that entitled him to live and work without the need to maintain his status as an international student.

It happened just at the right time! He had been summoned to urgently meet with Dr. Goldman, the dean of the San Antonio School of Economics, and the meeting did not go very well.

Dr. Goldman appeared to have been carved out of piece of hardwood for his role. His emotionless expression never changed. He was still a staunch believer in the economic theories of Adam Smith and others that rested entirely on the assumption that self-interest was the central spring of all economic activity in any human society. These early scientific economists believed that this assumption was just as important to economics as natural selection was vital to Darwin's understanding of natural science or the idea of gravity was key to Newton's physical science.

Initially, the belief in the righteousness of the "invisible hand" that Adam Smith and his fellow economists relied on to explain the merits and inevitability of laissez-faire capitalism was as fervent as that of the most devout followers of Christianity. Perhaps that invisible hand was, in fact, the hand of God blessing personal enrichment!

Later, Keynes and many other notable economists, realized that a more palatable set of economic principles had to be devised and articulated to resolve some of the systemic excesses intrinsic to a system that relied entirely on the assumption that self-interest and selfishness were the rightful basis for the economic decisions of a nation.

Today, modern economics has become a system of complex theories about the efficient allocation of resources, marginal utilities, and maximization of profits. However, modern scientific economics still conditions all the political and legal infrastructures at every level of society that disrespect the basic economic rights of the have-nots of society and legitimize their current exploitation by those who selfishly control most of the major resources of land, raw materials, and accumulated capital.

This was the economics taught by Dr. Goldman's faculty to those who sought to understand how the economic system works, including those who, like Mário, would like to see it work equitably for everyone.

Dr. Goldman was sitting in his office with his glasses on top of his nose as he looked at Mário's file.

After Mário sat down, Dr. Goldman said, "Mr. Garcia, several years ago, when you came to San Antonio College, you started taking courses in sociology, community development, and the like. Then you moved on to adult education. After that, you began taking economic development courses, supposedly to help you when you returned to your country. But then again, more recently, you decided to start auditing environmental science courses. I called this meeting to ask you to get serious about economy and to choose what kind of an economist you wish to become … if you wish to stay in my school."

"Dr. Goldman, I came into your college to learn about economics, but I never wanted to become an economist. I took courses in economics because I thought they would give me the skills to achieve my goals. I have decided to dedicate my life to working with and trying to help solve the problems of poverty, not just in my country, but also right here in the Flatlands where I now live. In order to do that, I realized that I had to learn many things, including theories about sociology and community development. Also, I thought it would be essential to understand something about adult learning in order to help unemployed adults develop skills and motivation to successfully enter the labor force. Much of what I have learned here has already proved to be helpful in my activities in the Flatlands! I took all these courses for good reasons, Dr. Goldman."

Dr. Goldman said, "Do you think you are ever going to save the poor without understanding economy, who makes it work, and how growth and prosperity are achieved and trickle down to help the poor?"

"No, Doctor! I am fully aware of the fact that in today's world, only the rich owners of the earth can save the poor … if they choose to. They have all the necessary means tightly under their control. They literally own the earth, including the tiny pieces the poor desperately need to survive on."

"Then you should work with the rich, shouldn't you, so you can help the poor?"

"Unfortunately, all that I and the people of the Flatlands see is the rich using every means at their disposal to make themselves richer, and they are doing it by destroying the earth through unsustainable economic growth and overconsumption in order to make always larger profits out of an always more impoverished planet."

"If that is what you believe, why are you in my school?"

"I came here, to this Christian college, hoping that I would learn how to make the American dream come true for everyone, including the least among us, but I realize that what I can learn here is merely to perpetuate a system that is at odds with what I consider to be fundamental American and Christian values."

"How frustrating and disappointing it must be for you, Mr. Garcia, to be here," said Dr. Goldman with sarcasm dripping in his voice.

"My frustration, Dr. Goldman, began when I realized the true spirit of Jesus had been mostly taken out of the so-called Judeo-Christian culture ever since the Roman emperors converted their armies into religious Crusaders for the Roman Empire, a tactic that has been imitated by the leaders of Western Christian nations to this day.

"All of them found it convenient to be associated with Christ while, so unlike Christ, they conquered and plundered and enslaved people everywhere. Despite all these lessons of history, I invested all my hopes again on the promise of the grand social experiment of this country and its Constitution that enshrined the principles of equality, fairness, representative government, freedom of religion and expression, and other concepts that are consistent with my Christian faith.

"I assumed that such a system would also allow for the fair sharing of the bounties of this land so that everyone would have their basic needs—food, shelter, health care, education, and employment—satisfied and life with decency and dignity guaranteed. But, here in your school, Dr. Goldman, I came to realize that the government has been bought by the laissez-faire greedy capitalists who have no intention of sharing fairly the earth they now own with all their constitutionally equal citizens, least of all with the poor who have no means to buy, rent, or lease anything from them!"

"Mr. Garcia, if that is your attitude, perhaps it is best that you withdraw from this college!"

That evening, fresh from the bitter feelings of humiliation and rejection that he felt after leaving Dr. Goldman's office, Mário went home and shared his unpleasant experience with the collectivists, and they talked all night.

The chili con carne was eaten right out of the can, and no other house chores were performed that evening. The conversation took a life of its own and headed in a very certain direction, though through very uncertain and untested paths. At the end of it, a summary of their ideas and decisions covered the full width of the white wall in permanent markers with what amounted to the group's mission:

> We commit to take charge cooperatively of our own economic affairs here in the Flatlands. By so doing, as Americans, we show our neighbors practical ways to exercise fully our constitutional right to life, liberty, and the pursuit of happiness!

And the collectivists began to disseminate their ideas throughout their neighborhood.

The *Flatlands Journal* was one of the platforms available to them. Mário, who enjoyed writing, became a frequent contributor. In his first article, he wrote:

> Money is what makes the world go around, we all know! Consequently, all those who were born into this world with an economic birthright to a fair portion of the earth need to have access to some money in order to activate their right to live with dignity today.

Yet in the hands of today's monopolistic money handlers and their political partners, worldwide capitalism has become a way to deny equal and just access to money to one-third of humankind, thereby perpetuating injustice and poverty. This is why elementary justice toward the poor requires that current capitalism must be restructured to treat money primarily not as the monopoly of a few but as a common asset to all. The welfare of today's human family demands that money and credit be used according to equal access rules developed for and applied to all alike, by responsible politicians of all nations and their international organizations.

In America, it should be normal to hold this view on behalf of the poor because most of us have benefitted from an economic system that has given us access to a reasonable mix of capital or other resources (land, education, skills development) sufficient to participate in this system and live within it with some comfort.

Our current question therefore is this: If capitalism has been good for so many of us in America, why not for everyone? Why shouldn't the poor among us be empowered to combine their labor with the capital resources they need to get better housing on their own, better neighborhood services, better health care, and better education—the same as other fellow Americans do?

If they were given fair access to money (appropriate training, job opportunities with living wages, equal access to credit, and knowledge to start a business), would it not allow them to run their own economic lives so that everyone could benefit and have a decent level of life?

All the answers given by traditional capitalist ideology to these challenges so far have not worked. They have led to our current reality: the profit of those who own everything also at the expense of keeping the poor as have-nots, dependent and sometimes prey of the haves.

We are still waiting for the day a more cooperative capitalism becomes our economic system. It should put the right value in the hands of those who create it through extending equal economic opportunity to all. There should not be a need any longer for some to have to pay a "poverty tax" that keeps them forever "dispossessed" at the end of legally designed, but unjust credit leashes.

This is why I think that the only way to win the anti-poverty war is for our politicians and economists to redesign the system so that it ensures fair universal access and utilization of capital, taking away unearned privilege and putting opportunity and responsibility equally in the hands of everyone, including the poor.

Mário Garcia
Santiago Flatlands, January 1967

Despite the initial skepticism to their ideas, the collectivists began to sense that they were indeed on the right track, but they had to demonstrate the practical validity of their economic approach. Collectivists had to show Flatlanders how they could improve their standard of living by together making a more cooperative capitalism work for them.

The collectivists started by first pooling some of their savings. Then, Tony Santos went to his father and asked him to cosign the mortgage on the huge old house they were renting for eight hundred dollars per month. His father accepted, and in this way, the collectivists bypassed the redlining practices of the banks regarding loans on Flatlands properties and the collectivists' poor credit histories.

They became the proud owners of their home at a considerably lower cost than the rent they were previously paying. However, they decided to continue making the same monthly payment into what was previously just their housing rent fund. The extra money kept accumulating into a savings account, which each one could use for a personal emergency or a spontaneous vacation. They began to enjoy the security of these savings instead of worrying about whether they would have enough money to survive until the next paycheck.

This arrangement worked out so well that they also applied it to their food budget. With such small but radical changes, the collectivists were learning how to become businesslike—while improving their quality of life.

Sharing these experiences with their Flatlands community put them in a position of leadership in the "crusade for better economic opportunities."

Joe Young and Lucy Eagle Feather also decided to buy and remodel their future family home in the Santiago Flatlands.

Mário, with his adult education academic preparation coupled with his practical field experience in all kinds of small remodeling projects, made himself available to help Joe and Lucy directly. In addition, he organized a training project for the group of Flatlanders who volunteered to help the couple. It wasn't long before Joe and Lucy's house was totally renovated. To celebrate this important occasion—and to thank everyone who had helped them achieve this economic milestone—Lucy set up a teepee in the backyard to show everyone how the earth can be used without harming it. The teepee, she was proud to explain, would serve as a space for environmental awareness activities for neighbors of all ages.

When Lucy was done with her inauguration speech, Mário said he had one more contribution to this project and unwrapped a piece of old cedar he had brought with him. He said, "I would like you to hang this piece of wood outside your teepee's door, Lucy. It was your grandfather's gift to me. When it opens up like this, it looks like an eagle, and when hung high, it will appear to glide like one. Your grandpa explained that the eagle symbolized the Great Spirit, who sees everything from above and sometimes reveals to us some of the things we really need to know down here."

The collectivists continued to train other people to remodel their own homes, with the additional help of experts from local construction companies, which eventually provided expert consultants and the use of otherwise unaffordable tools.

Periodically, a fresh-painted façade began to show up here and there throughout the neighborhood, and the bright colors of the owner's choice carried a message to all: "It's ours! We made it!"

~

Despite his outward appearance of being a laborer in his worn-out work clothes and long hair, Mário continued as a regular contributor to the *Flatlands Journal*, aiming to spread the collective's message and commitment to economic change.

In another article, Mário explained the practicality of "cooperative capitalism" and its benefits:

> For many people, the mere mention of cooperatives conjures up the image of an organization that is not very businesslike. Business is supposed to be competitive and fast-paced to respond to the consumer. Cooperatives, it is said, don't work because they are not efficient, and they are slow to react due to laborious committees and decision-making processes.
>
> For us, however, cooperatives can become true businesses with a broader and better social impact.
>
> The members of our collective, through our cooperation, have achieved greater financial security and attained the comforts of a good life in accordance with our individual preferences, all of which would not have happened if we had tried to do it each on his own. Our cooperation has already proven to be good business, and it has already led us to a better life, without any loss of security or responsibility for our own personal finances, which we manage scrupulously and professionally.
>
> Besides being financially profitable, our cooperativism—within the capitalist system—is based on a set of values and a way of life that are compatible with and generally considered basic to all the world's

religions and humanistic traditions. In addition, our cooperation enhances our humanity. When we genuinely cooperate, we do so voluntarily and without co-option or mutual exploitation. This leads to personal achievement, personal fulfillment, and the well-being of everyone.

Why is it then, that in our Santiago Flatlands community, we as neighbors have not always tried to achieve our individual and common economic goals through cooperation?

Personally, I am convinced that we can meet most of these needs if we manage to bring together our community resources, including personal skills. This is exactly what the Economic Opportunity Act of 1964 is designed to help us achieve.

In 1964, riding on the wave of empathy generated by the assassination of John F. Kennedy, Congress approved the Economic Opportunity Act, much like JFK had proposed it: "to eradicate the paradox of poverty in this land of abundance."

At its signing, President Johnson said proudly and without ambiguity, "Today, for the first time in all history of the human race, a great nation is able to make and is willing to make a commitment to eradicate poverty among its people."

The Economic Opportunity Act stated with equal clarity:

It is the policy of the United States to eliminate the paradox of poverty in the midst of plenty in this nation by opening to everyone the opportunity for education and training, the opportunity to work, and the opportunity to live in decency and dignity.

In a national climate of optimism, nearly one thousand community action councils were formed throughout the country to coordinate on the ground the allocation and spending of the new federal poverty-eradicating resources. They were to be used to close the existing gaps between the local public and private programs to irradiate the last pockets of poverty.

In this context, the Santiago Community Action Council was formed, and it sponsored the formation of many neighborhood councils within the county, such as the new Flatlands Neighborhood Council, in order to create and operate poverty-eradicating projects under local leadership. The announced new strategy for the neighborhood programs was exactly to put new opportunities in the hands of the poor persons themselves.

For Mário and the members of the collective, who believed so profoundly in the moral imperative of striving for the implementation of fundamental economic rights for everyone, the Flatlands Neighborhood Council looked like the ideal vehicle for the final eradication of poverty from their midst.

From now on, public works projects could provide new employment opportunities for the underprivileged as an alternative to welfare, and those with any entrepreneurial abilities could have access to start-up capital and advice from the Small Business Administration and other government agencies to help establish minority-owned-and-operated businesses. At last, those who owned very little or nothing and previously had been barred from participating in the free enterprise/capitalistic system could get a foothold on the ladder to climb out of poverty!

The neighborhood council had a board of directors formed by one-third official government appointees, one-third representatives of community service organizations, and one-third representatives of the poor chosen by neighborhood residents. Once selected, the board of directors would elect its president.

In this new context, the collectivists and other local leaders thought it was of vital importance to select the five residents who could best represent them and ensure that the changes they desired for the neighborhood would actually happen. Ideally, one of them would become the council's president.

Initially, there were two strong contenders for the presidency. Arthur Sims was a respected fifty-five-year-old African American who had moved from the South into the Santiago Flatlands to work in shipbuilding during the war. Due to his association with the Baptist Church and the new ecumenical parish—as well as his rich human qualities—he had become one of the neighborhood's most preeminent leaders.

The other candidate was Brandon Brown, a local teacher who tried unsuccessfully to become a city councilman and then became a part-time realtor while waiting for another opportunity at political leadership. He continued to enjoy some popular support in the Flatlands, where he maintained ownership of his old family home. He had also continued to cultivate his relationships with city hall and the executives who led the organizations that operated on a large scale in the Flatlands, including Goodwill Industries, the Red Cross, and the Catholic Charities, all of whom would have a representative on the council's board of directors. Based on these ties, Brown was confident he would be easily be appointed to the council and elected as the president, which would become the desired stepping-stone to higher office.

As the result of the involvement of activist groups, at the well-publicized meeting where the five local representatives of the poor were to be selected, more than seven hundred Flatland residents showed up, but they did not elect any of the candidates proposed by Brown.

When the five newly elected representatives of the poor residents of the area joined the other ten officially appointed members of the Flatlands Neighborhood Council Board to elect their president, they declared their unanimous support for Sims.

The officially appointed members that Brown had counted on saw the writing on the wall and quickly shifted their votes to Sims.

When elected, Sims immediately called on the collective and the other activist groups for assistance to draft the Flatlands Neighborhood Poverty Elimination Plan, a policy document to guide the Council's efforts "to alleviate poverty and bring residents of the Flatlands into the mainstream economy."

Mário and John Gray became nearly full-time contributors and threw all their energy toward this end. Sims realized, from the start, that one of his most important functions was public relations, and he frequently called on Mário and Gray to accompany him in order to explain to the public and the media the more technical aspects of the council's various proposals and applicable regulations.

Many members of the establishment's old guard—who made their living from being poverty concessionaires and had a vested interest in maintaining the status quo—kept themselves informed about the community through reading the *Flatlands Journal*, and they tended to view these detailed project presentations as harmless, inconsequential, and overambitious dreams of inexperienced idealists.

To their immense surprise, three months later after an exhaustive process of gathering and processing input from residents, the *Flatlands Journal* published the final proposal.

~

The Flatlands Poverty-Elimination Plan

Introduction

We, the elected members of the Flatlands Neighborhood Council, in close consultation with the residents of the Flatlands and the organizations providing services in our area, propose, as the core of our poverty-fighting strategy the formation of a legally independent nonprofit corporation to be known as the Flatlands Corporation. The Flatlands Corporation shall be controlled by the residents of the Flatlands, through their Flatlands Neighborhood Council, and it will implement the economic poverty-eliminating projects approved by the same council.

The officers of the corporation shall be selected by the neighborhood council from among qualified residents of the Flatlands in order to take advantage of their knowledge of our community. Because they live here, they will also benefit from our community's efforts to improve our economic conditions, and that will further motivate them.

The corporation's ultimate purpose is to provide the economic tools necessary for all capable residents of the Flatlands to achieve the economic self-sufficiency promised to all Americans by the

Economic Opportunity Act passed by the United States Congress.

The creation of this corporation does not replace or minimize the role of the existing network of governmental or nonprofit organizations that provide the services needed by those persons among us who are unable due to illness, disability, or other incapacity to provide for the basic needs of themselves and those who are dependent on them.

General Objectives

The corporation aims to be the vehicle through which the residents of the Flatlands will achieve the following major objectives:

1. To empower unemployed residents to solve their own economic problems through the creation of concrete employment opportunities.

    To this end, we will make proposals to government agencies to provide a proportional amount of their services to our community through direct standard subcontracting to our corporation, which will deliver them using local manpower, thus adding their salaries to the money circulating in our midst.

2. To help residents achieve homeownership, thereby also helping the community to own itself.

    To this end, we will make proposals to the City Housing Authority and other government-supported mortgage holders, who are now our absent landlords, to create lease-to-buy programs designed to transform us into the owners and caretakers of the houses we now pay rent for without ever being able to call them our own.

3.   To help residents start or obtain local businesses, thus also empowering the neighborhood to own and revitalize itself.

To this end, we will create a space in our area where the Small Business Administration and all the financial service providers that are mandated by the government or wish to participate in our economic growth may come to provide their services in cooperation with our own credit union.

4.   To create a residents' group of technically capable leaders to support our corporation in the creation and maintenance of a self-sustaining community. To this end, we will seek to have an active voice in the selection of public employees who work exclusively in our area, and we will propose and firmly advocate that a willingness to move into the Flatlands be an important condition for public employment in our service.

The specific project proposals designed to achieve these objectives emphasized the need for local autonomous leadership as well as the mobilization of circulating capital to the area as top priorities.

The government and business leaders' reaction to this manifesto coming out of the most problematic area of the city of Santiago was one of bemusement, and they all went about their regular routines with their normally complacent attitudes. They were convinced it was just talk. It would all fizzle out when it crashed against the firmly installed outside bureaucracies and the financial interests of those who owned most of the ground the Flatlanders had always lived on—but the Flatlands Poverty-Elimination Plan was not just talking this time!

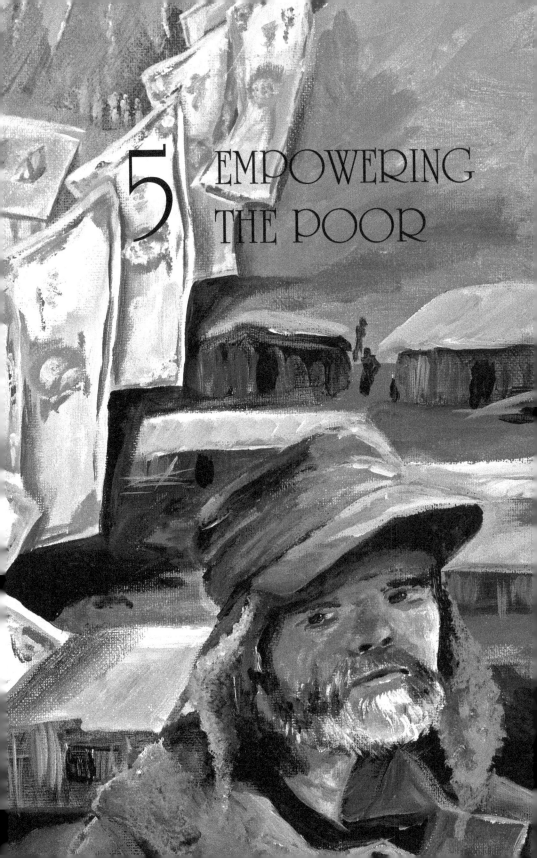

5 EMPOWERING THE POOR

The
Flatlands Corporation was formed, and not long after it began functioning—and at the suggestion of its leaders—about half of the tenants in the public housing project decided to start paying their rents into an escrow account instead of directly to the City Housing Authority (CHA).

The corporation proposed to residents that this action be taken in order to compel the CHA to enter into serious discussion with the tenants of public housing on how to create a path to ownership of their apartments instead of keeping them as perpetually subsidized renters.

At the same time this action was taken, the corporation also proposed to the CHA that it be contracted to administer all the services in its Greenwood Gardens City Housing Project, including full administrative responsibility to enter lease-to-buy agreements with tenants and collect from them monthly payments on behalf of the CHA. At the end of the lease-to-buy period, the CHA would transfer title of the property to the individual tenants, who then became responsible members of the Greenwood Gardens Owners Association.

In addition to creating a mechanism to enable residents of the Flatlands to become homeowners in their community, the corporation put forward another proposal designed to create a food cooperative, which would enable residents of the Flatlands to buy nutritious food in more cost-efficient ways.

The initial funds for setting this up would be raised by offering founding membership rights to one thousand Flatlands residents for one hundred dollars each. Upon the opening of the food cooperative, founding members would recoup their initial fees through a special discount.

Flatlanders willing to pay a five-dollar monthly fee to cover the operating costs could also begin to shop at the cooperative, enjoying significant savings in their food budgets.

The corporation was responsible for contracting professional management for the coop and ensure that it functioned as a nonprofit in the true sense of the words. The corporation would also provide the necessary guarantees for a line of credit to be established with local lenders to expand food offerings at favorable prices throughout the Flatlands as required by growing demand. This would end the needless spending of money on food provided by profit-maximizing businesses, thereby giving residents of the Flatlands healthy nutrition at considerable savings.

These proposals to encourage homeownership and access to cheaper and healthier food encouraged discussions about how the corporation could help bring goods and services to the Flatlands in a more cost-efficient way.

After these experiments took hold, the profiteering of external entities that simply sucked most of the money that came into the community right out of it again began to be scrutinized more realistically. In addition to the collectivists, a great number of Flatlands residents began to realize they had some power to change the rules of economic activities through collective bargaining—in areas that they previously thought were entirely out their control. For instance, many residents began to think that the time was right to insist to government agencies that the public sector jobs in the Flatlands be filled by qualified residents so that their salaries and talents could add dimension to community life by circulating within the area.

When the mainstream media started to publish and broadcast stories highlighting these developments, which challenged the normal activities of politicians, corporate bosses, and other members of the establishment, Mr. Sims made himself even more available as the official spokesperson for the neighborhood. His was an intelligent effort to create the necessary goodwill to make these activities viable. He continued to ask John Gray or Mário to accompany him and deal with some of the more technical questions.

Although John and Mário knew their place beside Sims and endeavored to be low-profile advocates of the corporation's plans, they were frequently quoted in the media because of their articulate, cogent statements, like the following:

- "The Flatlands is simply transforming itself in order to eliminate poverty as the recent federal legislation mandates."
- "The Flatlands Corporation is simply trying to harness the potential of the people and the resources of the Flatlands community to become a better participant in the arena of free enterprise in order to benefit its shareholders, who are the residents of this vibrant neighborhood."
- "The corporation recognizes that the political, business, and religious leaders of Santiago are the ones who currently hold the moral authority, the power, and the money necessary to eradicate poverty from the Flatlands. All we are doing is trying our best to empower ourselves to take charge of our futures and eliminate our poverty through our own collective efforts."

One of the unanticipated results of these information efforts was the sudden notoriety of the Flatlands Collective, which became identified publicly not only as the brains behind many of the corporation's projects but also their controversial proponent.

Many political, religious, and business leaders in the community lost no opportunity to focus on the negative side of every issue, and the collectivists were often the target of patently false attacks and extremely cynical criticism. Mário received several anonymous personal threats and insults on the telephone, mostly from public servants who felt threatened or annoyed by some of his words or by corporation activities they accused him of fostering.

He tried to remain calm, but there were situations that made his Latin blood boil, including when a certain anonymous Flatlands public servant wrote the following to the editor of the *Flatlands Journal*:

> Shame on you, Editor! You ought to be ashamed of yourselves for your poor judgment. How can you print the arguments of a "foreigner" who wants to decide where I should live and work in my own country? With a name like Garcia, he should pick up and go as soon as possible back to Mexico or Brazil, or wherever the h*** he came from, and practice there what he preaches here.

A few days later, Mário again lost his cool during a presentation by Sims at the Elks Club.

Mário knew that Sims was tolerated there as a guest speaker—but that he would have had great difficulty being approved as a member because of the color of his skin. In the past, he had already felt annoyed with the Elks Club's regular requests for the distributions of their Christmas and Thanksgiving food donations to the poor using the neighborhood council as its proxy, while receiving the recognition.

During the presentation, a member of the Elks Club said, "Let me give you some advice, Mr. Sims. With the help you receive from the Elks and other philanthropic organizations, you should concentrate on helping your own people—whom we have more than our share to take care of already here in Santiago. One thing you should never do with our help is give work to 'communist foreigners' who should be sent back to wherever they came from—and the sooner the better."

Mário immediately walked out.

Although he had to admit his emotions got the better of him at the Elks meeting, the next day, Mário had reason to feel optimistic. The Catholic bishop had invited him for a meeting in his episcopal residence on the Hillside, and Mário thought it might be an indication that the three Catholic parishes in the area and the Catholic Charities were ready to work with the corporation in the eradication of poverty and exclusion in the Flatlands. It was, after all, entirely in keeping with the teachings of Christ, was it not?

Before he left for the Hillside meeting, Mário told his fellow collectivists to keep their fingers crossed. "If all goes well today, this may be the day that I—and some of you—may need to take back all the bad comments we have made about our bishop! On the way up to the Hillside, maybe I should be preparing an apology!"

Bishop William Shannon was one of the most recognized leaders in Santiago, and the diocese, mostly through its philanthropic arm, the Catholic Charities, was already an active provider of services to the needy. Now it was being challenged by many to become a much stronger partner in the anti-poverty war in the Flatlands through its local parishes.

Mário had accepted the invitation for a meeting without hesitation. The collectivists knew the bishop was aware that the Flatlands Workers' Collective was initially the Young Christian Workers of St. Martin's Parish and that Mário had been employed there by Monsignor Cogan for some time. What they did not know was that the collectivists had often become a topic of discussion between the bishop and current civic leaders. They all saw them as the source of many of their problems because they were challenging the status quo and threatening the very lucrative operations that poverty concessionaires had providing goods and services to the poor in the Flatlands community. In this context, an organization of civic leaders and owners of the companies providing government-subsidized goods and services in the Flatlands wrote a letter to the bishop because they thought he would be the person to influence and possibly tame some of the more aggressive proposals made by the collective and the residents who were influenced by them.

Mário drove to the bishop's mansion expecting to discuss with him the goals and needs of the Flatlands Corporation—and to gain support for them. Despite all the difficulties they had faced, he was still optimistic that the political and business establishment would eventually recognize the potential of the corporation to alleviate poverty. He was also proud to be living in this new America where a community transformation, such as was occurring in the Flatlands, could happen.

Having recovered from the depression of the night before, Mário's optimistic attitude today could be summarized in the phrases used a few days before by a friendly reporter, quoting him at the end of the positive story he had written:

In spite of many remaining problems in the Flatlands, there is tremendous potential for improvement if we harness our resources and provide an opportunity for people to pull themselves out of poverty. I am finally finding what I, as an immigrant, came to this country looking for: the American dream, in the form of the grassroots movement, now afoot, to remove the social and economic injustices that originate and perpetuate poverty just as much here as in my own country. This gives me hope that, led by the United States, the whole world may still learn to share the earth's resources and return to environmental sanity.

The bishop received him in his official robes in a room overlooking the city, but there were no initial niceties—not even a handshake. He went around behind his desk and said, "Mr. Garcia, have you altogether lost your faith?"

Mário was not cowed. He said, "That is very direct, Excellency! Let me be equally direct. My experience of the last few years, since I left one of your parishes where I worked for a time, has restored much of the faith I was beginning to lose while I was there."

"I was not referring to your faith in Marx and communism, more appropriate for those living on the other side of the Iron Curtain," the bishop stated sarcastically. "I was referring to your faith in our church—and the place that the churches in general occupy in this community and in this country. Your public utterances are often blasphemous! The time has come when, for the welfare of my own flock, I must condemn you and your fellow communists personally and publicly if you continue to promote your godless ideology. I called you here to warn you and to give you a chance to retreat and retract. I am talking to you not only in my name but also in the name of other civic leaders with whom I often meet."

Mário got up and said, "I appreciate the warning, but I have no intention of retracting a word of what I have said both publicly and privately regarding the plans I support to alleviate poverty in the neighborhood where I live. I don't care what you say about me, but I hope you do not malign the friends I live and work with. They are practicing the faith that you preach in your church by helping the least amongst us improve their existence. I wish you a good afternoon!"

As Mário made it to the door, the bishop said, "You don't understand, Mr. Garcia." His tone conveyed a certain sense of urgency. "Your actions are undermining business leaders, elected officials, and public organizations—who all strive to help and keep alive those residents of the Flatlands who are indigent, sick, and sometimes criminal. You are targeting those good people because of the way they live, for where they choose to live, and for where they spend their hard-earned money. Are you not aware that what you call the establishment is building up resistance against you and your new neighborhood corporation on all sides? Do you understand now why I was asked by some community leaders to convince you to retreat before this situation escalates into full-fledged social disorder? You and your collective members are perhaps the only ones who can roll back this insane movement—and you must! If you do not, I am here to tell you that there are those who will not hesitate to stop you—even if it means using force!"

Mário was still standing at the door. "I don't comprehend you, your complicity with the establishment, or your false accusations! I do not comprehend the hypocrisy of the Catholic Church's public statements promoting the Word of God, but in some of its private practices, doing very little to help those less fortunate. I do not understand either your government that also preaches equality and freedom but does little to help its people achieve it. My coworkers and I have simply come up with ideas to enable the residents of the Flatlands to help themselves, and we are halfway there. I have nothing more to say to you."

Mário drove home, perhaps for the first time feeling bitterness so deep that it came close to the boundaries of hatred. Right then, he was totally unable to see much good in the people who led the public and private institutions that claimed to be the saviors of the low-income or indigent residents of the Flatlands and the rest of the country.

It felt like the silent majority was back. It had unsuccessfully tried to put Richard Nixon in the presidency in order to silence the voices of those who were speaking out in favor of civil rights in the South and elsewhere. However, it seemed to be back again and turning its attention to those who were fighting the "war against poverty."

Not even the assassinations of President Kennedy, Dr. Martin Luther King Jr., and Senator Robert F. Kennedy could make the again vociferous silent majority pause to think that perhaps the established social order needed reform! That economic justice was a right!

For Mário, being a Flatlander wasn't going to be easy.

Often unaware of Mário's troubles, I was also living my life in Santa Cruz in the midst of growing difficulties and challenges.

As I mentioned before, after my father's assassination in 1963, I inherited the family's fortune and abruptly became a Latin American businessman. My life for the next five years became a merry-go-round of exhilarating and, at times, nerve-racking activity, with drastic impacts on so many people that I was often at a loss as to what I could and should do.

To help you understand my life during this period, I must share a few things about the realities of the city and the state where I lived.

My city, Santa Cruz, is also the preeminent capital of the Brazilian state of the same name. It is a typically beautiful Latin American city, still loaded with influences from the time of the Portuguese colonization. It is now a sprawling metropolis at the mouth of a wide canyon between coastal mountains, and it stretches inland for several miles.

Seen from my red-tiled, centuries-old mansion, built on a choice spot halfway to the mountaintop, my city is enchanting. Watching it painted in soft light and shadows in the evening; breathing deep the scented breezes sweeping up the mountainside; and observing the contrasts between the old city on the riverfront, the shining new skyscrapers extending out from it, and the mantle of luscious green around the mountainside is something I never get tired of. This has been the background for many an evening of complete relaxation and undisturbed quietude looking out from my marble terrace, protected on the backside by a traditional glass-picked rock wall against intruders.

Further inland from the city, zigzagging away from the deeper canyon, several beautiful narrower valleys run between the hills and connect to the immense fertile and mineral-rich highlands. It is through these valleys that the resources of our land have flowed into the city for centuries, and wherefrom, for the past several decades, the "sem terra" (landless people) have also come by the thousands, adding to the exponentially growing urban population. Unable to find an empty space within the city, these newcomers are progressively forced to climb up the mountainsides, where they live in sordid favelas, which you, dear reader, would describe as slums or ghettoes in America.

This teeming population had begun to occupy the hillsides in my direction, well beyond the municipal sewer and water lines, the paved streets, and the electrical services. Sometimes I began to wonder whether the tranquility of my terrace could be assured for long, and the memory of my father's assassination also became a nightmare to me.

Let me share with you now a very personal experience to help you understand the pressure I lived under. Imagine me, one evening, walking into my terrace alone and exhausted. I threw myself on the soft armchair, closed my eyes, and fell asleep.

But even asleep, I could not relax because a uniformed, athletic, bearded young man jumped over the wall onto the terrace, covered my mouth with one hand, and pressed his revolver to my ear with the other. I was paralyzed by fear. I stared at the man, and I saw determination and hatred in his eyes. I felt power in his grip as he spat on my face.

"Get up and stand against that wall, you spineless gringo lover. Do not think about shouting for help unless you want to die! You and I are going to transact some important business." He cocked his gun as he let go of me, completely certain I would obey him. Then he put his finger carefully on the trigger, pointed the revolver steadily at my heart, and sat down.

"Relax! I come here today for your money and not for your life. My fellow guerrillas and I wish to enter into a partnership with you. We want to clean this country of idle parasites like you and return its resources and its government to the people to whom they belong. We cannot do this without money to buy what we need to live on and fight with. So, what we want you to do is use your cleverness and your fortune, as you always have, to make money from your gringo friends and then pass some of it on to us regularly. It won't be so bad, at least for a time, because we will end up buying bread and guns from your corrupt friends and give them back some of their dirty money again. Not a bad plan! You agree? And at least, for a while, everyone will be happy … and alive!"

"But I can't … no … listen, let's both talk … I am sure you will find me in sympathy with many of your just demands … and I am willing to …"

"Fine! I will tell you another way for you to start exercising your sympathy. Tell your gringo friends up north to stop sending our dictators their old planes, their guns and ammunition, and their dirty self-multiplying investment dollars. That will reduce our guerrilla costs by half and improve our immediate chances of success by 80 percent. Until you do that successfully, you will just have to pay us according to our contract. You keep us fighting, and we will keep you alive. If you don't accept our generous offer, we will consider that you are of no further value to us and to the coming generation, and we will see to it that you join your God-fearing, Christian, capitalist, parasitic forefathers in the bliss of their Christian heaven."

This man was dead serious. I realized in fear, recalling that my father had to buy his safety from political ambushes and blackmail with large portions of his fortune and was shot dead when he refused.

"But won't you hear my side? I—"

"Listen, you spineless capitalist puppet. I am not here to argue with you. There is only one good thing you and the likes of you can do before your day is over: you can pay us, willingly or by force, to rid the country of the mess you and your ancestors have created for us all." He stuck his gun under my chin, grabbed me by the collar, and said slowly, "Thirty million *reais* this first time. Meet us after sunset, at the cemetery, behind your father's chapel. You come alone, as if you were paying the old man a visit. If you tell the authorities, we will know—and your life will be over. From now on, we will have you covered from all sides, everywhere. You will be perfectly safe, as long as you do what we tell you."

He made me repeat his directions, and then he almost begged, as if he really cared for my safety. "André, don't fool yourself. We are dead serious!"

The use of my name made me recognize my assailant. The young man grabbing me by the collar was none other than Antonio Torres, the wiry little orphan of one of my father's miners who died because of the poison that went into his lungs while working in our mines to make my father rich. He was the little guy I used to love to take for a spin on my motorcycle when I was at Minas, just for the pleasure of seeing his enjoyment of it.

I said, "Antonio, I knew you as a child, and you liked me then! Do you really hate me that much now?"

"No, André. I do not hate you! The happiest and the saddest day of my life was the day I shot your father. The happiest because I was striking my first blow for justice. The saddest because it was your father I had to kill!"

In those few seconds, I realized how my father—and all those who caused men like Antonio's father to work themselves into an early grave in order to satisfy their greed—sowed the seeds of revolution right around them. I was facing the inevitable consequences of the sins of my father as well as my own because I now was the one prolonging the same system of oppression.

António removed his gun from under my chin and played with the trigger for a second. Then he let go of me and disappeared as quickly as he had arrived.

And that's when I woke up looking at the ceiling in panic. Now you know how sometimes my life became a nightmare. And what surprised me most was that my brain, even asleep, could understand so well the mind and the motivations of the guerillas.

Fortunately, this time, the ceiling I woke up looking into wasn't in my vulnerable terrace or even in Santa Cruz. Indeed, I was very safe and well installed in the fifteenth floor of the Hilton Hotel in Santiago, California.

Yet my nightmare forced me to confront once more the thoughts and emotions that I had tried so hard to ignore since my father's violent death. It made me realize that, like my father, I now lived in fear for my life.

My life! I had come from hating the luxurious monotony of my life in my early teens, to feeling challenged by it in my college days in Atlantica, to falling into selfish love with its pleasures in my university days in Santiago. I had reached a new crossroads, and I needed to make hard choices. I could continue to live a life of material luxury, constantly worried about my personal safety while perpetuating an unjust and corrupt system, or I could use my wealth to try to reduce the world's miseries as my good friend, Mário Garcia, and I once dreamed about in our school days in Atlantica.

In my better days, back then, I imagined my privileged life as the boosting power that could send me—and many of the people of my country—into a better world, humanized and just, where our rich land was revered and shared in dignity and brotherhood.

Though these wonderful thoughts about the magic possibilities open to a privileged person like me still had a hold of my mind, the harsh truth was that my life had become no more than the fuel of another replaceable human vehicle, carrying an attaché case full of papers for an international economic conglomerate, designed to take as much of our rich land as possible out of the reach of my fellow countrymen and my own.

Indeed, that is what I was doing in Santiago. I had been summoned to render my regular reports to Fred Gilmore on the status of the iron ore-mining operation that he and his investors financed in my land for enormous profits.

I was determined, however, to take my first opportunity to visit Mário Garcia, whom unfortunately I had managed to see very seldom in the last few years. So, as early as I could, I got into a taxi and gave the driver Mário's address in the Flatlands.

"You sure picked a lousy neighborhood to visit, mister!" The taxi driver started whistling some flat tune. When we got to the block, he stopped his whistling and said, "You could have saved yourself a fare, mister, if you had told me what you were looking for. I could have told you that the joint was burned down to the ground last week."

"It was what?"

"You don't have to believe me, mister. Take a look!"

And there it was. The Flatlands Workers' Collective residence and the two old houses next door, home to the new neighborhood corporation and its credit union, were all reduced to a gutted heap of rubble.

When I finally found Mário at a friend's crowded apartment, he was unrecognizable. He stared at me vaguely after we embraced emotionally, both of us unable to speak. For the first time, I saw in Mário the look of a man who desperately needed help.

I could easily have broken into tears were it not for the presence of his friends and the fear that I might increase his distress. Mário was beyond crying. I could see rage and bitterness in his face such as I never thought possible to exist in one of the best human beings I ever knew.

Finally, in a sad monotone, he said, "The bastards first threatened us, and then they did it! They really burned our house down to the ground. They came damn near burning Rebeca Williams down with it. She is still in the hospital. All the dreams we were building, all the hope we had brought here, all gone in a cloud of smoke.

"It took the firemen half an hour to travel fifteen blocks, because, according to the fire chief, they 'were given the wrong directions!' Everyone knows it was because we were proposing to discuss, at the neighborhood council level, whether all firemen and other public servants working in this area should be residents. Of course, they claim their delay had nothing to do with that.

"A few days before, the cops arrested Tony Santos for disturbing the peace, when all he was doing was conducting a corporation-sponsored workshop for teenagers in the park, and he refused to leave when they asked him to without providing any reason.

"The next day, I was stopped and searched on the street, and I was found in the possession of drugs, which they found exactly in the pocket where the cop searching me planted them. It didn't matter that I never touch the stuff. It won't matter to the Immigration Department to whom my infraction was immediately reported, according to an anonymous call I received later. Now the Immigration Department must be considering declaring me an 'undesirable alien' any day and deporting me! Prior to all this, I had also received death threats over the phone! As you can see, André, I am a mess. I need help. It would be suicidal to go on, and it would just bring about more distress to those around me. How did I come, André, to believe so naively in the essential, down-deep goodness of all human beings? Right now, I am full of contempt against the people who did this to us. What is worse: I feel hatred burning me inside, and I can't let go of it because if I return to my usual naivete, I will make myself an even easier target for those bastards! What do I do, André?"

"My friend, give yourself time! Most human beings are not this perverted. You'll find a way to turn it all around yet, and I am here to help. Come with me! We have a lot to talk about."

Eventually, Mário relaxed after we had sipped a couple of martinis at the bar of the Hilton. Some color came back to his pale and emaciated face, and the deep, dark circles around his eyes, caused by lack of sleep, seemed to lessen. But he still sat there disheartened and quiet as if there was nothing in his mind worth the effort to say it.

~

As we sat there wordless, my partner, Fred Gilmore, walked into the bar. He made it a habit to wine and dine me during my business trips, as if to make me more pliable to his business schemes. Gilmore had never met Mário. You may recall that it was at my request, many years ago, that Gilmore helped get him accepted to San Antonio's College, so that he could come to the United States on a student visa. All it took was a call to his buddy, the San Antonio College president!

Gilmore ignored Mário as he handed me the usual packet of tickets for the best sporting events, theater, and clubs in town, and three postcard-sized autographed pictures, with names and telephones on the back, so that I could visually select my preferred escort for the night.

Gilmore's personality and manners disturbed me even before we hassled over mine output projections for the coming year, my percentage of the anticipated profits, the settling of past accounts, additional capital investments needed, and many other hard negotiations. Once again, I began to feel pressured, colonized, used, and abused by this smiling, quick-talking, bulky man sitting down uninvited at my table as if he owned both the table and me, while overlooking altogether the friend sitting next to me.

Gilmore was the quintessential ugly American. He did to me personally what the United States in general was accused of doing to

Latin America: he controlled through investment and cunning, he collected dividends, he bought cheap and sold dear, he overreached his boundaries, and when it suited him, he dictated the way things were to be done.

He was in his early fifties, a tall man who bragged about lots of things, especially about his Catholic college football career. Regrettably, it had not instilled any of the qualities of good sportsmanship or fair play in him. His hair was now gray and thin on the top, his hairline receding, his once flat stomach now hung over his large belt, adding bulk to his massive structure. His shoulders were still big, and despite his tendency to hunch his back, he still stood up to over six feet tall.

Gilmore was a man who enjoyed talking, or rather pontificating, which he normally did unchallenged, due to his controlling posture and attitude within all his circles of activity. Often, I had been the quiet audience of his unending platitudes. He liked to talk especially about the ills of the world—as if he were the top authority on how to fix them. He behaved as if he knew it all!

With his personally constructed sense of Anglo-Saxon superiority, his status as a successful businessman, and the millions he had amassed by exploiting the natural resources that my family and others like us had made available to him, Gilmore always appeared overpowering to me, and my resentment was reaching the level of unqualified hatred.

So, this time, I decided not to accept the "pleasure pack" he was handing me. I returned it to him with assertive pleasure and said with contrived politeness, "I appreciate your thought, Fred, but I won't have time for playing around during this trip. I need to be in shape to compete with all those vultures sitting in your office, ready to devour me. This time, I'll just limit myself to a few relaxing walks in the park."

"Well, you sure don't take after your father. As for your walks in the park, leave your wallet in your hotel room and be careful. Our beautiful park is now full of lazy bums from the housing project and the Flatlands, and it is no longer safe for the likes of us. I wish people like that would stay in their place!

"Where is their place, Mr. Gilmore?" Mário asked quietly, but his tone was bordering on menacing.

"Oh, don't misunderstand me. I am not a racist or anything like that. I just think that the park should be enjoyed by the people who contribute to it through the taxes they pay and not by a handful of lazy bums who draw on the charity of others for everything and don't work like the rest of us. If a man wants to work, he can have everything in this country—but he can't have it served to him on a silver platter, like these scumbags want it."

Both Mário and I remained silent.

Gilmore saw condemnation, which enraged him, and it made him go on to say even viler things about minorities who live on welfare and "infest" public spaces like the park, making it unpleasant for people like him to enjoy.

Mário had begun to gulp another martini, as if he had a fire to quench inside of him. He began to shake his head and mumbled to himself, "I don't believe it! I just don't believe it!"

"You have something to say, young man?" asked Gilmore.

"I said you are unbelievable!" Then he turned to me and said, "I hate to do this to your business associate, André, but I cannot leave the barbarities he just said unanswered! Not tonight! Not now!" He turned back to Gilmore with fire in his eyes. "You are either a damned bigot or else you are just plain ignorant: probably both! It's not a handful of minority problem makers but thirty million Americans of all colors, many of whom are white, caught in a cycle of hunger, poverty, poor health, and unemployment, which you ought to worry about. Tens of thousands of people are living in ghettoes without any access to any share of the resources in this most powerful and wealthy country—resources owned and abused by people like you for merely your own profit with absolutely no concern for the human and environmental toll it takes. There are people in this wealthiest of all nations who are homeless, hungry, sick, and destitute through no fault of their own. There are others working two or even three jobs, but they cannot afford the most basic necessities for their families. The laws of this country protect the rights of private property owners, but they do not protect the economic rights of those who have no access to any of the means to acquire the most basic of human needs, including food, shelter, health care, and education. That, sir, is your main problem: lack of any understanding of what those who weren't born with your advantages have to face every day. Yet, you are ready to punish those who do not work without any concern for why they aren't working."

Gilmore said, "This land is, and has always been, the land of freedom and opportunity for those who are willing to work!" He separated each word as if no more needed to be said.

"Freedom? Let's consider how the Native inhabitants of this land feel about your concept of freedom," Mário responded. "Your forefathers arrived here many thousands of years after they did, but they forced them into reservations after killing millions of them and taking away the very best of the land they had always lived on. After that, many of your white ancestors enslaved other newcomers to cultivate the land and make it productive. Anyone who was not able to acquire land or was not competitive or strong enough to work was pushed out into the small spaces between the fences dividing the personal economic empires of a few. And now, true to tradition, you want to throw the poor out of a public park, the only patch of grass they can sit on without trespassing on private property!"

I had never seen Mário out of control like this; the martinis may have been a factor, but after all he had been through in the past few weeks, I understood why.

Gilmore turned to me and said sarcastically, "I don't know where your friend is from, but there are a few things I need to teach him, don't you think?" He turned to Mário. "My friend, you need to learn a lot about the spirit of American capitalism and free enterprise: the two ingredients that have made America the greatest nation on the face of the earth. When you do, maybe you will quit generalizing and begin to make some sense!"

Mário became enraged. "Yes, indeed, let's quit generalizing right now and become very specific! Just give me time. Look outside, sir! Look at what your uncontrolled free enterprise system has done to it all. Look at your air-polluted surroundings! Free enterprise has devastated much of your country and half of the world to acquire the resources you burn and overuse each day. The United States alone—now, in 1969—causes 60 percent of the pollution that now engulfs the planet. Each American now produces as much pollution as thirty-five people anywhere else on earth! If you could contain all the pollution you produce inside your borders, you would probably have already all died from suffocation. Is that specific enough, sir? Your 'success' would have already killed you, but you won't learn! You keep warming the earth at an unsustainable rate, aging it faster than it otherwise would, and bringing it closer to ecological disaster for all of humanity. Despite all the patent-protected and profitable new technologies being created, Americans are becoming more and more prone to coronary disease and lung cancer, but your free enterprise system allows corporations to promote smoking to the young and old regardless of its impact on public health. This free laissez-faire system and its near-immoral consumer brainwashing is well on its way to destroying this country and, unfortunately, much of the earth with it."

By then, Gilmore had drunk a few too many martinis, and he had no energy to respond to Mário, who had much more to say.

"Your political and business leaders generally profess to believe that by Manifest Destiny, America's place is above all the rest. But they callously overlook those who, through no fault of their own, are too poor, too sick, too old, or too unlucky to play in this harsh and unforgiving arena of the superior American way of life. To make it even worse, Americans like you think of them as losers! That, sir, shows an intolerable and sickening sense of indifference for the poor of this world!"

Gilmore was apoplectic by the end of Mário's tirade. He was practically frothing at the mouth, and he said, "Your statements are an affront to the democratic spirit and the values we inherited from our founding fathers. God ought to strike you for your ingratitude to those who have welcomed you to their land. You are just a mad dog biting the hand that feeds you!"

"That's more the hand that burnt my house down and almost killed one of my housemates! The same hand that would snuff out my human spirit if it could."

"What spirit?" Gilmore shouted, causing several heads in the hotel bar to turn toward us. He was fiery eyed. "Your spirit is sick or dead! You must have lost your religion, if you ever had one. America can only be understood on a background of spiritual values, which you obviously haven't got."

"Bravo! Finally, you and I agree. Religion! Organized, institutionalized religion is right at the core of the American system.

Judeo-Christian religion, to be precise! It legitimizes it, baptizes it, and, as one should expect, lives off of it. It is this religion and the establishment together that lay the heavy burdens of economic injustice on the backs of the poor, but, unlike Jesus and the true prophets of all religions, they are not willing to move a finger to change the current unjust economic and social conditions that hang upon them. This American religion you speak of, sir, is more concerned with preserving intact the privileges it shares with the establishment, along with the phony mottoes, written on your monuments and on dollar bills, such as 'One nation under God' and 'In God we trust.' Yes, sir! I agree! In America, membership in a church is one of the most acceptable ways to swear allegiance to the economic and political establishment. And it is indeed men like you, church-blessed and self-justified men before God, who have been the most destructive, as much in this country as abroad. From the beginning, it has been your kind of God-fearing, self-enterprising men who have destroyed many of the earth-loving native cultures of this world. It was religious men like you who, indifferent to the trail of devastation left behind, traded slaves for profit in Africa and often baptized them before they forced them to produce the yet more profitable sugar and cotton that they loaded into the same slave ships on the return trips to Europe. What outrages me most today is that men like you continue to use Jesus's message to justify their selfish interests and call it religion!"

Gilmore seemed to have lost his ability to speak. His brains must have been rather fogged up, judging from his glassy stare. He tried to focus on Mário. It looked like he was trying to recognize him. "Be quiet! Be quiet! You, insolent and faithless bastard! Who are you anyway to dare speak so much rubbish?"

"My name is Mário Garcia. I thought, erroneously, that after you cooperated so religiously to help me enter San Antonio's College, years ago, you might still remember my name."

"Oh yes! Now I know who you are! No wonder even the bishop is against you! No wonder they have burnt down your communist lair. It's too bad they didn't burn you down with it!"

The bartender came over to the table and asked Gilmore to lower his voice.

Gilmore threw his glass into the fireplace and left without another word.

After a cup of coffee, Mário looked calmer and more at peace with himself. I walked him to my room upstairs and told him to use one of the beds in the room.

I lay down on the other and tried to calm the turmoil inside my head. I realized then that in the four years that I had spent in America, I had been oblivious to a large part of America and that only tonight I had come to see it clearly.

Back then, I had swallowed all the standard, mainstream theories about the "greatness" of the American way of life, as lived at the university and all around me. Indeed, I was there to absorb and replicate the image of America in my country.

But I did not realize so poignantly that the system of capitalism and free enterprise, embraced by most Americans and supported by all their public and private institutions, was not designed to lift the powerless and disinherited out of their poverty. It was built on their backs and their fair share of the earth to the benefit of the wealthy and powerful!

Moreover, I was also groomed to be used mercilessly by this greedy capitalist system to facilitate in my poor country the cheap acquisition of the raw materials needed to satisfy the insatiable consumerist appetites of well-to-do, wasteful Americans.

And the scheme worked on me, didn't it? That's what I was here in Santiago to do once again!

I eventually fell asleep, but not before asking myself a question many times: How can I, in good conscience, continue to participate in this unbearable cycle of exploitation and injustice?

The next day, after a giant Sunday brunch, Mário and I headed from the hotel toward the Windmill Park, which extended for more than a mile down to the sea.

As we entered, the sight of lush vegetation, the smells and sights of summer, enhanced by the bright midday sun and the breezes playing on each branch and blossom, made it all shimmer and come alive. It felt like we had entered a different world.

Both of us began to relax as we observed the variety of people enjoying their surroundings with their pets. The soft sound of a distant drumbeat reached us. It was not unlike the sometimes festive rhythms of the favelas of my country. Several athletic, talkative, young black couples followed the drum call beyond the woods, while confirming to each other their mutual approval of the beat.

"That's real stuff, man! Let's check it out, man!"

"Yeah! It's boss! Listen to that! It swings, man! Let's go!"

These rhythms in the meadow were reflective of the new spirit of self-esteem, especially among Afro-Americans who were now asserting their own identity as black men and women. Through leaders like Adam Clayton Powell, and more recently Malcolm X, Huey Newton, and his Black Panther Party, they came to believe they were Afro-Americans by right, and they affirmed it with pride. Could it be that these assertive young blacks would soon be to the Gilmores of

America what the guerrillas of my country had become to me and the other "owners" of Latin America?

As I walked beside a quiet but apparently relaxed Mário, I noticed children flying kites, and I nostalgically recalled the freedom of my young years, the freedom to run in the wind, to fly a kite and roll on the grass. I envied the grown-ups who were doing just that along with the children.

At the end of another open meadow, perhaps one hundred young men and women were engaged in various forms of conversation and intimacy with their friends. The kaleidoscopic colors and shapes of their clothes allowed them to blend in perfectly with their surroundings.

A woman, in her early twenties or so, was dancing away to the strumming of her boyfriend's guitar while holding her baby. She was graceful and lithe, a piece of flowery and nearly transparent cloth wrapped around her waist and hung over her shapely legs. Her top half was covered only by abundant blonde hair through which her breasts took turns peeking out at the crowd.

This young woman represented well the young people that throughout the United States were referred to as flower children. They were dancing to the new rhythms of the sixties, and they were challenging all the political, social, and cultural norms that the likes of Gilmore held so dear. They were rebellious, defiant, and unwilling to accept the status quo when it came to poverty, racism, war, and all the other negative effects of the policies that the establishment imposed on their country and the planet.

I felt this new spirit of the sixties permeating me too. I felt good and invigorated by it. Maybe there was still reason to hope for a changed world after all. I wanted to surrender to this new hope that was embraced by what came to be known as the hippie movement.

Mário and I strolled on without much conversation; I think we were both realizing that we were each at a crossroads and that the decisions we were going to make regarding what to do next were going to have profound and long-term effects on our lives.

When we got to the beach, Mário took off his shoes and stepped out into the surf. He played with his hand in the water as if performing a magical ritual, and then he looked at the horizon for a long time as if he could see past it. It was as if he was trying to send a hug to Monica through the oceans embracing all the lands of this world, including Atlantica.

Much had changed in Atlantica, but not much had changed in Portugal. The country was still under the dictatorship of António Salazar and was at the peak of its colonial wars in Africa and the Indian subcontinent. Within the borders of Portugal, the last surviving European colonial power, the state police suppressed any sign of political or social opposition to the government. Mário realized that, if he was to be deported back to his country, he would either be conscripted to fight unjust wars or, if he resisted, he would be jailed for treason and/or sedition.

When he finally came out of his stupor, I put my arm around his shoulder and said, "Mário, let us go home!"

"Home?" he asked distractedly. "Where is that?"

"Home is where I live! Home is in Santa Cruz. My home will now be your home!"

Mário looked me straight on for a minute with a mysterious glow in his eyes. "I think you really mean it! You know I'd make a lousy miner, and being around you, I am likely to get you into trouble with your friends because of my strong views."

"I don't need you as a miner! As it is, I have got too many!" I laughed. "However, it would not be such a bad thing for my friends in Santa Cruz to hear some of your views on a variety of subjects. Think about it!"

Mário and I walked away from the quiet and peace of the park into the hubbub of the packed sidewalks.

It was clear to me that, given what had happened, it was no longer possible for Mário to continue to live in America. The dream of a land of freedom, equality, justice, fairness, and basic human dignity for everyone had turned out to be an illusion. It was equally clear that he couldn't return to Portugal.

Indeed, the only practical alternative was for him to come to Santa Cruz with me.

So, later that day, when Mário and I sat down for dinner, I asked him again, "Mário, will you come to Santa Cruz with me?"

"How could I not go? By now, I must be officially an 'undesirable alien' in this country. As much as I would like to stay and continue to sing 'We shall overcome!' with all the good persons in this country who are trying to change it, I know I will eventually be forced to leave. Anyway, what I sought here is not yet available to be duplicated in our countries as I naively dreamed. Maybe it will in thirty years! After unrestrained capitalism finally burns itself and the world's resources into the ground, and if some of the nonconformists we saw in the park today manage to survive, maybe a new America will rise from the environmental and social catastrophe that now seems inevitable.

"At that point, I hope to be able to return to a new nation where some economic and environmental sanity is restored, where the color of the skin of fellow citizens doesn't determine the course of their lives, and where poverty doesn't condemn someone to choose between eating or being warm in the winter or between getting medical care or giving a child a good education. For right now,

André, I accept your generous offer! I can't think of a better place to go than to your home, and in your company, my brother! If you will have me!"

"You know I will!" I felt relieved from some of my fears for Mário— and for myself. I knew, from experience, that together we could each be strong enough to overcome our current problems.

6 LATIN AMERICA

We

had decided to go south, but before we could leave, Mário and I still had several very difficult things to do.

For the next week, I had to get through arduous meetings with Gilmore and his bespectacled accountants in Santiago. He seemed to have conveniently forgotten the painful encounter with Mário at the hotel bar, but he was true to his usual self. He acted like a bulldog with every aspect of our business negotiations, biting into every issue and holding on to it with such ferocity that you eventually gave in. When it finally was over, I was ready and anxious to go home.

A couple of days later, Mário was ready too. He had faced no legal problems leaving America or obtaining a visa to enter Brazil. The painful part of his departure was leaving his friends at the collective; they had become his family. I could see from the look on his face how hard the goodbyes had been.

Finally, we boarded the Varig flight that would take us first to a stop at San José, Costa Rica, on our way to Brazil.

In normal circumstances, for Mário, who always loved flying, this opportunity to be in the air over Latin America would be an exhilarating experience. He would be super excited, anticipating the breathtaking views of ancient Aztec and Mayan territories where large populations have now built modern Mexico and the new countries of Central America, studded with large metropolitan areas, and linked through land and water the Atlantic and the Pacific Oceans. He would have anticipated his adrenaline-charged sensations over the Andean Mountains and the immense Amazonian basin, but today his emotions seemed to have been drained out of him. He was exhausted, and he fell asleep soon after we got into the plane.

As I sat beside him, I became increasingly concerned about his future, especially given his state of mind due to recent events and the crude realities he would have to face when he landed on Latin American soil.

Let me tell you about some of the crude realities of Latin America, the ones Mário already knew and more importantly, those he didn't know yet. Despite our long-lasting friendship and his work for years with Mexican immigrants in the United States, Mário certainly wasn't fully aware of the great cultural divide between the two Americas.

After he had secured his permanent residency status in the United States, Mário could travel in and out of Mexico without a visa, and he had once spent a three-week vacation in the city of Mexicali on the border. He lived in the heart of a shantytown of around fifty thousand floating residents, much of it built out of irregular pieces of wood and cardboard boxes made into shacks, which were originally meant to provide temporary shelter. Many of them, however, had been converted through additional layers of plastic into permanent housing for a succession of floating residents. In fact, there was a constant interchange of persons in this shantytown, most of them arriving from other parts of Mexico and from countries farther south.

Practically all the new arrivals were waiting for a chance to get into the United States and make their way into an agricultural bracero camp somewhere. A good number of them came back to Mexicali after having been picked out of the bracero streams by the authorities in the United States and later dropped over the border. They were waiting for another chance to get back in—or else they were penniless and had no means to go any farther. Some of the more permanent residents included mothers with children, waiting for husbands whom they hadn't heard from in a long time, and some elderly who simply didn't have the strength to go anywhere else. They all had physical misery, very little money, and never enough for food. An army of inter- mediaries promised them opportunities to sneak back into the United States. Mário had not seen such distress and despair in the Flatlands or even in Atlantica's Vila Miséria slum. This was his first glimpse of the vast socioeconomic problems of Latin America.

In contrast, the following year, Mário went farther south into Baja California, Mexico, to participate in a harvest festival with some Mexican friends. There, he was able to observe, firsthand, life in an ejido, a characteristic planned community initiated through government-sponsored land reform. Here, economic security and social services were provided to a significant number of families, who clustered their houses around their school and the health services center, not the traditional community church. The climax of their community life was the harvest festival, which celebrated the positive achievements of the year. There was happiness here!

Mário was so impressed with the contrast between these two Mexican communities we had just flown over, which were sepa- rated by less than one hundred miles, that he decided he had to try to understand the reasons for these different outcomes. He made plans to spend some time at the Intercultural Documentation Center (CIDOC), in Cuernavaca, Mexico, which was ostensibly a language and research center for social service volunteers, missionaries, and other well-intentioned persons who wanted to help in the developing world.

CIDOC had been established by Ivan Illich, a controversial man who was of the opinion that the social service volunteers and missionaries going to Latin America in the 1960s ran the risk of doing more harm than good there, walking in step, as they often did, with the greedy American investment capitalists. So, he aimed many of CIDOC's activities at convincing those who came south ready to apply Northern recipes to Latin American maladies, that it was as important as their volunteer work to stay home and help reshape the hearts and minds of Northern capitalist investors in questions of applied socio-economic justice before they came south. When potential volunteers couldn't be convinced to stay home and effect change there, CIDOC tried to help them understand Latin American languages and cultures better, particularly the causes of current guerrilla movements in several countries.

After his stay at CIDOC, Mário left Cuernavaca convinced that the best course of action for him was to return to the Flatlands and use his talent and energies to continue effecting change there. He was also convinced that the battle for social justice in both Atlantica and in Latin America was best fought by the people there rather than well-intentioned outsiders trying to do it for them.

But despite his efforts to understand the intricate economic and political realities of Latin America, Mário did not have the direct knowledge that people like me do. He hadn't yet experienced, on the ground, the vast systems of corruption in both the public and private sectors of Latin American countries. He did not know the history of foreign investment conglomerates that enriched themselves exponentially in Latin America with complete disregard for the welfare of the local countries and their citizens.

Historically, this foreign manipulation had gained strength at the turn of the twentieth century with the giant wave of British-led foreign investments. Later, and with still greater impacts, came the American "dollar diplomacy" of the 1940s. In recent years, American involvement became even more aggressive through the current government's aid programs, which were entirely subservient to laissez-faire capitalist interests.

It was through these recurring waves of foreign investment that the economic and political reality of the Latin America of the 1960s became what it is: a vast web of international investment networks controlling regional and national institutions so closely that they all became an inseparable and practically indestructible single structure, designed to identify and suck out all available resources.

A typical example of this is my own state of Santa Cruz, where Gilmore's investments and other conglomerates were firmly established. Directly or indirectly, they derived profits from everything they touched—from the machinery needed to extract natural resources for export to the building and operation of local infrastructure. These included the building, operation, and maintenance of railroads, roads, power grids, and factories and the buying and selling of the materials and equipment necessary for their business ventures.

In situations such as these, the government and all levels of the public sector are often so dependent and powerless that they are, for all practical purposes, controlled by the giant foreign corporate entities. In this context, government leaders are generally unable or unwilling to counter an investment conglomerate's corrupt and destructive practices because in many instances, those interests have also become their own.

Knowing Mário as well as I did, I knew there was no easy way to introduce this new level of socioeconomic injustice to him. I was worried.

As we flew over the Andes and the luscious Amazon rain forests, Mário began to look more like his usual self. It was as if he had finally found his way out of a dark tunnel and suddenly seen the light. He glued himself to the plane's window and peered down over the vast mountainous territory, which extended as far as the eye could see, crisscrossed by river canyons. He was awed by the hugeness of the territory and mesmerized by its beauty. His love for flying and the wide panoramic views combined to activate his emotions and his sentiment of joy. Apparently, he began to feel his soul stretching out again. He turned to me and said, "Thank you, André, for bringing me into your beautiful land! Here, a paradise is still possible. A land like this should be more than enough for all life forms—human, animal, and vegetable—to live in sustainable harmony forever.

"Thank God!" he said a bit later as we flew over a green carpet of the still unbroken Amazon forests. "The senseless pollution caused by the uncontrolled use of fossil fuels in North America does not appear to have affected this corner of the Amazon yet. Perhaps we can still stop the unsustainable and ultimately suicidal race of global investors to turn natural resources into short-term financial gains."

I smiled wanly because I could see in the far distance the rising smoke of our rain forest being cleared by burning in order to make room for export-oriented agriculture along the new Amazon highway, thus speeding up the destruction of this last healthy lung of our smoke-smothered planet. Worse yet: those financing that new highway would like nothing more than to wind it around the whole Amazon basin, opening it to even larger-scale exploitation of its remaining forests and its untapped mining subsoil in order to feed the insatiable global markets.

By the time we arrived in Santa Cruz, we were exhausted. We bypassed the city and wound our way up the mountain to where my home was located. From there, Mário observed—in awe—old Santa Cruz, which was built by the Portuguese in their best colonial style with the immense profits from the exportation of the abundant resources from the hinterland. He noticed how the old city had been surrounded by a huge modern metropolis, formed by a ring of modern buildings and residences, but what struck him most was how all the empty spaces between these newer buildings and the sides of the canyon were covered by favelas.

The next day, the ever-curious Mário found his way to public transportation and began to explore the entire city alone, sometimes quite aimlessly, in an effort to become familiar with this amazing concentration of humanity.

What he found was a city of contrasts, the likes of which he had not seen before. Mário went from the decaying colonial core into the newer and wider avenues, which run out of it like spokes in a wheel through the shinier ring of new constructions. From there on, the streets lost their size and their sense of direction until they fragmented into a maze of zigzagging, mostly unpaved, paths designed to give access to every inch of flat space that could be carved out on the lower mountainside. The shelters, built from all sorts of discarded materials, were the homes of destitute people of all sizes and descriptions. For Mário, the favelas bore no resemblance to even the worst of what he had seen in the Santiago Flatlands or in Atlantica's Vila Miséria. Here, the sheer misery and stench of the most desperate of human conditions were present everywhere, and the things that could elevate and give meaning to life were nowhere to be found.

Mário walked around as if he were sleepwalking. He automatically skirted around puddles; he avoided beggars because he had nothing left to give. At times, he stopped and stared at another miserable construction that passed for a home but was no more than pieces of cardboard and metal forming an enclosure. He bumped into people pushing into overcrowded buses, heading back into the city from their turnaround stops. He smelled the stench of open sewers and garbage piles everywhere. He was overwhelmed by the sheer numbers of people of every shade having in common only their extreme poverty. Obviously, the favelas here, in 1969, were not a point of passage to a dream of a better life on the northern side of the border, as the Mexicali shantytowns he had seen in Mexico in 1965. In Santa Cruz, the favelas were the only ground left for the have-nots between the land of the haves and the solid granite mountain.

How can there be such poverty and congestion in a country that is so land rich? Why are so many people moving into a city where they have to live like this? How and why does the leadership of a nation tolerate such destruction of nature and such misery and injustice for so many millions in order to secure monetary profit for a small number of landowners, industrialists, and corrupt politicians?

To save himself from this overwhelming feeling that was sucking him in a downward spiral into a murky pool of hopelessness, Mário thought, *In this dark situation, there is only one thing for me to do, and that isn't to curse the darkness! I must at least light one candle!* And that was the only perceptible message that Mário could still hear clearly from the deepest layers of his consciousness.

At that precise moment, he was approached by a man in his thirties. His face was drawn, his straight black hair was cut elliptically around his forehead and down to the back of his neck, and his face revealed a rich mixture of racial features from different continents. His pants reached down to his shins and were held up by two handwoven pieces of rope over a faded shirt. He clutched a straw hat, which he pressed to his chest as he stretched his right hand to Mário begging for a coin.

A younger woman hung onto his arm, her forlorn eyes piercing Mário's. Behind her, hanging on to each other's hands, three small children were each carrying a small bag containing perhaps all they had on this earth. Obviously, they were extremely poor and all of them looked like they were starving.

Mário stopped. Once again, he sunk his hands into his pockets, and this time, they came out empty. He was also empty of words. He was exhausted mentally and emotionally; tears ran down his face, and his arms suddenly reached forward and embraced the man as if he were a brother he had lost and did not expect to find again.

As I sat at the terrace that evening, I saw the six of them slowly walking up to my lower gate and went down to meet them.

Mário said, "This is Joao and Filomena Soares, and these here are Joãozinho, Pelé, and Rosalina."

The whole Soares family was frozen in position, standing close to Mário, who was apprehensive as to how I would react to these unexpected guests.

I waved them in. "Come on in. Dinner must be ready by now. If it isn't, we will cook it ourselves. The kitchen is this way." I wrapped my arm over Mário's shoulder to convey a clear message: "No explanations are needed, my friend!"

He smiled with relief and gratitude.

Over hot soup and sandwiches, which were consumed with unseemly haste, the Soares reluctantly and sparingly detailed the circumstances that had led them to Santa Cruz. They had been pushed out of the land where they had been squatters for the past several years. They rode produce trucks, walked, hitchhiked, and worked their way over the thousand miles of country that separated them from Santa Cruz, where they hoped to escape hunger, the drought, and the lack of means to grow food or find employment. They scavenged, bartered, and worked for food in an all-consuming effort to survive, which left no time or money to look for shelter of their own, steady work, clothing, or any other basic necessities. They had to beg for all those things daily, in small doses. If they had any luck at all so far, it was that they were still together as a family.

After they finished their meal, Filomena looked at Mário and me with an earnest look on her face. As she held on tightly to Joao's hand, she said, "Would you, sirs, for the love of God, help us poor sem terra find some work so that we can buy some food and maybe save a little money to help us go back home again?"

Mário looked at me because he knew that I was the one to answer that question.

I said, "But, Filomena, you have said that you have no home. You told us you were squatters, and the *fazendeiro* sent his guards to chase you off his land. Clearly, you traveled with three small children, over a thousand miles, to escape that life. What can you hope to gain by going back there again?"

"We will go to another fazenda at harvest time," said Joao. "Maybe another fazendeiro will hire us a few days and let us raise some food on a small piece of his land, as we did before. Maybe the drought will not be as bad next year, and there may be some more work somewhere. We might even be able to find my father, if he is still alive, and he may have some friends who may help us with some food to make the children grow strong again."

Mário put his hand on Joao's shoulder. "There may be some friends here if you stay a while. Someone here may be willing to help you and your family." As if to give strength to his argument, he sat on his heels two steps from little Rosalina and smiled at her intensely until she smiled back at him shyly, initially trying to hide behind her mother's skirt. Then, slowly she came forward and stood in front of

Mário, letting him take her hands in his. She made no effort to get away and giggled a little, proving she was still a real child.

The rest of us were staring at them.

Mário gently looked into her eyes and said, "Rosalina, I am very sad and lonely today, and I need a friend. Will you stay and be my friend?"

Rosalina giggled again, raised her little arms, wrapped them around Mário's neck, and kissed him repeatedly.

Mário and I let the Soares family rest, and we organized the room where they could spend the night. We were both impressed with the fact that, after a life of misery at the hands of a fazendeiro and after a failed effort to improve their lives in the city, the only hope still left in them was to go back to the earth and find a little corner of their own to put down some roots.

"I wish I could go back with them," said Mário. "Maybe going back to the earth is how I can also find the healing I so much need now, André!"

Mário and I talked through most of the night, and the conversation had a sense of direction. It pointed back to the earth.

As a result, the next day—to my own surprise and against my better judgment—Mário, Joao, and I negotiated a loan of two thousand dollars for the start-up expenses of moving back to the land, to be paid back by Joao and Mário in equal small amounts, starting one year later. In addition to the loan, I donated three acres of land to the Soares family and two to Mário, in a location of their choice on my Minas estate in the hinterlands of Santa Cruz. This had once been grazing land that had not been leased or utilized since my father had negotiated a joint venture for iron ore exploration with Gilmore. Next came the building of a railroad spur, through which thousands of tons of mineral had now been brought to shipment.

Days later, when we were rested and our negotiations were

complete, we all climbed into my jeep and drove away from the city. Once we had driven over the mountains, we advanced into the interior plain, which had been overgrazed in past generations. It had lost its native vegetation and now had a desertlike quality, made worse by years of drought that were frequent in this part of the country.

When we finally came to the area of Minas, we stayed for the night. The next day, we went into a range of hills surrounded by some clusters of trees, which were evidence that occasional rainwater had been collected near their roots by temporary streams, which though gone underground, still kept them green.

Mário became even more enthusiastic. He took the wheel from me and drove around every hillock and into every meadow and small valley, surveying the land to find the right location to build shelter and start growing some crops.

As we were driving around, the children giggled and played with each other like children do when they are particularly happy. Joao and Filomena had lost any resemblance to the two fearful, desperate people I had opened my gate to a few days earlier. They were excited beyond description as they began to realize that they had been singled out by fate to become owners of land and make friends with a rich fazendeiro and a man from an island they had never heard of, way across the sea, but a man who had shed tears when he could not help them with money and now was ready to be their friend, partner, and neighbor.

Mário stopped the jeep at the entrance of a wider valley, which was walled in by an exposed granite ridge on the south side and spreading its fertile-looking ground to the north from where the winter sun would shine, keeping it warmer for year-round crops. He scooped up a handful of dirt and let it run through his fingers, and it was obvious it felt good to him! He quickened his pace toward a grove of greener trees near the granite ridge; they were evidence of a nearby source of mineral-loaded water. From behind the trees, he shouted, "We have water!" He pointed to the rock face, a few meters above the ground, and we could see a wet strip all the way down to the ground.

"Let us go for a drink!" Mário waved at us to follow him.

On a ledge in the granite, six or eight feet above the ground, tiny puddles were continuously being refilled by the few drops dripping down the rock face.

Mário climbed to the ledge and stood up; he could see the whole valley from that perch. His eyes ran back and forth over the land, as if feeling all its bumps and caressing it, testing its moisture, and measuring its potential.

Perhaps he was feeling now what he felt when his father took him to what would become his *quintal* (a mini farm) in Atlantica at the age of eleven. They were there to pick a spot where he would start planting and caring for the trees whose fruits he would eat when he grew up. Obviously, Mário was feeling the pleasure of touching the earth again as he waved us to join him on the ledge. "I like it here," he said. "What do you think, Joao?"

Joao looked out upon the land as if it were sacred, and with his eyes brimming with tears, he said, "Yes! Yes! Yes!" He was overwhelmed with the idea that he finally had one small piece of the earth that would be his to cultivate, care for, and live on! After he showed his agreement to Mário, he turned toward me with an appreciation and love such as I had never seen so clearly stamped on a man's face before.

At that moment, I also knew that something altogether new was born inside of me. It was a sense of a new worth, conferred on me not by my peers, not by my governor or my president, or even by my foreign trade partners or by my church, but by a humble sem terra. I had just provided a key to a fellowman that gave him and his family the means to survive, perhaps even thrive. What Joao had given me was a special kind of fulfillment such as I had never experienced before. And then there was the sudden realization that I held in my hands, potentially, hundreds of such keys to a better life.

In order to appreciate the uniqueness of this occasion, you would need to observe—like Filomena, Joãozinho, Pelé and Rosalina did— what the three grown men did next. This pedigreed aristocrat, his friend Mário, and a landless squatter, first embraced each other as if they were brothers, and then arms wrapped shoulder to shoulder ran down into the open ground and raced back and forth on it several times. Then, joining their hands, they made a circle. They called Filomena and the three children into it, after which they started making music at the top of their lungs and danced around them to the evening sun, in front of a rocky cliff on the backside of Monte Queimado, near Minas, in the state of Santa Cruz.

The next few days were spent shopping for tools, cooking utensils, some pieces of canvas, dried fish and flour, beans and potatoes, and a variety of other necessities for the new pioneers, including a couple of live goats, rabbits, and chickens. The excitement of it all was indescribable for me, and it lasted well beyond the time Mário and the Soares family drove off to their new homestead in the jeep they had borrowed from me.

Approximately one month later, in the spring, I returned to Monte Queimado, and I was greeted as a most welcome friend. Rosalina took me by the hand immediately and led me to a bush where a mother canary was hatching her young. Mário and Joao, not unlike the children, were anxious to take their turn showing off their accomplishments to me.

They had not only excavated and protected the spring, but also built a covered two-meter water reservoir near the bottom of the granite rock face, which was now filled to the brim with drinking water. They diverted the overflow to irrigate the garden plot, which they were now busy preparing. Some plant seedlings were already beginning to pop through the freshly spaded ground, and Joao's skill as a vegetable grower was beginning to show in the way he prepared the furrows and planned to plant the various kinds of vegetables in an intricate companion gardening scheme, which he had learned from his father.

He was still acting as if he did not have more than one hundred square feet of ground to grow on instead of the three acres I had given him since he was used to being a landless squatter. This frugal arrangement worked well by concentrating the available compost and water and making the best of it, proving again it doesn't take much to change the life of a man from misery and hunger to a sustainable living.

Mário had left the farming to Joao; he had begun to gather stones and clear the place for their permanent houses. He had already dug a hole and built a small outhouse, which functioned has an ordinary outdoor bathroom, and he had built an outdoor kitchen next to the tents, which protected their things from the occasional rain and from the animals at night. He used all the subsistence skills he had learned from his family in San Lucas and the planning skills he had learned in his many community development ventures in Vila Miséria and the Flatlands.

Mário said, "Within one year, we plan to be self-sufficient in food and housing, and we will have repaid some of our debt to you."

"I will hold you to that, pal!" I replied as I left that peaceful place, which was beginning to gain identity and character through the stewardship of the persons who lived there. They were integrating themselves into it with thoughtful and imaginative action.

I have never been the typical outdoorsman, but when I was in Monte Queimado with my friends, even I felt a desire to work with my hands, to be exposed to the elements, and to feel one with nature. Those back-to-the-earth desires felt like seeds beginning to bud forth from the ground of my arid consciousness.

7 NOSSA TERRA

One

year went by quickly since Mário and the Soares had moved to Monte Queimado. During that time, my business activities intensified. I had to meet with Gilmore in Santiago a couple of times to discuss proposals to modernize and expand the mining operations on my lands.

Something about the plans just didn't feel right to me. I decided to visit the operations at Minas to have another look at the situation on the ground and think again about my options.

As I paced through the debris around the mine, listened to the noisy equipment, observed the miners in their routines, surveyed my surroundings, and discussed Gilmore's plans with some of my key people, I felt a growing sense of dissonance and confusion.

I was painfully aware that the hills that surrounded the mine were stripped of any vegetation. The lush green forests that had covered these hills had disappeared. In their place were artificial mounds of debris cut with bulldozer trails where not a blade of grass could survive. The air over the miners' village was permanently hazy with mine dust, which covered all the rooftops and remaining vegetation.

Standing there, I had no choice but to confront the dilemma before me. On one hand, the income from this mine was the source of my comfortable living. It also provided my government an enormous amount of revenue from export taxes, and it provided income to two hundred employees whose families were dependent on it for their survival.

On the other hand, I had to continue to allow the digging of wound-like holes into the land and depleting my country of valuable and finite resources to enrich myself, Gilmore, his investors, and a few corrupt politicians along the way. *Why should I increase production, thus more rapidly depleting my land of its natural resources, just for a fraction of Gilmore's profits? Why should I allow Gilmore to bring in more expensive and newer equipment and thus grant him more control over more of my resources and cater to his limitless greed? How could I justify this profit-motivated escalation when I knew that a more domestically directed national-development program could extend some of its benefits to millions of my impoverished fellow citizens?*

On the other hand, what would happen if I didn't accept Gilmore's proposal?

He said, "An opportunity we can't afford to lose will pass us by because the European countries are in need of mineral imports in larger quantities now, the mining consortia are ready to provide the capital necessary to exploit the full potential of the minerals buried in this land, and all the infrastructure of hydroelectric dams, roads, railway lines and harbors for large tankers have already been built with foreign aid funds.

"Now we can also become partners with and benefit from the mega-investors who are building gigantic ore-processing facilities including the new three hundred-mile pipeline that will carry the ore slurry to the coast for shipment. Additionally, André, your State of Santa Cruz and its people will also benefit from all this investment!"

"Certainly!" I could answer to the suddenly philanthropic Gilmore. "Santa Cruz and its people will benefit from all this generous investment: after the investors have recovered their loans and the exorbitant interest they charge for them; the foreign suppliers of the machinery needed for extracting the mineral have been paid their inflated equipment prices; the consultants at Goldman Sachs have been rewarded handsomely for their wisdom; and many of our corrupt politicians have pocketed their bribes. Then, if there is anything left, and only then, dear Gilmore, will the people of Santa Cruz get something from this host of foreign benefactors, who will make another generous offer: to sell to 'the Natives' the excess electricity from the conglomerate's central, which they built on our river with other countries' foreign aid."

And what would I get from Gilmore's generosity? I certainly would end up with a much bigger hole in the ground, I would be able to build a higher defensive wall around my house on the mountainside, and I would be ensuring I would live a privileged life like my ancestors and pass it on to my children until the end of our days.

On my return from the mine, Mário was waiting for me in Santa Cruz. He had come to visit and to pay his and Joao's second instalment on their loans. He looked healthy, happy, and relaxed. I could not help but envy him. As always, we talked far into the night.

This time, I found myself sharing Gilmore's latest proposals and how conflicted I was about them. Mário became visibly tense as he listened to me and realized how troubled I was.

"Mário, I need to take a fresh look at my problems. Help me figure out what I should do! I need to see my situation from all angles because if I don't watch out, I could soon be faced not with one Gilmore, but with an army of Gilmores. I value your opinion and your insights."

Mário leaned back on the sofa and looked at a fixed point on the ceiling. "André, we are brothers, and I know you respect my opinions. For this reason, I know my words may have serious consequences, but remember that they are born from my life's experiences and my personal mission. As you know, my beliefs on economic development matters are diametrically opposed to those of most economists, including Dr. Goldman, who kicked me out of his school of economics. Nonetheless, let's talk seriously about the economic issues deeply affecting you personally and your state.

"André, you know better than me that foreign investors do not come to Santa Cruz to help its people even when they are cooperating with the World Bank or the International Monetary Fund, supposedly to assist underdeveloped economies. If they really wanted to help your state and your country, they would be transferring their technical business know-how to you or your country in the most efficient way possible to enable you to be as successful as they are. In addition, they would provide investment capital that would not require you to give up control over your resources. In other words, they would empower you to become like them, and consequently, they would be doing business with you as an equal! Right? Instead of this, take a look at what happens! They demand that you adopt the rules of 'free trade,' which supersede and overrule the business laws in developing countries, like yours.

"As a consequence, the most powerful and cost-effective free traders, such as the giant, predominantly American and European, multinational companies, will have an automatic advantage right inside your country's borders from the start. Indeed, these companies expand their business's interests into your country, competing favorably from the start with your less-equipped and less-experienced local counterparts, which often go under, leaving a new market open for their increasingly exclusive free trade! The only way this is different from old colonialism is that old colonizers often had to risk their lives and fight hard for the lands and resources they stole from the Natives!

"André, I don't have to tell you that international free traders are here to serve their own for-profit interests first, to control the rich resources of your country, and to keep you poor and dependent. When that happens, for every dollar they invest in your poor country, they will reap exponentially growing revenues. These include your high interest payments on huge debts, profits from their growing new markets, increased control over globally scarce raw materials, and the exploitation of local cheap labor.

"In your case, André, you can be sure that Gilmore and his associates are simply trying to acquire the largest quantities of iron ore possible for the cheapest price possible so they can sell it for huge profits elsewhere. They are simply not trying to *help* you or your country!"

I said, "There is a lot about your understanding of international economics that is undeniable, but I cannot undo the past, and now I am entangled up to my neck with my government, which owns and operates at a loss, the railroad that was built on my ancestors' land at the public's expense, supposedly for the benefit of my family. To keep it running, the governor now needs to acquire, for a price, immense quantities of fresh investment from those you call 'neocolonial' investors. They offer to provide the financial backing needed because the operation of the railroad is essential for their profit-making enterprises here. Moreover, I am not alone in this predicament! All my fellow fazendeiros need this railroad to maintain their inheritance and lifestyle. You see, Mário, like my father, I have been selling my soul to the devil, and a badly calculated action on my part now can have serious economic, political, and social repercussions far beyond me and my own personal interests.

"Without the tax revenues that the state and the country earn from mining operations, the economy will come to a standstill—and we would risk causing an economic depression. If I interrupt this kind of international 'investment and trade' and encourage others to do the same, I will become the scapegoat who brought about the ruin of the state—and perhaps even the nation!"

"That's obvious to me also, André!" Mário said. "But this system in its current form keeps the lion's share of the money and power in the hands of external investors and profiteers, and that will keep your country poor forever. Why should you have to accept the onerous terms that these outside investors impose on you? Your country and its people would benefit much more if you chose to develop your industry at your own pace, apply more appropriate technology, and invest within your means in clusters where you have an advantage either to serve your own market or to export.

"It seems to me, André, that to truly develop your country and uplift your people, the government should be focusing on projects like land reform; small development initiatives that use appropriate technology and minimize environmental damage; small loans to local entrepreneurs that provide local employment and secure a sustainable future for themselves and their families. These kinds of development strategies would encourage the formation of local talent, promote innovation, and stimulate new business activity.

"Most importantly, any profits derived from these efforts would remain in the country—and not be siphoned to a bank in New York or London! It would most likely be reinvested in the local businesses and communities, providing improved housing, education, health care, and transportation. Don't you think that this is what the state of Santa Cruz needs to do?"

"Mário, I follow your reasoning, but I am afraid the forces that control the economic engines of the very interdependent global economy are unstoppable. Against these realities, you and I—and even countries like mine—are powerless."

Mário closed his eyes again in full concentration. "André, regardless of what your state can or will do, you and I are not powerless! At a minimum, we have the power to withdraw our voluntary participation in a corrupt global economic system. That's what Gandhi and the Indians did until the British Empire had to give up their monopolistic control of the cloth and salt trade, which allowed England to siphon out massive amounts of money from the poor in their colony. Thankfully, there are still parts of your country where resource-wasting consumerism has not fully taken hold yet. Your personal land patrimony, which is not near the mine, is a good example of this.

"There, you still have the opportunity to make sensible, sustainable decisions that won't destroy the environment and will allow people to live and work with some dignity. You have already seen it work! You gave me and the Soares family a small patch of land and a small loan, and within a year, we are thriving, using up very little of the resources of the earth, and using it in a way that doesn't destroy it and leave it barren. We eat well; we have stayed healthy and busy in daily contact with nature. We have sold and bartered the produce of our land to obtain other necessities, and we are beginning to repay your loan. This payment is small because our loan was small. Because our payments are small, we can make them without destroying or abusing our resources. Nothing but your goodwill and our natural wisdom launched us into our new and much more contented life.

"Imagine the impact it would have on this country if it decided to initiate a countrywide land reform designed to replicate our success with every poor and willing family now living in the favelas? Isn't this what you and I imagined together when we were at the San Luis College in Atlantica fifteen years ago?"

The next day, Mário left to return to his little patch of land and the simple, peaceful existence he enjoyed. There, he could live out his fantasy of combining the best humanistic learning of the ages with the more appropriate miracles of technology and science in order to heal the wounds of the industrial age and help create a better and more humane society, integrated in a more sustainable world.

As always, Mário's visit helped me.

He left me with a clear vision of alternatives and a challenge to be as true to myself as he was. He always managed to put before my eyes the best version of myself, not the businessman or the Latin American tycoon I saw when I looked in the mirror.

As I lay awake that night, I knew in my heart that, one day soon, I would have to choose between continuing to collaborate with Gilmore's exploitation and joining Mário in his quest to help create a human family of brothers and sisters with rights, sharing an economically just and ecologically sustainable earth.

Several months passed. The lucrative mining operations resulting from the partnership between Gilmore and myself continued to overrun my land in order to feed the multinational corporations' hunger for cheap iron ore. I continued to play my role to facilitate this enterprise, but I did so with increased reluctance as each day passed. I had managed to resist Gilmore's demands to expand production, but the pressure was taking a toll. I realized that I needed to take a break.

So, one day, still wondering what I should do about Gilmore's proposals, I rode out to Minas on the other side of the mountain, my jeep leaving a trail of dust behind me. Finally, I arrived at the village, as parched and dried up inside as the terrain I had just driven over.

Once again, I drove past the ramshackle cabins, where two hundred miners and their families lived. The cabins were built around the fazenda's store, which was where most of the salaries I paid them ended up in exchange for the food and a few other essentials they needed that were trucked in from the city.

The miners were trapped in this cycle of hard labor, paying high prices for poor-quality food and living in an environment that offered their children no opportunity other than eventually working in the mine themselves. I was perpetuating a system started by my ancestors that trapped these families in this barren place, and the sad part was that I also felt trapped.

To give my father his due, I recognized that he had been sensitive to some of the miners' human needs. He had built a school for the children and hired a teacher. He had also brought electrical power from the mine into the village and made some occasional improvements on the roads and houses. Compared with the squalor of many of the favelas around the city, Minas wasn't bad. Yet it was still a depressing place.

Nonetheless, as I drove through, I couldn't escape the sight of many underfed children. An unusually large number of frail men sitting in front of the cottages appeared to have aged prematurely. The dust in the mines had probably lodged in their lungs and brains and turned some of them into not much more than vegetables.

I felt depressed when I left the village and climbed up to the scrub brush-filled higher lands that had been a fertile pasture before it was mercilessly overgrazed under one of my grandfather's thoughtless schemes. As I descended into Monte Queimado Valley, the only green left was a row of deep-rooted trees, which wound their way down the center, showing the course of the creek, which had gone underground for the summer.

I zigzagged around it, for a long while, going north toward the green trees on the subirrigated mountain slopes that formed the beginning of the narrower canyon where the dry creek came from.

As I got closer, their houses became visible. They were clinging to the rocky cliff, as if growing out of it and facing the sun. I was seeing them complete for the first time. They were an environmentalist's dream, a masterpiece of simplicity.

To start with, they had picked and prepared the spot best suited for their houses, and they used the natural shapes and the materials of their land. These ingenious upstart builders had no habits of conventional construction or architectural training to prejudice them when they started their project. So, they were free to be creative and to analyze and respond to their essential shelter needs unimpaired. Nature, as always, was willing to cooperate with her friends, and they too welcomed her as a partner in their venture.

The rocky cliff facing the valley at the bottom of the mountain ended on a granite protrusion, windswept and rain washed, sticking out like a large boot resting flat on the valley's floor.

The boot's front end was nearly rectangular, six to eight feet high, and it extended for about forty feet on an almost straight line. To Mário and Joao, it looked like a ready-made back wall for their new homes. So, with the abundant pieces of granite, broken off from the surrounding mountainside over the ages, they built the front end of the granite boot to a leveled eight-foot wall. The large gutter behind it was designed to drain both the runoff that could come from the mountainside on the back and the water from the roof of the houses they were going to build in front of it.

With the back wall built, they leveled a fifteen-foot-by-forty-foot rectangle of ground in front of it to become the floor of their twin houses. Then they constructed the front wall at the front edge of the cleared area parallel to the granite back wall. This front wall had two separate entrance doors, each with a window at its side, and it was built tall enough to accommodate a row of small square windows running the full length of the houses above the doors. They were placed so that the low winter sun shining through them would hit the granite back wall and warm it up.

The roof, framed with long timbers cut on the nearby mountain, was built to drip into the gutter behind the back wall and to climb gently to a few feet beyond the front wall of the houses, a length calculated to shade the row of small windows over the doors from the hot summer sun.

To complete the structure, a solid interior wall divided the two houses. An end wall closed in each house, with side windows open to the outside to provide light to bedrooms and baths.

A common patio was cleared on front of the two houses, and it was already planted with flowers in full bloom. From both ends of the patio, paths ran around the corners of the houses into the tool sheds, which had also been built hugging both sides of the granite boot.

As I approached, the noise of my jeep's engine brought Mário running out of his door to embrace me. Joao stuck his shovel on the ground and rushed to meet me. His face still showed the same happiness I saw when I gave him and Mário the land. Filomena and the kids got in at the end of the noisy *abraços*, and I felt the welcome of a homecoming.

Although the hot summer sun was beating down on the valley, the houses were cool and comfortable inside, closer to the ground temperature of the granite back wall. Plentiful indirect light flooded the interior and enhanced everything from the simple wooden furniture to the structure of the chimneys built over the cooking stoves.

The roughness and naturalness of the walls were softened by

many colorful children's drawings and other artsy pieces carved by the adults in their spare time. They included a stunning piece of art, carved by Joao out of an ancient cedar root, hanging from a nearly invisible fishing string right outside his house's front window.

Everything about this living space was comfortable and inviting. It was truly nice to be here. Our conversation was about the small but satisfying accomplishments of these new settlers. That night, on the bed that Mário prepared for me, the quiet of my surroundings was so peaceful, and I slept better than I had in years.

The next morning, I got up at sunrise and walked to the spring for a drink. It was overflowing with a steady, small run of clear water into the gutter, which made it flow to the garden's network of pipes placed all over the ground so they would deliver a few waterdrops to the various points in the soil. A variety of leafy vegetables were growing freely toward the morning sun.

I was still thinking about how little one needs to be happy when I saw Mário sitting on the ledge above the spring.

"Good morning, André! Come on and join me!'

"Good morning, Mário!"

"You know, this perch reminds me of Miradouro—a vista back home in Atlantica, overlooking the beauty of San Lucas Valley. It was at that location that Padre José inspired me as a young person to think about my life's purpose. There, he encouraged me to contribute to make this world a better place and to help create a happier and just human family. If we think seriously about it, that's the only plausible reason why persons like us should have a headful of dreams of justice and happiness for all, along with the wisdom, know-how, and determination to figure out ways to accomplish such dreams.

"Today, André, I compare this perch to Miradouro because I have begun to dream again! From here, I can take a look around me and imagine myself helping to transform this valley into a beautiful living place for others like me."

"It's so good to see that you have become your old self again, Mário! I was worried that now that you had created your own little paradise here, you might have given up trying to change the world."

"This place has healed me, André! I no longer feel that it is futile optimism to continue to be an activist for social and economic justice, as I was inclined to do after the burning incident in the Santiago Flatlands. It is reenergizing to feel intense hope again! Instead of clinging to my good life here, I want to share it with those who are not as lucky as I am."

"That's the confident Mário I knew!"

"Yes, André, I feel upbeat again! Indeed, every time I look at this empty valley and I think of all the sem terra persons not far from here, I envision a world of possibilities! André, don't you see what I see from here?"

I laughed. "Mário, I do not have your vision or your imagination! My thoughts have all been wrapped around financial statements and projections for days in a row, in order to prepare for my next encounter with Gilmore, in California!"

"Relax, André! Forget Gilmore for a little while. Look at the beauty and the potential of the valley before us. Those green elms along the creek bed remind us that that there is running water by their roots. Many small springs just like the one running down this cliff are feeding that underground stream. Like the elms, we figured out a way to capture one of those springs and were able to grow healthier lives here and make our world better. André, don't you see how many opportunities such as ours there are just along this creek?"

"Mário, my mind is just as numb as my body! Come on! Just

tell me what is in your mind and quit trying to make me guess your visionary ideas."

"All right! That creek is to this whole valley what this spring is to our garden and our homes, André! With your help, and the help of any smart bank and a good government—the same kind of help you alone gave Joao and me—all your workers at the mine could become self-sufficient house builders and food growers on this valley, just like we have done.

"Within a couple of years, that creek could be dammed at the rock gate up there and capture all that wasted underground water, plus the rain overflow collected by the mountainsides. That would be enough to provide domestic and irrigation water all year round for hundreds of people. The whole valley down there could become a garden producing healthier food for all the people of Minas and perhaps many more!"

I sat quietly, with my elbows anchored on my knees, my head stuck between my hands, and my eyes staring at the bone-dry valley, trying to imagine it turning green.

"Mário, are you telling me to kiss the mine and Gilmore goodbye? The mine has been the miners' livelihood for decades as well as my family's ticket to our well-to-do traditional way of life. It has also been the source of untold riches to Gilmore's investors and the source of large amounts of taxes to my country!

"Next, you want me to come out here to this edge of nowhere and build a dam, sell or donate this land to the miners, so that they can build their homes and grow their own food here? You are a dreamer all right! To start with, the miners are not people of the earth the way you imagine them. They are not builders or farmers. They make their living by destroying the earth with picks and machines, and they probably hate it with a passion. If I quit paying them, they will all end up in favelas in the city as soon as they can get there with all their possessions in a little sack on their backs."

"André, one year ago, I would have agreed with you that the probability of the miners wanting to do what the Soares family and I did would have been close to impossible, but I have witnessed that their attitudes have changed now. Some of the miners, who have seen us in the mine's store and at the cantina's tavern, have become curious about us and what we are doing out here. Therefore, we invited them to come and see our rock houses and our gardens as we were building and developing them. Initially, they didn't believe we would survive long and stay, but now they come and buy our vegetables and corn, and they admire our houses, which they can see are much better than their cottages.

"They often express a certain envy when they see us and the children living a free and full life. So, as you see, André, some of the miners have changed their attitudes, and most of them would be willing to learn from our experience, become self-sufficient farmers, and sell the product of their land in the nearby markets."

I laughed again. "Mário, you are still the incurable dreamer I befriended as a teenager! Yet, I am happy that you haven't lost the ability to turn hidden opportunities into challenging dreams!"

"André, what you call 'my dream' of transforming this valley and its people into a thriving community is possible because you could actually make it happen. You could be to your Minas estate what Dona Olivia[3] was to the town I grew up in—but without resorting to

---

[3] D. Olivia was the countess of San Lucas, in Atlantica, until 1908. In that year, under the weight of her responsibilities after the death of her father, in a fit of despair, she committed suicide by throwing herself into the sea, after she had made a will leaving all the lands of the county to the people of San Lucas, including Mário's ancestors.

her tragic methods. By donating her lands to the people of San Lucas, she practically eliminated poverty there and made the community I grew up in possible. And the beauty of it, André, is that you are alive and can experience the positive transformation of your land and its people!"

"You make your vision appealing, Mário, but what you don't see is that greedy foreign investors and our corrupt politicians could easily turn your visionary's dream into a nightmare."

Mário smiled wryly. "I don't blame you for thinking that. I know you have already experienced more than your share of nightmares, but you still survive and thrive because you are strong and immensely capable. And you enjoy making other people's dreams come true, including mine!

"You taught me math and science and helped me pass the entrance exams back in our school days in Atlantica. Without your help then, I would have failed those exams and gone back to San Lucas. That would probably have ended my dream of being an active participant in the building of a better Atlantica and a better world. Later, when my dream became impossible to achieve in Atlantica, you helped me come to the United States, and I was able to study and work on the transformation of the Santiago Flatlands. And when I was pushed out of the United States, you brought me to your home in Santa Cruz, gave me a homestead, and loaned me the money I needed to make it the sustainable success you are looking at. As you see, dear André, you are the one who has made my dreams come true repeatedly! If I am an incurable dreamer, as you say, you have no one to blame but yourself! The truth is that you genuinely thrive on making dreams come true. I am inclined to think that right now the Soares family and I are not only fulfilling our dreams—we are also fulfilling yours!"

There was a long moment of silence as I absorbed the words Mário had spoken. I couldn't find words of my own to respond. Overcome by emotion, I reached out and grabbed him in my arms, speechless.

Over the years, time and time again, when I looked at Mário, I felt that he reflected back to me the image of my best self. He did that because he always believed in the best in me as no one ever did—including myself most of the time.

As I drove my jeep back through Minas, I realized how sterile my life would have been without sharing some of Mário's unrestrained optimism about life and its possibilities. And all I did the rest of the way home was dream about how I could use the small candle of those homesteads to light a much-needed bonfire in the state of Santa Cruz.

A few days later, I left for my meetings with Gilmore in Santiago. This time, however, unlike previous occasions, I went into the negotiations with confidence and a markedly different sense of what I could do. I bargained aggressively for a favorable settlement of current issues, and I avoided all attempts by Gilmore to accept his proposal regarding the new capitalization plans for the mine.

I knew that I was definitely getting to Gilmore, when, at the end of our negotiating sessions, he changed his manipulative tactics and threatened me rudely. "We are running out of time, my boy! No more delaying! It's getting to the point where you have to shit or get off the pot!"

"Well, Fred, right now I feel like doing neither!" I left him stewing in his own bad juices, totally befuddled at his failure to intimidate me as usual.

The reason I was able to resist Gilmore's pressure tactics was because I no longer felt that his plans were the only option I had for securing my future. I had taken a fresh look at my assets, and I knew I could survive comfortably on my other investments, particularly some ecologically sound tree farming, which I had begun to develop on the higher mountain areas of Minas. I decided, therefore, to study seriously the feasibility of closing the mine and giving the miners and squatters on the land an opportunity to gain title to some of the land they had lived on for years.

This wasn't a small project by any means. It would amount to initiating on my own a genuine land reform program for the first time in the state. It would also return to some of the descendants of my Native ancestors and many other sem terra some of the land that my Portuguese ancestors had appropriated and kept by force, thus transforming most of its inhabitants into squatters for centuries.

As soon as I got back to Santa Cruz, I announced my intention to an overjoyed Mário, and together we made plans to announce to the miners in Minas that they would be offered an opportunity to own a piece of land where they could farm and build homes of their own.

With this decision, I began the most exciting and fulfilling period of my life. I do not want to elaborate on what impact this decision had on me personally because it is Mário's story that I am here to tell, and he is the one who made the project possible. He approached this new challenge with the same zeal and dedication that he had shown in the Flatlands of Santiago or in Vila Miséria in Atlantica. This time, I had the privilege of being involved. I worked very closely with him and the mine workers, and I witnessed a group of disorganized, dispirited, skeptical, tired people beginning to develop into a highly motivated, vibrant, and enthusiastic community.

I recall as one of my fondest memories the Sunday when a group of miners came to Mário's house for one of his literacy classes. It was one of those winter days when the air outside was crisp and made you pull up your coat in spite of the bright sun. The men came in groups of three or four, rough hands in their pockets, some wearing rough rubber sandals made out of old tires and no socks. Some of the younger ones who couldn't even afford those came barefoot.

There were about twelve men in this group. They spread out comfortably throughout the one large room that comprised Mário's home. That one room served as a living room, bedroom, and occasional kitchen. Mário's bed doubled as couch for some, and a few rough benches around an equally rough table accommodated the rest. The low winter sun shone straight on the granite back wall through the row of small windows below the roof overhang. It felt really comfortable.

Initially, the men had looked askance at me because they associated me with the low wages from the mine and the high prices at the company store. However, my regular attendance at the meetings changed their attitude toward me, and I now felt at home and accepted by them. That meant a great deal to me.

This Sunday, Mário had written on the makeshift blackboard the word "Minas." Each of the men went up, one by one, and copied the word, some erasing it several times until each was happy with his penmanship. Suddenly, Mário raised his voice so the whole group could hear him, and he said, "I have been wondering if Minas or Monte Queimado will be the right names for this valley from now on."

They all nodded and murmured their agreement to Mário's sentiment. One of the men said, "Did you hear that, guys? One of these days, we will be able to rename this valley!"

"Truly!" said another. "By moving into this land and owning it, it becomes our land, and—"

"That's it!" shouted one of the men, jumping to his feet with excitement. You just named it! This land will be *our* land! We will call it 'Nossa Terra'!"

All the other men stood up clapping their hands in approval, unable to contain the joy born of the idea that they could lay claim to a small patch of dirt on the backside of Monte Queimado. Most of them never imagined that one day they would have that privilege.

I will never forget the day when what used to be a useless piece of empty land for me became Nossa Terra for those men. It became a historical day for all of us.

The miners, with Mário's help, formed a credit union and began to deposit their savings for a down payment on the land, which I had promised to sell to them at a fair price. It was understood that the proceeds from this sale would be used to build the essential infrastructure for the new community (roads, irrigation channels, etc.). I also promised collateral to guarantee a bank loan for the materials necessary to build a small dam on the upper creek that would be big enough to store an ample supply of drinking and irrigation water. The users would eventually repay the bank loan over several years.

Once that loan was negotiated, I engaged an engineer to develop a technically sound plan for us, and the work began with a combination of voluntary labor from the men on weekends and holidays and the free use of mine equipment in order to make the project more affordable.

In less than one year, the dam was built.

In the meantime, Mário and a team of technicians, including surveyors, a soil specialist, and my attorney, laid down the boundary survey plan for the new community, including roads, water, irrigation lines and other relevant markings.

The area that I had agreed to sell to the miners was divided into two hundred plots of different sizes and characteristics in order to satisfy a variety of personal needs, ambitions, and individual capacity.

The miners were then invited to bid for particular parcels of land; the intensity of the bidding depended on the quality of the soil and potential for subsistence farming. The team of surveyors and soil specialists did an excellent job, and at the end, just about everyone was satisfied. They could hardly believe that they were becoming landowners.

Once the contracts were signed, payments began to be made to the credit union's investment fund regularly. This was necessary in order to build a healthy reserve fund and to start paying back all-important community investments, such as the connection of Nossa Terra to the electrical grid, the buying of essential farming equipment, and the acquisition of a truck to carry fresh produce to the market. These homegrown financing schemes were the creative product of necessity because these miner-farmers would never have qualified for individual loans from conventional banks.

I also handpicked a capable management team to run the credit union and ensure appropriate financial control of all community-funded operations.

The miners and their families lost no time in starting their vegetable gardens and building their homes as soon as they were given possession of their land. Within two years, some were doing so well that they started quitting the mine—with my encouragement—as we began to wind down the mining activity.

Nossa Terra had truly gained its place on the map!

In the meantime, despite my joy at the great strides being made in Nossa Terra, I knew that storm clouds were gathering—and that soon it might rain on my party.

~

Finally, when I knew that the Nossa Terra project was well on its way, I informed Gilmore that I was going to close the mine.

He was furious.

This time, he did not demand that I come to Santiago immediately to discuss the matter, which was his habit in urgent situations. Two days later, he was in Santa Cruz, and when I refused to reconsider my position, he started putting pressure on me from all sides.

First, he went to the governor and told him that if I closed "this important mine in Minas," he would have to break his contracts for the utilization and maintenance of the railroad spur, which served the mine in Minas and the lumber and cattle country in the interior of the state. Without the Minas shipments, Gilmore's other ventures would become unprofitable, which he explained to the governor.

And after going to the governor, he went to a source of real local power: Don Jorge Rodrigues. Don Jorge's father and my grandfather had joined forces to bring the railroad spur up the San Gregorio Canyon into the interior forests and grazing areas controlled by them at the turn of the century. As a result, Don Jorge had already moved the edge of the forest many miles back by cutting down huge numbers of trees for sale to the construction and paper industries. He needed the railroad to continue making his obscene profits.

Before he was done, Gilmore visited the chamber of commerce in Santa Cruz and warned its members that my attitudes and actions were sure to jeopardize future investment projects in the state. He insisted that the best way to encourage new investments in the whole San Gregorio region was to point to the volume and variety of the existing high-profit-generating enterprises. Without an intensified mining activity in Minas, his investments there would come dangerously close to losing the necessary critical mass. If I were to close the mine, he claimed, it would be seen as a signal that investment opportunities in the state were on the decline.

It was not long before the governor, Don Jorge, and the officers of the chamber of commerce were all summoning me to urgent meetings.

The chamber knew that Gilmore was bluffing when he made the threat to move all his investments out of Santa Cruz. They knew that Gilmore and his associates would not abandon a region that was currently making them millions even without the proceeds from the iron ore coming out of my mine. What worried them was the negative impact that an upset Gilmore would have on the terms of future negotiations.

The governor however had more immediate concerns. The state budget could not afford to lose any revenue from exports and other taxes that the foreign investors were providing to the public coffers. He and the domestic oligarchs like Don Jorge were concerned that all the bad publicity about the investment climate in Santa Cruz would drive the multinational investors to more promising regions, and they were critical partners in their business ventures.

At my meeting with the governor, he insisted that my decision to close the mine was placing in jeopardy the long-term sustainability of the already shaky economy of the state.

I respectfully told him that I was as concerned about the long-term sustainability of our state's economy as he was. But I added that I was aware of all the studies that indicated that iron ore was a strategic resource for our future—and that giving it away cheaply now was stealing from that future to support our current bad habits. Therefore, I could not in good conscience continue to be part of this wasteful exploitation of resources that left me, my heirs, and my state with nothing but a hole in the ground instead of the iron ore we would need to build our future.

As for my ancestors, I explained to the governor that I felt a much stronger obligation to honor them by restoring my environmentally degraded land through reforestation and active farming, which I believed would be of greater benefit to the state and its people, both in the short term and the long term.

Needless to say, the governor was not happy with my explanations, and he expressed his displeasure in somewhat threatening terms. He said I was playing with fire and that he sincerely hoped I wouldn't get burnt. "André, by engaging in your dreamy adventures against the economic interests of your peers, you forfeit the role your forefathers occupied in their midst. You will lose their goodwill and gain their unforgiving animosity."

And this didn't end with the governor's reprimand and warning. My bankers, who were aware of my recent actions at the mine and all the other changes I had initiated regarding my business interests, were no longer willing to extend to me the credit that had never been denied before. As a result, in order to finance the necessary infrastructure investments for Nossa Terra, I had to free some of my personal funds.

The disapproval from my fellow oligarchs was even more difficult to bear; their workers began to organize and demand similar concessions to those my workers had obtained from me.

And to rub salt in the establishment's wounds, there were signs of division within the local Catholic church between those who subscribed to a new movement called liberation theology, which called for the involvement of the church in political and civic matters in order to help the poor obtain social justice, and those who felt comfortable with the status quo and its traditional charitable ministry. In the minds of the oligarchs, Nossa Terra and I were associated with the new rebellious movement.

What saved me from caving in under all these pressures was the conviction that I was doing the right thing. I felt an inner peace and satisfaction, which I had never known to exist before. For the first time, I was doing what should have been done all along: I was using my fortune and my position of privilege to make positive change in the life of others less fortunate.

As Mário often reminded me, I was becoming the person I had always wanted to be. But the pressure grew stronger. As I mentioned before, my fellow oligarchs had an all-powerful state association. It's raison dêtre was the preservation of moral values and the social order, meaning essentially, the preservation of their power and influence over the entire state.

The association's clandestine committee, known as the Iron Hand, was rumored to have been deployed to carry out political purges—and even assassinations—in order to remove threats to its power and wealth.

In the early 1960s, during President Joao Goulart's left-leaning term of office, it was often whispered in private that the American CIA often relied on the Iron Hand for many of its information-gathering and other anti-communist Cold War activities, clearly indicative of the sympathies of its members and the strength of their capabilities.

With the attention focused on my new ventures, I began to neglect attending this oligarchs' association meetings and social events. I finally decided to stop paying the customary dues, which my father and my ancestors had always done.

It should come as no surprise therefore that my total withdrawal from the association was interpreted as opposition to its agenda and refusal to pay for its activities. And it wasn't long before the initial subtle pressures turned into serious warnings that I was treading on a minefield, followed by some anonymous death threats if I didn't cease my shady communist activities.

I also received notice that I was no longer a member of the religious retreat association, of which I had also inherited membership from my father. This organization represented the alliance of the traditional church and the aristocracy and included many of the most powerful men in our state, including many of the descendants of the Portuguese nobility, like myself. In today's Cold War environment, it provided a religious justification for the ruling elites' posture of spiritual and physical preparedness against the godlessness of communism.

On the third anniversary of the establishment of Nossa Terra, the community celebrated the completion of the local school, and the last families from Minas were moved into their new homes and small farms.

The project was proving to be a success. Fifty-seven more homes had been completed in just the past year, two more cooperative trucks with "Produtos da Nossa Terra" written on them had been bought, and sizable contracts for the sale of Nossa Terra products had been made with several urban supermarkets.

I was invited to the Nossa Terra anniversary celebration mostly as a friend but also as an important person whom the community had chosen to honor on this special occasion. I participated fully and enthusiastically in the festivities, and I took immense pride in their success.

In four years, the Nossa Terra Valley had been totally changed. Small, well-kept dirt roads now crisscrossed the valley, connecting 156 new homes and as many families. A simple but functional school had been built. A small clay factory produced bricks and tiles, a mill prepared the lumber, and a tool-renting shop provided the tools needed for all the new construction. All the essentials for the building of family homes, community buildings, and irrigation projects were easily available and could be purchased or rented with the help of small loans from our own credit union.

On this celebration day, what impressed most the more than two thousand visitors of this innovative community was the beautiful healthy vegetable fields and orchards, which provided the residents of Nossa Terra with appropriate food supply and filled the Nossa Terra Cooperative trucks, which produced a reasonable income for nearly everyone.

Indeed, the Nossa Terra experiment had become well-known particularly among organizations of rural workers and *sem terra* squatters throughout the state of Santa Cruz. Many of the leaders of these organizations were invited to be on the stage that had been built for the celebratory occasion. One by one, they stood at the podium and made passionate speeches congratulating us eloquently on our success. Naturally, some of them even used the occasion to launch their own grand ideas to an obviously supportive audience.

Inspired by the Nossa Terra initiative, one enthusiastic young leader invited all the people present to march to the governor's mansion with him on the following Sunday to demand a share of the state's unused land to the landless sem terra where they could build "thriving, self-sustaining communities, such as this one." The idea was loudly approved.

This was more than a spontaneous expression of enthusiasm. As I discovered later, the proposal had been discreetly discussed among these leaders. They knew that if they had planned such a demonstration openly, it would be stopped by the authorities.

~

A few days later, I joined the demonstrating crowds of people as they walked along Santa Cruz's main avenue to the governor's mansion. I couldn't believe how large the throng was. I expected a few hundred to show up, but there were thousands of people filling the streets, much to the chagrin of motorists in the city.

There was a clear message from the sem terra to the governor and the state oligarchs written meticulously in a designed sign: "Esta Terra Também é Nossa!" (This land is also ours!)

The governor wasted no time in calling law enforcement to put a stop to it. Within minutes, men in uniform began to block side streets to keep additional groups from joining in. Quickly, the police blocked the leaders of the crowd from getting closer to the executive mansion and ordered everyone to disperse.

Much to my surprise, the organizers of the march had come prepared to counter some of the police tactics. When the marchers encountered police with fierce dogs, they released the cats they were carrying in bags. This provoked such a reaction from the dogs that controlling them became a bigger challenge to the police than controlling the crowd. Also, many apparent innocent bystanders cut some of the hoses hooked up to the water cannons with well-hidden machetes before a drop of water ever came out of them.

These tactics allowed the crowd to get a little closer to the mansion, but by then, the governor had already called in the military. With a few shots into the air and several tear gas grenades into the crowd, the police and the military had no problem dispersing the demonstrators before they got within sight of the governor's mansion.

The demonstration leaders were quickly taken into custody and driven away with sirens shrieking.

Initially, Mário and I were herded into the city jail with a large group of marchers, but a short time later, we were taken to the high-security state prison on the outskirts of the city. We were immediately separated and isolated for interrogation along with a select group of other leaders.

Before I was taken to an interrogation room, I was given an opportunity to talk privately with a senior member of the oligarchs' association. He started by accusing me of deeds that were an affront to the culture and traditions that were "so carefully nurtured by your own forefathers." Moreover, he added that many of my activities were illegal, treasonous, and undermining the institutions of government. Nonetheless, he assured me, I could still be quietly bailed out and my name kept out of the press if I would put an official end to my public support of the land reform movement, which I had "initiated alone" at Nossa Terra. "Your peers are, without exception, disgusted with your recent actions. We have left you alone so far—out of the respect we still have for your father—but today, however, you have gone too far. You must quit now—or you will suffer huge consequences."

I responded, "I feel that I have only begun!"

The oligarch grimaced and walked away without another word.

The next day, Mário and I were charged separately in court with a variety of crimes, including organizing an unauthorized and illegal demonstration against the state, inciting a riot, and disrespecting and violently attacking the forces of law and order.

I vaguely recollect hearing them talking of subversion and disloyalty to the state, and as I later found out, Mário was also accused of violating the terms of his resident visa.

After pleading not guilty, both of us were sent back to the high-security state penitentiary, and we were kept in isolation a few doors from each other.

My cell measured approximately eight by six feet with a bare wooden cot, a water faucet, and a toilet hole. The iron door had a rectangular slit in the middle, which allowed for the only light and ventilation.

That's where I began telling you about Mário's journey through the Americas.

Now, one year, two months, and seven days later, this is still my residence. This has been, without question, the worst experience of my life. The total isolation and boredom of the first few months were relieved a little bit after Mário made an uneasy alliance with the warden, whom I introduced to you at the beginning of this book as Toro. It was through him that Mário got the brown paper bags he used to write his thoughts on.

First, he wrote *Guided Tours to San Lucas* about San Lucas and his life there before we met at the San Luis College, in Atlantica, as teenagers. He did this because he wanted me to know how he came to be the kind of person he was and because, as he said, "I do not want to lose sight of my upbringing in San Lucas and what's best in our Latin Christian culture, in spite of its historical misapplications."

Sometime later, he wrote *The Dream of a Flight over America*, which I shared with you as I began to write. By that time, Mário had convinced Toro to bring me a supply of used paper bags and pencils, which I still use to continue to tell his challenging life story. It still has an unforeseeable ending.

During this past year, Mário and I have managed to meet occasionally for brief moments. This happens mostly before or after Mass, which is celebrated in prison once in a while by a Franciscan monk who, among other things, reminds Mário of Padre José of San Lucas. Both men aimed their lives at rediscovering Christianity as Jesus and the early Christians lived it in order to help create a better world for the human family.

As a consequence of his vision, this Franciscan monk, Padre Custódio, became a fervent proponent of liberation theology, which advocates a radical reinterpretation of Jesus's teachings from the perspective of the poor and disenfranchised. He, and others of like mind, are constantly asking themselves not what Christians must believe in but what they and their church must do, here and now, to bring about social and economic justice. According to Padre Custódio, the church must be like Jesus of Nazareth and make its ministry to the poor its essential mission.

We convinced Padre Custódio to be a regular visitor to Nossa Terra, and he is our emissary and keeps us in touch with our friends there. The most important help he has given Mário and me has been the opportunity for our short occasional meetings.

I still remember the first such meeting, after six months in separate jail cells.

"André, I am so sorry for all the things I have brought upon you," Mário said after we embraced, choking up in our own tears.

"Sorry for what?" I said, trying to keep a brave face.

"Mostly for bringing you here! A country boy like me can survive here. But you? You were hardly prepared to tolerate this hell on earth. This isn't fair! After all you have done to help so many!"

It is typical of Mário to worry more about the well-being of others than about his own—even when he is in the same dire situation. He continued to do his best to encourage and motivate me. "Don't lose your courage, André! Without men like Padre Custódio in the church and you among the rich, practicing the social justice that many Christians profess but few live by, the favela dwellers and the sem terra of this country will never be able to call this land Nossa Terra."

By now, eighteen long months have passed. Initially, we had reason to fear that our fates would be like those of the supporters of Joao Goulart's agrarian reform who—after being kidnapped and jailed—often became the disappeared. The uncertainty of our situation often terrorized us.

However, after a while, we concluded that, as long as we were still alive, our best strategy was to remain as positive as possible and look for every opportunity to improve our dire situation. And that's what we have done.

At first, I was terribly worried about what would happen to my properties and how I would manage my affairs from prison. That nearly drove me to despair until one of my most trusted managers found a way to meet me with my lawyer so that I could give him power of attorney to act on my behalf. Later, he also found a way, through one of the prison guards, to send me occasional reports, which enables me to accompany the life of my enterprises and to be sure that my assets are secure.

Unlike me, without business affairs to worry about and unable to engage in anything worthwhile outside the walls of this prison, Mário has continued to express in his writing his strong resilience, even though he sometimes acknowledges some despair.

Just a few days ago, a miracle began to happen with a letter he received from Monica.

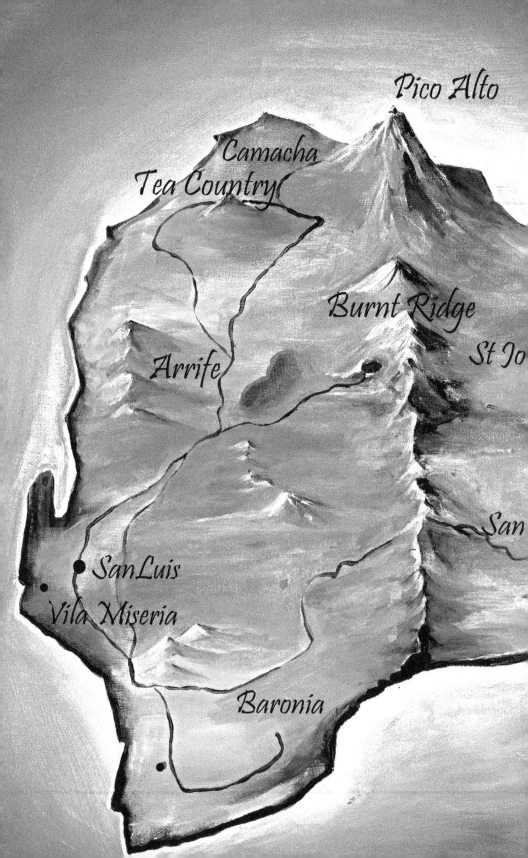

8 ATLANTICA

April

26, 1974

Mário, my dearest love,

As I wrap my arms around you and
hold you tight, I have the greatest
of news to share with you. Yesterday,
instead of going to the university,
I spent the day with my fellow
countrymen in the streets of Lisbon,
celebrating our democratic future!
Yes, love! The dictators have fallen!
We are finally living in a free
country! Our day has come! We will
soon be together!

This might be hard to believe, but
it is the plain truth: the soldiers
are parading themselves through
the streets of Lisbon with red
carnations stuck on their carbines,
and no one here fears their bullets
anymore. Only yesterday, they were
preparing to be sent to Africa to

213

214 ~ Manuel Januário

maim and kill other human beings whose only sin was wanting to be free in their own lands!

The state secret police (PIDE) has been disbanded; many of its chiefs are in jail, and the Revolution Council has promised that all political prisoners will soon be freed.

The government has fallen to an organized group of captains of the armed forces, who had been planning a coup for months. They neutralized the PIDE, took over many military installations and the national TV, and calmly escorted the prime minister to safety after obtaining from him a renunciation of his power. Soon after, the people began to fill the streets to the sound of Zeca Afonso's "Grândola Vila Morena" singing that "the people have the power," and from now on, the political power will come from them—and not from on high through a dictator like Salazar or Marcelo Caetano!

Monica went on to write in great detail the news of the 1974 Carnation Revolution, which, after forty years, finally allowed the Portuguese people to live in a free democratic system. Such had not been the case since

1933, when António Salazar installed the repressive, fascist Estado Novo Regime that ruled the country with an iron fist, while enslaving the overseas colonies of Angola, Mozambique, Guinea-Bissau, Cape Verde, and more, under the pretense of being overseas provinces of Portugal.

Salazar's government had managed to maintain Portugal as the last anachronistic European empire, against total international disapproval, including regular UN condemnations. In the latter few years of this regime, the country barely survived by spending practically all the ill-gotten resources that Salazar had amassed during the Second World War by staying out of the conflict and trading with both sides.

The fighting against the African freedom movements continued only at the expense of the total impoverishment of the country in order to send larger and larger numbers of soldiers into more difficult conditions.

But finally, the nightmare seemed to be over for the country.

For Mário and Monica, this was also the signal that their time to reunite in Atlantica had finally come. She ended her letter with the following:

> You will certainly be coming out of that prison soon, and there is nothing to stop you from returning to me and begin now in Atlantica the work you have been preparing for all your life. How I yearn for that day! Come soon, my love! I desperately need both you and your help.

It was not only Monica who needed Mário's return. Atlantica also needed the help of all its citizens to help change the antiquated systems of landownership, as well as the unequal and unfair distribution of resources practiced since the 1500s.

Now the power was no longer exclusively in the hands of the owners of the land, mostly of noble descent like my relatives, the Barbosas of Atlantica. Salazar's Estado Novo regime had created industrial monopolies, which had become the new centers of power controlled by a dozen superrich families, and they owned most of the national industry and soaked up its economic benefits.

With the Carnation Revolution, the heads of these oligarchies and superrich families would lose their grip on power, and the national stage was set for a complete change of paradigm.

The euphoria on the streets of Lisbon turned into a climate of hope for the development of effective democratic institutions and practices.

Eventually, many political parties came into existence, reflecting the spectrum of ideologies that had given rise to the Cold War. They proposed an array of choices to the Portuguese people, which served as the foundation for serious political debate. The excited masses of people had never experienced such freedom before.

In spite of the initial challenges and some confusion, the revolutionary Movement of the Armed Forces (MFA) and the political parties agreed that there were two top priorities: to write the new constitution and to negotiate the immediate cessation of the colonial wars in Africa.

Negotiations with African freedom fighters began rapidly, resulting in the eventual independence of Angola, Mozambique, Guinea-Bissau, Cape Verde, and São Tomé e Principe. However, the status of the Atlantic islands, including Atlantica, was different.

Let me explain the unique situation of Atlantica before I go into its current politics. The island of Atlantica is geographically a peripheral, oceanic region of Europe. It has an area of slightly more than four thousand square kilometers (2,500 square miles) and a population of around 550,000.

Deep under its volcanic soil, there are remnants of some European clay, perhaps brought there on the edge of the Eurasian tectonic formation, which grinds into the African and American plates under Atlantica.[4]

Atlantica was discovered in the early 1500s at the beginning of the Portuguese maritime expansion. Since the beginning, it was the Portuguese who settled there, along with a mixture of people from other national and racial origins, including adventurers and fugitives from various countries, and a few descendants of African slaves and shipwrecked pirates.

In great measure, today's diversity of Atlantica's population is due to its location at the crossroads of the sea routes to the Orient, to Africa, and to the Americas, which were followed by the Portuguese explorers and by various European colonial empires that, in later centuries, sailed the Atlantic in search of overseas trade and pillage.

This explains why Atlantica has developed a unique culture with typical Portuguese/European characteristics. Understanding these demographic and geographic factors, the new democratic Portuguese regime recognized that Atlantica was not just an oceanic Portuguese region. It was a special case with three possible solutions:

- Should Atlantica be administratively integrated into the new Portuguese Democratic Republic?

---

[4] Atlantica is a fictional, peripheral, and isolated autonomous region of Portugal. It is created here to serve as an example of what needs to be done in today's world by good politicians and economists to create a better world. However, Atlantica's geographical, historical, and cultural parallelism with the actual autonomous regions of Madeira and the Azores is real, and it is not irrelevant to this story.

- Should Atlantica's unique culture be recognized and become independent?
- Should Atlantica become an autonomous region of Portugal?

Given how divided Atlanteans themselves were on these issues, the new leaders in Lisbon decided, wisely, to allow Atlanteans to have a referendum to determine their political future. This decision provided additional incentive for all the political forces that had an ambition to shape Atlantica's future to start mobilizing.

It was clear from the beginning that the Atlantica referendum was not just important to Atlanteans but also to the two world superpowers, which were then at the peak of their Cold War struggles. This interest was primarily due to its geographical position. While the American government's priority was to maintain their air force base on Atlantica's soil, the Soviets saw Atlantica as an opportunity to gain a convenient stepping-stone to communist Cuba—at the backdoor of the United States.

In this Cold War environment, it came as no surprise that the front-runners in the political dialogue in Atlantica were the two pro-independence parties, appropriately named the Republican Party and the Atlantean Liberation Front (ALF), supported, at least covertly by the United States and Soviet Union, respectively.

The Atlantean Liberation Front was the first party to be registered as such on the island. Their leadership was encouraged by the early success of the fiercely competitive Portuguese Communist Party (PCP), which had been formed underground during the Salazar regime and included many active political outcasts. These forces now emerged on the scene with an appealing popular agenda and strong organizational skills, which were developed during their most difficult days of exile, sometimes in Russia.

The ALF strategy for an independent Atlantica was based on what one would call an ideologically Marxist agenda. Its promises included immediate reforms similar to those so successfully carried out in Cuba: universal health care, nationalization of large land holdings and businesses, housing for the homeless, and full employment for everyone.

The most visible face of this movement was Noe Montes-Claros, a man who had first studied in France but soon found his way to Moscow, where he was indoctrinated before he established his headquarters in a North African country. There, he associated with other Portuguese university students forced into exile by Salazar's repressive dictatorship. He was inspiring in his speeches and totally committed to the job of building a pillar of a new communist world order in the North Atlantic.

The leader of the Republican Party, Dr. Figueiroa, a man who had been educated in American universities, had come to believe that America was the prototype of what any modern nation should be. In his opinion, there were no problems in Atlantica that the sound application of a good dose of American capitalism would not solve. So, he formulated a clear, foolproof winning strategy, which he proposed to Atlanteans everywhere, particularly those already living in the United States with relatives in Atlantica.

Figueiroa understood that it was of strategic significance for the United States to keep its military base in Atlantica. It was essential for the projection of its military power into Europe, the Middle East, and beyond. He also knew that the Carnation Revolution in Portugal was perceived by the Americans as containing a serious threat of communist infiltration in Europe through its Portuguese Atlantic front. Figueiroa assumed that this fact alone would motivate Americans to sooner or later offer covert or even open support for an independent Atlantica under the rule of a pro-American Republican Party.

Accordingly, he wasted no time in associating the communist ALF with godlessness, making him the champion of most of the tendentiously religious Atlanteans. Next, he mobilized the support of the most influential Atlantean emigrants in the United States while reaching out in every way possible for the support of the American government.

But these two pro-independence parties were not the only political forces in Atlantica. There was the Atlantean Socialist Party, the only large political force that didn't advocate for independence. Ironically, it was poorly supported by the national socialists in Lisbon, who were particularly busy with the transition from the Estado Novo regime to a functioning democracy.

The Atlantean Socialist Party contended that separating Atlantica from Portugal would separate it from its mother culture and the roots of many of its traditions. It would also throw it right into the exploiting hands of the international Cold War giants, to be eventually used as best suited them in their drive for global supremacy. In fact, the Socialist Party proposed to Atlanteans that becoming an independent nation would be the shortest route for Atlanteans to totally lose their independence and identity. They would become either a communist outpost in the Atlantic or another US-subservient banana republic, unevenly divided between foreign investors and poor natives, these latter cheaply employed or without jobs at all.

In the absence of foreign sponsors, the socialist movement had few resources, and its leadership was poorly equipped to help Atlanteans understand the importance of keeping whatever little control they still had of their traditional way of life.

As it happened, the leader of the Atlantean Socialist Party was none other than Ricardo Antunes, a classmate of both Mário and mine at the San Luis College in Atlantica some eighteen years earlier.

Having already been forced into military service in Africa and having actively participated in the Carnation Revolution and its aftermath, Antunes was convinced that the new Portuguese Democratic government had learned its lesson and would never again abuse the basic rights of the Portuguese people, including Atlanteans. He shared the democratic vision of the socialists in Lisbon, and he believed they could be trusted to respect Atlantica as an autonomous region, empowered to control its economic future and maintain its cultural identity—within a free and democratic Portugal.

Antunes was a well-intentioned man, with a message that should have been attractive to the majority of Atlanteans who lived mostly as small, rural landowners. But as an ex-military man with no experience in rural-development issues, he was at a huge disadvantage to the other two political parties, who unintentionally combined their extremely opposed independence forces to defeat the Socialists, the only pro-Portugal significant adversary.

In a desperate effort to seek help for his party, Antunes often traveled to Lisbon in search of both financial and political support. He also thought that as the leader of a party that supported the regional autonomy, he should be listened to by the mainland government, while the practical details of regional autonomy were still being defined in the national Parliament. This was the time to ensure that the regional autonomy statutes delegated to the new Atlantean government primary responsibility over internal political, economic, and social affairs, with the least interference possible from the national government in Lisbon, in accordance with the principle of subsidiarity.

As it had become his habit, whenever he was in Lisbon, Antunes met with a group of well-placed Atlanteans to raise their awareness of current regional issues and prioritize their political activities. He knew that, despite everyone's best intentions, all Atlantean talents combined would scarcely be enough to address the challenges ahead.

Monica, still a student in Lisbon, was usually a part of this select group.

Antunes was as frustrated as she was with the lack of success of the official Portuguese efforts to free Mário in Santa Cruz, and he always asked Monica for updates on his college classmate's situation. This time, he was particularly intense. "Monica, we cannot allow Mário to rot in a dungeon when we need him here so desperately. Mário is, in fact, one of our first exiled rebels, thanks to your aunt's personal resentment. His triumphant return to rural Atlantica to continue the work he has done abroad could mobilize thousands of Atlanteans in our favor, and we desperately need that to happen before the referendum!"

"I agree," answered Monica. "But how do we go about freeing him from a Latin American fortress?"

"What do you think of a 'Free Mário Garcia' petition, signed by thousands of Atlanteans and directed specifically to the governor of Santa Cruz through official channels, but accompanied by a threat to take Mário's case to the 'court' of international public opinion, if he continues to ignore it?

"The Carnation Revolution has put Portugal on the headlines and therefore, well-organized popular action might make the governor fear the world's attention and act to free Mário."

Antunes and Monica decided to seek an audience with the Portuguese minister of foreign affairs, and he agreed to discuss Mário's case directly with both the Brazilian government and the governor of Santa Cruz before the Free Mário Garcia campaign petition was sent directly to the governor.

Monica returned to Atlantica immediately to help organize the petition. Many parish priests who had been students in the San Luis College with Mário and others, including the activist Padre Elias of Vila Miséria—with whom Mário had worked prior to his going to America—began to vocally support the efforts to get signatures for this petition. The Atlantean Socialist Party put all the weight of its organization behind the campaign as well.

It was only a matter of weeks before two boxes full of signatures were collected and made ready to be sent to the governor in Santa Cruz, attached to the Free Mário petition. The last thing the Santa Cruz governor wanted was to deal publicly with a petition that would bring back to the front lines Mário's imprisonment and mine, which he had kept deliberately under wraps. He ignored it at first, but when faced with the threat of international bad press by the Atlantean Socialist Party, the governor became apprehensive and issued a careful statement: "We are now studying the Mário Garcia case in consultation with our Ministry of Justice, and we hope to find the appropriate solution as soon as possible."

With the Free Mário campaign, the Atlantean Socialist Party had finally captured the attention of many voters in the rural areas of Atlantica, and with clever prompting by Antunes, the local newspapers and television associated the Free Mário campaign with the Socialist Party. As a result, there was hardly a day without some public comment by Antunes on the generally watched nightly news.

On October 10, 1975, Toro opened the door to my cell in the Santa Cruz state prison, ordered me to get up, and manacled me. "Follow me," he said with his usual rancorous demeanor. Then, he led me to a small room furnished with a table and two chairs. He left, locking the door behind himself, without an explanation.

Ten minutes or so later, he came back with Mário, whose arms were free to embrace me.

"Take your time. I will wait as long as you wish," said Toro, this time showing an uncharacteristic kindness.

I raised my manacled hands over Mário's head, and after a long, wordless embrace, Mário finally said, "André, I am free!" He did not smile. His face did not beam with joy. His eyes were fixed on mine where he could see my reaction of genuine happiness, but he remained somber. "Words will never adequately convey what I feel at this moment, my brother," Mário said. As he did often in difficult situations, he spoke quickly and with an earnestness that was palpable. I listened attentively with tears in my eyes. "You literally picked me out of the ashes I was buried under in Santiago. You brought me to your home, and then you gave me a home of my own when I was homeless. You allowed me to grow roots into the earth, and I became alive again. You made it possible for my dream of an earthbound life to become real, my brother!

"Later, I pushed you hard to choose the well-being of the poor squatters and dispossessed workers on your land over the expectations of your peers and Gilmore. That was easy for me to do. I had nothing to lose! But you, my brother, were confronting the interests and threats of powerful business partners and your own government! André, as your brother, I am proud of your courage, but at this moment, I feel great pain that I am free to go, and you will be staying here." He choked up.

I took the opportunity to raise my manacled hands again above his head, slide them behind his back, and press him hard against my chest for a long hug.

I hoped that on his departure from the Santa Cruz airport, he would be able to see Nossa Terra and feel as proud as I was of the project that he and I had engineered under the light of Padre José's singular vision of economic and social justice, which he was now going to take back to his native Atlantica.

~

Mário peered down from the plane's window. It was fall in Atlantica, and the sun was shining in a cloudless sky. Flying to the San Luis airport, over the hills and valleys, he could savor the memories of the homeland he had been away from for so many years.

Although Atlanteans loved to spend such a beautiful day outdoors, the Atlantean airport was not where people usually gathered. Today was obviously an exception. People from the rolling inland hills, and from Vila Miséria on the edge of the city, were all converging to a large open space outside of the landing strip area at the airport. They came in cars and pickup trucks and on foot—as if they were going to the annual fair. Some were curious first-time visitors, observing the occasional takeoffs and landings with excitement. Others talked enthusiastically.

The plane touched down on the runway, coasted to a shrieking near stop, and then continued to move on toward the terminal and the huge crowd. The airplane's door opened up, and about three dozen tourists and businesspeople walked down the outside stairway.

Finally, a thin, pale-faced man with a two-day growth of dark whiskers and wearing worn-out jeans appeared at the doorway. He had nothing to carry, which left his hands free to hold on to the rail as he walked down haltingly.

At his sight, the crowd broke out into excitement, giving voice to the slogans they had unfolded in front of them:

Viva Mário Garcia!

Viva Nossa Terra!

Viva Atlantica!

Esta terra também é nossa!

Mário stopped halfway down and looked at the people in total disbelief. Then he zeroed in on the small group at the bottom of the steps, and he practically fell into their arms as they surged to meet him halfway up the stairs.

When the hugging and kissing stopped, they moved a few hundred yards out of the fenced area to a small stage with a podium prepared by the socialist organizers.

Mário walked over, bent down, and grabbed a handful of soil from the ground. He raised it above his head, held it tightly, and walked to the microphone.

"Obrigado! Obrigado! Obrigado por me trazerem de novo a casa! A este solo atlântico que estou segurando na minha mão e que nos une a todos. É este solo que agora devemos aprender a compartilhar uns com os outros como irmãos e irmãs. Eu estou muito grato e muito feliz por terem encontrado uma maneira de me trazerem de volta para que eu me junte a todos vos e participe na criação de uma nova Atlântica. Obrigado! Obrigado! Obrigado por me trazerem de volta a casa. Viva Atlantica!"

(Thank you! Thank you! Thank you for bringing me home! It is this Atlantean soil I am holding in my hand that binds all of us together, and it is this soil that we now must learn how to share with one another as brothers and sisters. I am thankful and overjoyed that you found a way to bring me home to join you and participate in the creation of a new Atlantica. Thank you! Thank you! Thank you for bringing me home! Viva Atlantica!)

The surprising welcome at the airport made Mário realize that the Atlantean Socialist Party's campaign to free him had made him a symbol for the aspirations of Atlantean society. The resulting adulation of the crowd, the physical and emotional strain of the journey, and the reunion with his family and Monica brought him to a state of euphoria and joy, but that was also exhausting. So, they all headed to San Lucas almost immediately looking forward to the rest he needed.

When they got to San Lucas, knowing that the Garcia home was already too small for Mário's parents and for his sister's family of four, the town council offered the old monastery caretaker's small house to Mário and Monica during their stay. This was the simple residence where Padre José had lived.

Alone for the first time, they could finally confirm and feel through their senses the reality of their emotions and sentiments, of their love, for one another. They looked into each other's eyes, listened to each other's words, and constantly held and touched each other. They were tasting their mutual desires and allowing their bodies to melt into each other and create the unity they had longed for for so long. They could at last experience their love turning into pure pleasure and their pleasure turning into fulfillment. Their lives were now complete! It felt like heaven!

At the first opportunity, they went on a long walk up to St. John's Hill. It had been there that they had first openly declared their love for each other. Now it was the ideal place for them to renew their commitment under the same bright sky and to start looking ahead into their future as a couple and a family.

They realized that, being one rich and the other poor, they were in the best of positions to each contribute a half of what was necessary to the fulfillment of their shared humanistic dreams. And they decided confidently that that was the heart of their mission together on earth for the rest of their lives.

When they returned home, tired and hungry, Mário went outside looking for some firewood in the backyard. He lit a cooking fire where he had watched Padre José do it so many times before.

In the meantime, Monica stood with a teacup in her hand, deep in thought about this extraordinary man who from this place had managed to conduct a successful land reform against all odds, practically doing away with poverty in San Lucas. What had made him choose to live here like a farmer among farmers, a man of the earth, when he could have chosen a more comfortable corner of this huge monastery to be his home? There was surely a big lesson to be learned here.

Monica had also witnessed the poor people's struggles and misery while working with her father as the director of the Misericordia Hospital where she helped deliver emergency assistance to those in the greatest need. However, she had always felt frustrated because the fractures between the haves and the have-nots were never healed. Here, in San Lucas, however, that dire poverty had practically ceased to exist.

Now that she was ready to take the control of her aunt's fortune from the hands of the legally appointed administrator, Padre José was surely an inspiration to her. She turned to Mário and said, "What would Padre José say to me now? He must have been a man of great faith! What made him tick? He is surely a source of great inspiration to me."

Mário said, "Men of faith usually have great convictions and belief in the existence of God in heaven and what others teach in His name here on earth. I think Padre José was more a man of vision. He existed inside God 'knowingly.' He thought of God as an Intelligence capable of imagining the universe and then having the power to put His own existence and life into all the things that He had imagined, including us, marvelous humans, with whom He sometimes shares some of His dream plans! Usually the ones that are within our power to fulfill!

"Obviously, like Jesus, Padre José was a man of broader visions than those shaping the world of his day! As a priest and as a historian, Padre José saw Jesus as the man who two thousand years ago envisioned humankind as a family and challenged all men and women to take a conscious step to the next level of their evolution: consciously becoming and living as 'children' of the same God, wherefrom they all got their equal human dignity and their birthright to inherit a living share of God's earth. For him, it was all that simple!"

"And it was this simple and profound vision that Padre José shared with you in places like this kitchen that worked like a 'torch over your head shining on your path,' in places like the Flatlands in America and Nossa Terra in Santa Cruz, as you once told me!"

"Yes, Monica! It was in places like this, under the torch of Padre José's simple world vision, where I began to understand that I should see and treat every human being as a brother or a sister, though at times it wasn't easy, as when my brothers acted like bastards trying to burn us down to the ground in the Santiago Flatlands!"

"But, Mário, do you really think that a visionary's torch like Padre José's and yours can ever be lit brightly enough over the heads of those who own and control the earth today?"

"Yes! I think many more of us are ready to understand that the earth is our inherited homeland and that we should together find win-win strategies to share it as a human family."

"There is that optimism of yours again, and I love you for it! And now come here—under the torch of Padre José's vision and in his kitchen—and embrace me like a sister who is also your other half!"

The conversation stopped. It had once more helped them dive deeper into the meaning of their lives and the deep love they shared.

The fire died down before the water boiled and the potatoes were peeled. Instead, Mário and Monica laid in each other's arms again, making up for the years of forced separation. For them, lovemaking was not only the physical pleasure that they had postponed for so long, but it was also the expression of their vision for a life together in Atlantica, now turning into the better world they had dreamed about ever since they had met as teenagers in this extraordinary town of San Lucas.

For a few days after his arrival in San Lucas, Mário was jarred by the changes that had taken place during his time away.

The panoramic views of sea and mountains, the exposure of his body to direct sunlight after being in a dark cell for so long, the sultry freshness of the air at Ponta Negra, and the loving presence of Monica and his family, his friends, and his neighbors bred into him a great sense of well-being. In just a few days, his prison paleness was replaced by a deep tan closer to his physical appearance when growing up.

He accompanied his father to his quintal (small farm orchard) where Mário was first introduced to farming, and he hugged the grown trees that he had planted many years before.

His mother, Rosa, tenderly observed him and hugged him frequently. She couldn't help but run her fingers through his thinning hair. No words were needed for her to express her deep love for him. Obviously, she was overjoyed with his return.

For Mário and Monica, San Lucas had become a paradise where everything felt right after all the challenges of the past many years.

But they knew that this heavenly retreat was temporary. They would soon be called upon to return to San Luis and participate in the building of the new Atlantica, perhaps making it more like the San Lucas of Padre Jose, seizing the favorable conditions created by the optimism of the Carnation Revolution.

Days later, Mário and Monica offered a welcome in Padre Jose's kitchen to Antunes and two of his closest political associates for a serious discussion of the current political situation in Atlantica. "We, Socialists, only have six short months before the referendum to convince Atlanteans that we are the ones who hold the key to their better future. Somehow, we have to find a way to unmask Figueiroa—and the well-oiled political machine working on his behalf. He has the know-how that he acquired in America. He has money in abundance from hidden sources flowing into his campaign, and he knows how to buy people's attention and votes with it. He offers an American-like attractive dream to Atlanteans, many of whom see Portugal and Europe as the source of the exploitation they have been subjected to throughout their history.

"To make it worse, Figueiroa has the backing of a megalomaniac from California called Tony Matos, who is already investing his great fortune on a bet that Atlantica will turn into the next banana republic that is subservient to American interests. He is traveling through the countryside daily, making pie-in-the-sky money offers for the most desirable vacant lands.

Antunes paused and shook his head with frustration. "And we aren't much better off with our other independentist opponents. The communists have practically taken over Vila Miséria, and they are strong among the poor in general. Living in an ocean of needs, the poor are quite receptive to the communists' enticing promises. By now, many have come to believe that under communism, each one gives to the state only according to his limited possibilities, but in exchange, he receives from it according to his unlimited needs.

"The sad result of the well-organized aggressiveness of both our independentist opponents is that we are lagging behind everywhere. Even the enthusiasm we managed to create in the rural areas with the Free Mário petition has weakened. We desperately need a catalyst that is capable of galvanizing those who believe that the social, economic, and cultural forces that give Atlantica its unique identity, must be preserved."

Mário said, "Of party politics I know nothing, but there is one thing I am sure of: the worst way to preserve Atlantica's earth-based values and uniqueness is to place them in the hands of American capitalists or Russian-type communists. I am ready therefore to go to work on behalf of the socialist position, but perhaps not as another card-carrying socialist, Antunes.

"If I try to speak to either the Republicans or the Communists as a Socialist, they won't listen to me any more than they listen to you. I think we need to bypass party affiliations and speak to the inner soul of all Atlanteans and find the common denominator that binds us all to this land. Perhaps there is still time to start a genuine grassroots movement that encourages heretofore silent Atlanteans to take the future in their own hands and demand from all political parties clear commitments to their causes before they blindly offer them their votes."

This was not exactly what Antunes and his companions wanted to hear from Mário, and at first, it caused some apprehension. Obviously, they had hoped to integrate Mário and Monica's efforts directly into their campaign activities. Antunes eventually ended up seeing Mário's point, and they all agreed to work to achieve the same goals—but in different ways.

Mário and Monica wasted no time getting to work.

The following day, they headed for San Luis.

First, they met with the activist Padre Elias in Vila Miséria, and he confirmed what they already knew.

"The Communists have a strong foothold here, and they have not occupied your lands yet because the lousy administrator that your dying countess aunt appointed to manage your properties until now has let them all go wild. Yet, the Communists have already promised to nationalize all the tea country estates and give them to the workers if they vote for them. Most workers are ready to go with them.

"On the other hand, a few voters are willing to place their bets with the Republicans, whom they trust will bring from America the large-scale agribusiness investments that will provide them with better paying jobs. These are already singing victory every time they hear that Matos has bought another piece of the island."

"Do you think it is too late to find a middle ground?" asked Monica. "What if I told the workers that I am willing to start cooperative farming development in my aunt's tea country, following closely what my cousin André did with Mário in Nossa Terra, in Brazil? What if the Socialists promised a government-supported agrarian reform aimed at the formation of producers' cooperatives? Is it too late to pass that message to the workers?"

There were no easy answers to these questions. Padre Elias, however, was certain that smart political action was urgent if those who wanted regional autonomy were going to have a chance to win.

In order to be practical, they agreed to intensify discussions with all those who were in a position to sway public opinion and had not yet pledged their support to a specific party.

For the next few days, Monica and Mário had meetings in Vila Miséria and with key individuals and representatives of environmental and other nongovernmental organizations in the capital. Many of them were frustrated with the main parties because generally they were not listening to them. It was apparent that the issues raised by small organizations and interest groups were not big vote-getters, and the parties ignored them.

According to many uncommitted observers, Atlantica seemed to be headed straight into *partidocracia*, where the large-scale political power comes to reside in the hands of the party leaders who are subservient to the interests of the elites with the capacity to pay for slick campaigns with well-massaged messages with appeal to the largest possible number of voters. Naturally, once elected, the winning party will proceed to consolidate its position by protecting the interests of those who financed their way to victory.

Knowing this situation and hoping to find a way to make small interests also count, Mário kept asking repeatedly and insistently the following question: "What if those of us who simply want to be Portuguese Atlanteans—the way we have always been—agree on some basic values to serve as the basis for a coalition of small interest groups and individuals who are willing to vote together to defend them? I bet no party will ignore a coalition holding a large number of such votes."

After two weeks in San Luis, Mário and Monica headed out into the rural villages and towns, specifically to thank Mário's old college friends, many of whom had collaborated to make the Free Mário petition a success.

In Arrife, a town surrounded by fertile lands, evenly divided between a land baron and many small farmers, the Republicans were holding a political meeting in the large parish hall, which was conveniently scheduled to coincide with one of Matos' land-buying sprees in the area.

Knowing the quality of the land in Arrife, Matos made no pretense of his desire to buy out the whole town in order to duplicate his gigantic cattle and milk products empire in California. He had already begun to discuss land prices with the local land baron, and he wanted to entice the small farmers to sell.

Dr. Figueiroa was definitely working for him when he aligned his message totally with Matos's interests. "If you vote for the Republican Party, I assure you that Arrife will be unrecognizable in a few years. The Republicans will bring in heavy outside investment. Instead of the low-producing, hydrangea-fenced, small pastures, the whole mountainside will be deep plowed, fertilized, and seeded with quick-growth grass, which once established, will feed five times more cattle. All of you men, who now can hardly make a living on your small pastures, will be able to sell and immediately receive a good amount of money with which you can improve your houses and better your living conditions.

"It won't take long before you will have access to one of the many secure-paying jobs that will be created in pasture maintenance, cattle raising, road building, milk processing, and many other activities, such as feedlot and slaughterhouse operations. Arrife will finally get on the map as it deserves because of its famous Island Cheese, which in the future will be produced in much larger quantities. The superior quality of your salty pasture-fed beef will be recognized everywhere, and the quantity available for export will triple."

Mário and Monica sat among the large audience of peasant farmers at this open meeting and listened carefully.

The next day, at the suggestion of Arrife's parish priest, Padre Zeferino, Monica and Mário went back to the same parish hall for a smaller meeting with representatives of the local Small Farmers Association and members of the Farmers Credit Union. The men, who had listened to Figueiroa quietly the night before, tonight had plenty of questions to debate. It was obvious that Figueiroa's message was causing deep concern.

"If Dr. Figueiroa knows what is good for us so well and wants to help us, why does he insist that we must sell our land and plow our hydrangea fences under instead of joining the efforts of our association to make our land more productive in our own hands?"

"What do we do for a living while the big investors get themselves ready to operate full-scale?"

"How many of us are they really going to need as employees? I am now fifty years old. Will they really want to hire me?"

"My father left me this land, as his father left it to him before. What will I leave to my son?"

"What if we ourselves make all the improvements Figueiroa says Arrife needs, but at our own pace and within our means? Wouldn't that be the only way for us to increase our own personal profits?"

"I have always used my head, working for myself, my own way. How can I ever become just a pair of arms working for Mr. Matos?"

"What will happen to our native vegetation, our beautiful hydrangea fences, and the birds without trees to hide in and nest on?"

Mário and Monica were impressed with the number of relevant questions and the skepticism the farmers demonstrated. It seemed that Dr. Figueiroa had studied Arrife's problems so well that he already knew how to solve them all. It appeared that some Republicans were even willing to give up comfortable lives and successful careers in order to improve the lives of local small farmers. Surprisingly, in exchange for all this generosity, all they wanted from the people of Arrife was their votes.

Pedro, the president of the Farmers Credit Union wryly observed, "Paradoxically the Republicans' and the Communists' promises to us are completely different, yet the price they charge for them is exactly the same: our votes! That's why I am not willing to buy any of their promises! Another paradox related to Dr. Figueiroa is that he says he comes here to help us, but never once did he ask us what we needed from him!"

"That is an important point," said Mário. "Shouldn't last night's meeting have been primarily an opportunity for the Republicans to listen to what your needs were so that they would know how to respond to them?

"Mário, you know politicians wouldn't listen to what we have to say."

"I beg to differ, Pedro! If what you say was true, I would still be in Santa Cruz right now—in a lousy jail. It wasn't until many thousands of you shouted a message loud enough to be heard across the ocean that the governor of Santa Cruz let me go free!"

"You've got a point there, Mário! But that was a little different perhaps."

"I agree! It's very different! You did all that shouting to free just one prisoner. Now you need to free a whole lot of you and your families from those who want to kick you out of your lands, so that they can make huge profits out of them or else turn them into a state farm. It seems to me that you have to keep shouting, again and again and much louder, until they hear you!"

"Okay, you have convinced me that we need to shout louder for politicians to hear us, but I am not sure we would easily agree among ourselves on the message we want them to hear."

"Perhaps we shouldn't focus on the message right now. Listening to you here in Arrife, it's obvious that you already know what you want and need from politicians." Mário was choosing his words carefully. "Perhaps what we need to do first is build the megaphone that will allow us to shout louder and be heard. A megaphone can take the shape of a coalition of persons and organizations that have interests that are similar enough for them to work and vote together to protect them. Any politician will listen to any message that comes out of that megaphone if that message brings a few thousand votes attached."

For a while, the conversation had been between Mário and the young credit union president, while the rest of the farmers listened quietly. But now they wanted to talk too. And they did, for hours, until those present were sold on the idea of forming a coalition of politically uncommitted Atlanteans who wanted to assert their rights and be heard regarding their future.

So, it was in Arrife, in the defense of traditional and sustainable farming, that the idea of the Homeland Coalition took hold, the very same town that Matos had already chosen to become the headquarters of his new meat and milk products empire, in Atlantica.

The hard work of forming a region-wide Homeland Coalition began immediately and with the help of considerable talent, right from the start.

Monica and Mário committed to work full-time. Monica was very well qualified, well-known, and respected in all circles of Atlantean life. Her steady dedication to social causes was very relevant now—as was the fact that she had been away at the university studying the intricacies of rural development and sustainable agriculture in Atlantica. Besides, her friends and the workers in the lands that she had inherited from the countess knew that she had chosen the area of her studies deliberately to better prepare herself to understand and lead the needed land reform in Atlantica.

Monica and Mário got immediately involved with the Faia Environmental Protection Association, which was named after the indigenous tree faia da terra. The preservation of Atlantica's native species of fauna and flora was the association's priority. A staff of four specialists collaborated with prominent international research universities studying Atlantica's unique ecosystems. It was by far the most important environmental protection organization in Atlantica, with a large membership distributed throughout the island.

The Faia Association welcomed warmly the idea of the Arrife farmers to form the Homeland Coalition and immediately pledged their full support.

At Mário's request, the diocese of Atlantica, through its Peace and Justice Commission, also offered the coalition staff time and space in its facilities for meetings as well as the preparation of materials and mailings. This offer was particularly beneficial because the commission already had a network of active cells at the parish level throughout Atlantica, which offered immediate contact with the various cultural and social action organizations in each town.

As soon as local organizations and individuals began to see the alignment between the coalition's objectives and their own, they joined in and offered their contributions everywhere.

And so, the Homeland Coalition came alive five full months ahead of the elections—and because it had filled a gap in the current political discussions and offered much needed help in the registration of voters—it soon gained great visibility.

The most obvious sign that the coalition was having an impact was the fact that every politician interviewed on TV had something to say about it, and that kept increasing its importance in the eyes of the population. Let me explain why.

Television had just become a widespread phenomenon in Atlantica in 1976. There was only one channel, and Atlanteans watched it regularly with a genuine interest, especially the open political discussions taking place since the Carnation Revolution in Lisbon. For many, it was the first time they were able to watch a real political debate and participate in the open process of choosing their leaders.

Until then, the election process in Portugal was limited to the local leaders of the National Union Party showing up at each village, city, and town after Sunday Mass on Election Day to deliver the list of preregistered male voters and a corresponding stack of ballots. These already contained the name of the person chosen by Salazar's party to be elected the next president of the nation.

Once elected by a huge landslide, the new president's most important function was to appoint Salazar as the prime minister, once more. As prime minister, Salazar would then govern the country with his council of ministers—all appointed by him—until a similar election process was reenacted four years later.

On a particular Friday night, three months ahead of elections, the curiosity and excitement of the people in front of their TV sets everywhere on the island was palpable because the heads of the three main parties were going to debate each other face-to-face for the first time. Up until then, they had responded to the journalists' questions individually and unchallenged.

Moreover, it was announced that the opening topic of the debate was the "recently formed, politically unaligned Homeland Coalition," which the host described as an organization that was articulating "a new groundswell of voices that had not yet been heard from in the political arena."

At a first moment, the party leaders, like good politicians, all welcomed the coalition's arrival on the political scene and tried to find a way to identify with it.

The Republican candidate, Dr. Figueiroa, stated, "A coalition of independent voters is most welcome in Atlantica, and I am sure that it will become clear to its members that our party's proposals offer the best way forward for all their individual projects and goals." He went on to explain that choosing the Communist pro-independence party would be catastrophic. It would lead to the formation of a predatory centralized government in Atlantica committed to nationalize all private property and initiative, and it would destroy the democratic freedoms that Atlanteans were enjoying for the first time.

Next, Figueiroa said that choosing to remain under Portugal's thumb would be equally disastrous. Under the Socialists, Atlantica would remain a small part of a distant ancient state—and its limitless potential as an independent country aligned with the United States would be lost forever.

When the Atlantean Liberation Front's Noe Montes Claros turn came to speak, he said, "Not so fast, Dr. Figueiroa! A coalition of independent voters will not go knocking on your door because it will be obvious to them that the type of independence you offer Atlanteans will only make them more dependent on greedy foreign capitalists who will not hesitate in appropriating Atlantean resources and cheap labor to further enrich themselves. In contrast, with the ALF in charge, Atlantean resources will be shared by everyone alike—and we will no longer have the current inequality between the masses of the common people and the ruling elites."

"Thank you, gentlemen," Antunes said. "You have both proven the common sense of the Socialist position. The kind of independence you both promise is the shortest route for us to lose the self-determination we have managed to gain so far. The choice you offer to Atlantean voters is whether they prefer to hand over control of their current resources and economic affairs to greedy profit-motivated American-style capitalists or to a dictatorial Soviet-style government."

Antunes continued to argue that the true interests of Atlanteans, including the sense of cultural identity they had built over the centuries, were best served by turning Atlantica into a self-governing autonomous region of Portugal, totally dedicated to sustainable development, such as proposed by the new coalition. "Becoming an autonomous region will enhance our identity and allow us to remain true to ourselves. We are neither Americans or Soviets; we are Portuguese-Atlanteans, and as such, we are an integral and important part of Portugal!"

Although nothing more was said about the Homeland Coalition

at Friday night's debate, it was obvious that the stage was now set for coalition members to begin to take advantage of this newfound notoriety and bring their previously ignored issues to the forefront of the political debate.

For instance, an engineer with the Faia Environmental Association decided the time was right to rush the publication of his study about Atlantica's extraordinary potential for becoming an energy self-sufficient region through the sustainable use of its renewable resources. At a press release in the coalition's headquarters, the engineer challenged the party candidates to discuss their views on the development of Atlantica's unique geothermal, wind, and tidal energy generation potential.

"Given our exceptional conditions, we want to know whether the parties consider investment in renewable energy resources a priority in order to avoid the exploitation of our small economy by the big energy cartels of the outside world. We want to know also which parties are ready to start now with a realistic program designed to achieve renewable energy self-sufficiency by the year 2000, such as we have found to be feasible in our study."

Headlines in the media the next day read, 'Energy Self-sufficiency by 2000!"

The journalist wrote, "The Homeland Coalition demands a commitment by the political parties to make Atlantica self-sufficient in energy by the year 2000."

In another instance, a reporter was invited by the coalition to attend a meeting of farmers in Arrife, and Pedro Galvão, the credit union president, restated some of the points he had discussed in previous coalition meetings. "The fact is that 80 percent of us in Atlantica still live in rural areas, and there can be no sustainable development here unless farmers like us have an opportunity to make a decent living. Our priorities therefore are to have access to the means to improve our productivity without destroying our land and to improve our capacity to sell our product.

"We wonder to what extent the political parties understand this issue. Are they willing to set up the mechanisms that will install technical capacity for sustainable agriculture in the hands of Atlanteans? Are they ready to ensure financing for the development of rural producers' cooperatives and markets for their products?"

The next day the headlines stated: "The Coalition's Small Farmers Challenge the Republican Way!" The article said, 'Small farmers in Atlantica reject the Republican large-scale industrial farming approach to agricultural development. They demand that any future government be committed to preserve their property rights and implement policies that will assist them to practice environmentally efficient and sustainable agriculture in the hands of Atlanteans. They want to preserve traditional crops, native species, and centuries of farming practices that have served them well and enhanced product quality."

At the following Friday night's televised political debate, Dr. Figueroa began to display some cracks in his usually calm and scholarly demeanor. In order to attack Antunes, he came out fighting the coalition. By doing so, he played right into Antunes's own hands. "This coalition, which you, Mr. Antunes, seem to be developing such a liking for, is no more than a collection of losers and amateur scientists like you. You and your inexperienced friends have obviously put it together to use it against us. Your coalition has no financial resources and no competent leadership to implement their proposals. What the coalition proposes would cause Atlantica's economy to go down fragmented in an anarchic vortex of small interests still connected to the way things were under the collapsed dictatorship of Portugal.

244 ~ Manuel Januário

"The milk and meat production in large scale, which the coalition attacks as dangerous monoculture, is in fact the only way to efficiently utilize Atlantica's comparative advantages due to its climate and year-round pastures."

Dr. Figueroa was both wrong and unwise when he decided to attack Antunes through the coalition, which, having risen from the grassroots, was beginning to articulate the most authentic and urgent aspirations of Atlanteans. His angry denunciation of those aspirations only served to demonstrate how out of touch he was with many independent voters, and it alienated them from the Republican Party.

With only two months left to the election, independent voters and coalition supporters gained yet another influential ally, Antonio Moniz, the director of the regional television. Moniz was one of those frustrated journalists who, in the days of the dictatorship, had become best known and respected among his peers more for what he did not publish than for what he did publish. Salazar's censorship would cut so much out of his articles that the pages surrounding them were often filled with pictures put in there at the last minute to fill the empty spaces, so much so that he would say jokingly to his friends that in his articles, "Each picture was literally worth a thousand words!"

As the administrator of the only TV station on the island, he felt a genuine responsibility to play a role in the discussion of all issues important to Atlanteans, particularly those not yet given enough attention by the parties. He decided to dedicate the thirty minutes of prime time immediately after the news hour every Monday evening to interviewing one of eight personalities not officially attached to any party, whom he thought could best bring to the attention of all voters' public interest ideas that had not yet been fully discussed.

Moniz knew that practically the whole island would be watching these interviews, but he made it a point to announce it before the news to raise the audience's level of curiosity and give his program greater significance.

On this Monday night, he made his pitch as tantalizing as he could. "Welcome again to the News Hour, followed tonight by our elections feature: 'Atlantica, What Future?' Tonight, however, our theme should be more appropriately named 'Atlantica, What a Future!' Stay tuned after the news! See you in an hour."

One Atlantean who did not watch the News Hour this Monday was the most preeminent supporter of the Republican Party: Tony Matos.

Normally, he would have left his hotel room at eight o'clock and gone straight to Eusebio's for dinner, but tonight, he had many troublesome ideas running through his mind. He decided to mull them over with a cool head before he started pouring martinis down his throat. And there was no better way to do that than to take a stroll to the docks to see the six big tractors and two bulldozers that had just been delivered to him that afternoon from the United States. They looked disproportionately large and nearly occupied all the cargo area spaces.

This was a huge investment, the biggest any single individual had ever made in brand-new agricultural equipment in Atlantica. Matos did not usually buy so much equipment in a single time with his own money, and he had partially mortgaged one of his milk processing and distribution plants in California because he didn't want to share this particular project with his investment partners.

As he looked at the huge pieces of equipment in front of him, Matos thought, *This is really big stuff! It better work!*

As a young man growing up in Atlantica, Matos was obsessed with the idea that he wanted to become a rich man, but he didn't know how until he went into the military service in Portugal. There, he discovered the simple secret: to be rich, you become a businessman.

As a businessman, you multiply your earnings by the number of men you have working for you. Twenty men at your service will make you rich ten or even twenty times faster than if you work alone!

On his return to Atlantica, however, when he tried to put his get-rich formula into practice, he ran into two unanticipated problems. First, he had insufficient start-up capital for his business, and second, he discovered that all the best business opportunities were already taken.

Yet, just as he was about to succumb to the terrible fate of becoming just a worker making money for another businessman, he learned that there was still another secret to getting rich fast: You have to be at the right place at the right time, according to Frank Melo.

Melo was the richest man Matos's village had ever produced. He had immigrated to the San Joaquin Valley in California when it was still a near desert. When water became easily available—and the land was still very cheap—he had the good sense to grab as much land and water as he could. Eventually, he became one of the most successful cattle ranchers and milk producers during the agricultural gold rush.

Matos lived next door to Melo's vacation home in Atlantica, and for him, that meant being in the right place at the right time.

Mr. Melo had a daughter near Matos's age, and she found the army-trained physique and genuine good looks of her father's young neighbor of great interest to her. Matos wasted no time and courted her incessantly; before the summer was over, he had married her. After two years, he was on his way to becoming the foreman of his father-in-law's operations in California.

Five years later, Mr. Melo decided to retire in Pismo Beach, like many other rich Portuguese ranchers. But, unlike them, he did not sell his dairy farm to the giant companies that were supplying dairy products to the new supermarket chains because his son-in-law had learned yet another method for amassing an even greater fortune: using other people's money to expand your own business.

It's easy! All you have to do is convince investors to trust you enough to lend you the large quantities of money you need to double or triple your business and its profits in exchange for a reliable small share of those profits.

So, Matos joined all the exclusive clubs, where these potential investors played golf, tennis, and other rich people's games, so that he could win their confidence, and then he used their money to make himself wealthier by the minute. From this same group of new friends, Matos hired the best accountants and lawyers to protect his interests and keep it all legal.

This way, Matos secured his place among the elite, and he developed a sense of moral superiority and entitlement every bit as strong as that of the original immigrants to America in the *Mayflower*.

It seemed that Matos had finally achieved everything he had aspired to in his early days in Atlantica, and all he had to do now was be a happy man and rest on his laurels. Sadly, however, there was one trick to being rich that Matos hadn't learned yet: quitting while you are ahead!

As he was enlarging his dairy empire in the United States, Matos frequently came to Atlantica for vacations with his relatives. While he was there, he often rubbed his success in the faces of the merchants and bankers who had ignored him when he came home from military service. His pride and unquenchable ambition still demanded that he get even with them.

While on vacation in Atlantica in 1975, months after the Carnation Revolution in Lisbon, Matos ran into Dr. Alberto Figueiroa. The professor had spent a number of years as a university professor in California, but he had returned home to become the leader of the island's newly formed Republican Party, seeking to obtain independence from Portugal, just like the other overseas Portuguese territories had done.

In his conversations with Figueiroa, Matos realized that a politically independent Atlantica, economically dependent on the United States, was a perfect opportunity to create a new meat and dairy products empire on his native island. Once again, Matos felt that he was in the right place at the right time.

He began to buy land from impoverished land barons at bargain prices, and he became the most visible and influential supporter of the Atlantean Republican Party. His plan was to buy out as many of the small farmers as necessary to create a continuous landmass, free of any hydrangea fences so he could sow alfalfa and other fast-growing grasses for year-round pasturing of cattle. This would result in huge quantities of pasture-fed meat and milk products of superior quality.

As a pure business venture, the plan was ideal at both ends of the equation. On the marketing side, the established reputation of quality of Atlantean dairy products secured high demand practically without any publicity. On the production side, his cash-in-hand offers to broke land barons and poor small farmers would guarantee access to large tracts of fertile land at bargain prices. Cheap labor was also guaranteed, and Matos's own expertise in dairy business couldn't be matched anywhere on the island. There was no way it could go wrong!

So, when the Republican Party jumped ahead in the polls, relying on his instincts alone, Matos left his American businesses in the hands of his capable managers, moved to Atlantica, and dedicated himself totally to the immediate development of his new venture. He was way ahead of any competitors who might be having similar ideas. The speed at which he carried out his plans reflects the degree of confidence he had.

At the docks that night, looking at his disproportionately large pieces of equipment, he was experiencing intense doubt—an emotional state he had long forgotten.

From the moment he had married his rich neighbor's daughter, everything had always gone right for him, and he had come to believe it always would. However, what Dr. Figueiroa had wanted to discuss with him earlier in the morning had, for the first time, made him doubt the wisdom of his enormous gamble.

The questions Dr. Figueiroa wanted to discuss were serious: "Is an independent Atlantica really the preferred American strategy for Atlantica, as we were led to believe covertly, or would America really prefer to operate its strategic air force here under the terms of its current treaty with Portugal? Might this be the reason why the American ambassador in Lisbon is always so busy that he never has time to meet with me?" Figueiroa asked Matos and himself these questions.

He was also concerned that the lobbying efforts in Washington on behalf of an independent Atlantica had not taken off as planned. The agribusiness professional lobbyists in Washington were used to working with deep-pocketed investors in the Central American banana republics, and they didn't seem to be highly motivated to work on behalf of investments in cattle and dairy products in a still-to-become-independent Atlantica.

The conversation with Figueiroa in the morning had raised doubts in Matos's mind about his political capacities on the big stage. The significant decline of voter support for the party shown by the polls in this afternoon's paper added an even more serious question in his mind: *Will I be able to deliver the promised independence here in Atlantica?*

And right then, at the docks, Matos felt alone and totally out of his comfort zone. This was a situation he could not control with money and clever business schemes as he usually did. Indeed, when he took a last look at his shiny new tractors and bulldozers, he could no longer clearly visualize them churning through the hydrangea-fenced quilt of small pastures on the lower flanks of Pico Alto and turning them into a seamless mantle of green grass, dotted only with his countless beef and dairy cattle.

When Matos finally strode into Eusebio's for his regular steak dinner, dressed in his trademark American Levi jeans, his tight western-cut shirt, tucked under a wide cowhide belt encrusted with blue stones, he was as imposing a figure as always, but he felt out of place in the midst of all these mild-mannered Atlanteans.

A couple sitting at his regular dining table in front of the television got up and offered it to him politely, and they blended in with the after-dinner coffee- and beer-drinking group arguing over the weekend's football results, just shown at the end of the News Hour. Matos plopped himself on the stuffed armchair facing the TV and ordered the usual double martini to soothe his troubles. He even made a faint attempt to seduce the waitress, trying to calm himself down.

At the sound of the TV announcer's voice signaling the start of Moniz's highly anticipated elections program, the TV screen showed the words: "Atlantica, What Future?"

The crowd, still mesmerized by the magic of TV, quieted down immediately.

Moniz was already talking and raising his hands as a sign of victory as he walked into the studio. "My friends, after many weeks of trying, I finally convinced Mário Garcia to come here and get grilled tonight! Mário was born on the other side of Pico Alto thirty-nine years ago and was nurtured as a true believer in economic and social justice by the well-known Padre José of San Lucas, the only man who has implemented a successful land reform in Atlantica, and perhaps in the country.

"Mário learned the lessons of his mentor so well that at the first opportunity, he scolded none other than the owner of half the island, Countess Barbosa. He told her she shouldn't keep all that land for herself, and he challenged her to give some of it to the landless poor. Imagine that!

"With her oligarch's pride seriously shaken by his words and actions, she forced him out of college—and eventually out of the country—much like what happened to other young students who challenged Antonio Salazar back then in Portugal.

"Anyway, the years have passed, and he has come back like the political exiles of his generation, but this one, my friends, will have nothing to do with organized politics!"

Mário finally appeared on the screen in front of Moniz.

"Mr. Garcia, how do you explain this contradiction: a returned political exile who wants nothing to do with politicians?"

Mário smiled at Moniz's intentional provocation and said, "Mr. Moniz, you are mistaken about my attitudes toward politics and politicians. I respect and honor politics as an essential vocation to serve the community, and I also have every reason to like our politicians for what they honestly want to do to improve and change our future. I recognize that our destiny is in their hands, and it is through their leadership and wisdom that I trust Atlantica will become that paradise we all dream with!"

"Why, then, does your Homeland Coalition remain politically nonaligned instead of becoming a party and fielding candidates in this important election?"

"My coalition? Once again, Mr. Moniz your question is deliberately provocative! How can a coalition be mine or anybody else's if by definition it is a 'conglomerate' of many individual citizens and separate social interests? The members of this coalition have come together to articulate a common platform that ensures our separate survival and protects our rights vis-à-vis other stronger forces with greater visibility and power."

"And what is that common platform, Mr. Garcia?"

"Simply: Atlantica is our homeland! It is a place where Atlanteans have learned to live and survive together for centuries united by their common values as well as the soil they come from—in spite of their many significant differences and sometimes conflicting interests. Our coalition sees this cultural unity through diversity as the foundation of our common future to be passed on to our children."

"Don't all the political parties share those attitudes?"

"I hope all the parties understand that it is in their long-term interest to preserve the cultural values that unite citizens with the land in Atlantica and give us our unique identity. To the extent they do, all of us in the coalition will accept them. We will also not hesitate to give them our votes as our political leaders and the defenders of our individual legitimate rights and interests."

"To what extent have the parties embraced this coalition platform?"

"That is not very clear yet," replied Mário.

"Please explain!" urged Moniz.

"Let's review the position taken by the Communist Party. It has praiseworthy proposals in the defense of the basic economic and social rights of Atlanteans, such as the right to a job, a living wage, an education for all children, health care, and decent housing. And who in their right mind would disagree with the idea that everyone should be given an opportunity to contribute to the development of society 'according to his ability,' and in exchange to receive from it 'according to his needs'? Yet the same Communist Party parts company with the Homeland Coalition when it proposes that Atlantica should adopt the Soviet-style, state-owns-everything model and become a Soviet pawn in the Cold War!"

"And the Republican Party, how does it accept the coalition's platform?"

"On the surface, the Republicans want to implement policies that would help Atlanteans improve their standard of living. We need the better access to international capital and credit they propose to be able to import appropriate technology and the tools necessary to promote greater efficiency of our agricultural resources. It is only the efficiency the Republicans say we need that can lead us into the autonomous, self-reliant, sustainable, and environmentally sound future we seek. And indeed, in many of these areas the Republican Party seems to be the best positioned to provide the leadership we need to take us to the better economic future we all want.

"Yet, the same Republican Party also promotes policies that will be favorable to the large corporations that will destroy our diversified small farms to make way to a beef and dairy products monoculture. That will eliminate much of the biodiversity of our homeland—and the self-sufficiency and diversity of our food supply.

"Besides, all this will be done to enrich primarily the multinational enterprises, who will become the primary beneficiaries of our favorable climatic conditions and the reputation we have earned through decades of making our traditional products excellent, such as our 'Island Cheese.'"

"But don't the Republicans promise also good-paying jobs for Atlanteans?"

"Yes! But when the new owners of Atlantica promise us good-paying jobs in exchange for our lands, they do not say how many good-paying jobs. And we all know that any profit-first-oriented business will offer as few jobs as possible in order to keep production costs low and profits high. You can bet that the land bought from under our farmers will be used first and foremost for the enrichment of their new owners—and not to create jobs or to ensure the well-being of all Atlantean farmers."

There was no mistake about how strongly Mário felt about the impact of international corporations taking over Atlantica's agricultural infrastructure and how it would affect the people and culture of the island.

Moniz realized that Mário had more to say, and he said, "Please go on!"

"Mr. Moniz, these corporations will be literally taking our land permanently away from under us when the heavy equipment, already sitting on the docks, levels our gentle slopes, destroys our unique native flora and hydrangea fences, and corrals Atlanteans into crowded villages and towns.

"Farmers will have to rely on these companies to provide them with employment to support their families. But only the strong and the healthy will be hired to operate the equipment to harvest crops and prepare the produce for export.

"Atlanteans will lose the relative abundance of the seasonal crops they now collect in their cellars in exchange for a small paycheck to be used at the company store to buy expensive food and other necessities that will have to be imported from long distances. And, Mr. Moniz, there are others in our coalition who can explain with much greater authority than me the negative impacts on our water, air, and soil resulting from these changes to our traditional agricultural practices."

Matos could not stand listening to this persuasive indictment of his plans anymore. He got up and flung his still-half-full martini glass into the wall above the television.

The liquid showered down on the small crowd, and they were stunned at his behavior.

"I will kill that son of a bitch! You mark my words! Even if it is the last thing I do, I will kill that son of bitch!" He stormed out of Eusebio's with the threatening look of a genuine madman stamped on his face.

The patrons at Eusebio's continued to listen to the rest of Mário's interview—and so did thousands of other Atlanteans in the homes and community centers of Atlantica.

In the following weeks the political parties, joined by community leaders and opinion makers, continued to expound on what the future of Atlantica should be.

Television continued to air nonpartisan points of view, which contributed to the new and growing awareness among voters that they actually had a choice as free and independent individuals. No longer did they all have to toe a single party's line as in the past!

Paradoxically, this notion of each person voting their own choice created genuine uncertainty and encouraged each voter to stay involved, thinking that their vote could be the decisive one.

The coalition stayed politically unaffiliated, but it became increasingly obvious that its rise had given new life to and benefited the Socialist Party because their platforms were more closely aligned.

A few days before the election, the officials of the coalition announced that a picnic was to be held at the park in the center of San Luis to celebrate its successful voter registration campaign and to make a last public appeal for all Atlanteans to vote.

Many speeches were made.

When Mário's turn came, he said, "We came here primarily to celebrate, not to hear speeches! But I have been delegated by the San Lucas Town Council to invite you all to participate in our San Lucas Community Celebration, and that deserves a short explanation. As you might know, Dona Olivia was the last of the Count Vasconcellos who owned the San Lucas Valley for centuries. In 1908, in a fit of despair under the pressure of her responsibilities and feeling alone, she resolved that her way out was to commit suicide and leave the land to the people of San Lucas. The title to all the county's properties was then transferred to the same San Lucans who for many centuries had worked for her ancestors as near slaves.

"Padre José was the man she chose to execute her testament, but he did much more than that. He helped us in San Lucas understand that we were made to be and live as one with our land and with each other—much like a human family should. That's what we celebrate in San Lucas on June 24! I think that all of us in Atlantica are now learning to do the same! So, if you can join us at St. John's Hill, let's begin to celebrate together our newfound future as Atlanteans!"

After the picnic, Mário and Monica, exhausted from the demanding schedule of the past few months, left for San Lucas. They were tired, but they were also very happy because they had helped bring to the forefront of the political debate the need for preserving the environment, the culture, and the integrity of the Atlantean way of life.

Monica knew that Mário' happiness had roots even deeper than that. They were as deep as his conviction that Atlanteans today, like San Lucans many years before, were in the frontline of those trying to create a new model for shaping a better humankind living in a sustainable better world.

The day after they arrived in San Lucas, Monica and Mário decided to walk their favorite trail up to Miradouro. Dazzled again by its beautiful sights and their memories, Mário began to pour out what was going through his mind. "It was walking this trail, when I was merely twenty years old, that Padre José helped me understand in a mature way that I was just a tiny part of an unfinished world—and that the most plausible reason for me to exist was to help improve it as much as I could, until the whole of humanity became a family of brothers. I never forgot that!"

Monica embraced him impulsively and said, "Don't forget that some of your human 'brothers' don't think exactly the way you do, starting with Matos's publicly announced position!"

"True! But, in spite of Matos's primitive attitudes, most of us in Atlantica are ready to join other justice-driven societies and speed ahead into the fast-coming better world! What a joy!"

9 BUILDING THE DREAMLAND

Elections

finally took place on the June 21, 1976, and 90 percent of all eligible Atlanteans voted. That was the firm first step of Atlanteans toward their new Atlantica.

This was an astonishing accomplishment, considering the fact that many were first-time voters. These results would have been hard to achieve had it not been for the efforts of the Homeland Coalition, which coordinated voter-registration campaigns in every town and village on the island.

It was obvious that voting was a serious affair for Atlanteans. Some were still debating the issues as they walked to the voting booths to cast their votes for the first time.

Through their many heated discussions, they had matured in their sense of citizenship. Most Atlanteans had gained a greater awareness of their personal worth, their rights, and also their sense of belonging to a wider community, which they were now shaping through their vote.

This was progress for a people who had been living by a different paradigm for five hundred years, molded by the interests of colonizers who often claimed divine right to own and control their territories and the people living therein.

In San Lucas, on June 24, at 7:00 a.m., Mário and Monica, entered the stream of people headed toward St. John's Hill for the traditional community celebration of thanks for the ownership of their land. Many of them were out-of-towners who had accepted the invitation to participate. They had begun to arrive in San Lucas the day before by all means of transportation or on foot with tents on their backs. Walking up the trail, they were still talking about politics and the election.

If someone from the old days could drop in on the St. John's Hill trail today, they would not recognize these new Atlanteans. They were excited and talkative, but after every hour of climb, their conversations stopped—and they dedicated total attention to their transistor radios, hoping to hear the results of the final vote count.

The voting had taken place three days earlier, but the results were slow in coming because the elections commission wanted to ensure that the final count, when announced, was correct.

Mário and Monica followed the moving crowd calmly, involved in the conversations and feeling all the excitement until, three hours later, they reached the top.

It was a gorgeous sunny day with a blue sky dotted here and there with small white clouds born of the moist western breezes that traveled over the Atlantic Ocean and swept up the green slopes of Atlantica. The scent of the grass mixed with that of the ocean in the breeze.

By ten thirty, most of the crowd of San Lucans, swollen by perhaps a couple thousand other Atlanteans, had flooded into the flat bottom of the low-rimmed crater on top of St. John's Hill. Most were dressed in colorful traditional attire as a sign of the regional pride encouraged by the Socialists' campaign. Many wore *albarcas* on their feet and hand-knit wool caps on their heads. An exceptional feeling of popular celebration filled the thinner hilltop air.

Suddenly, when the watches marked eleven o'clock, the crowd went silent again. The Elections Commission was ready to announce the final results, according to the news broadcast!

The Republicans had 33 percent of the vote, the Communists had managed to reach 10 percent, and the Socialists had won with 52 percent. The rest of the votes had been divided between the Monarchists and the Greens.

For several minutes, it was absolute delirium in the crowd, which obviously had voted mostly Socialist. The crowd went silent again as Antunes was about to make a victory speech over the airwaves. All the radios were put at their highest volume, so everyone could hear him.

"In the months leading up to this election, all of us Atlanteans have been discussing how we should build our collective future. We generally agreed that we want to develop our common resources in a way that benefits all of us, so that no Atlantean is left behind. So, fortunately, our differences were not about our ultimate goals, which thankfully we all share, but about the way to achieve them. And even when we argued about the different ways to reach those goals, we found that, in many respects, our proposals were similar. So, my dear Atlantean brothers and sisters, we are all winners today! Congratulations!

"Now, in order to succeed, we must all work together! This is the time to join hands and activate all our energies toward the achievement of our common goals and objectives in life.

"My special congratulations and my appeal to unite go out to all the parties and to all individuals and groups of Atlanteans who worked so hard to make our first democratic election campaign such a success.

"As the president of the Socialists, I want to thank specially our hard workers. But I can't forget that it was the Homeland Coalition that was present to help register voters in places where even the parties didn't go, using volunteers recruited from everywhere, even from a Latin American jail."

Amidst the roar of the crowd that heard these last words, a group of enthusiastic San Lucas young men grabbed Mário, carried him to the center of the plateau, and clapped their hands. "Viva Atlantica! Viva Atlantica!"

When they quieted down, Mário shouted at the top of his lungs, "My friends, this is a day of celebration! Let's sing and dance! Let the music begin!"

The crowd was in a celebrating mood, and the musicians were ready.

After a strident trumpet call, the violins and mandolins began to play the joyfully festive melodies the older San Lucans had been perfecting for decades.

Soon all began to sing and form into the customary concentric dancing circles, starting smaller in the middle, each being hugged in by the next. They synchronized their steps to the music and moved to the same rhythm, each in the opposite direction to the next, forming a human kaleidoscope of color and harmony. And the gyrating circles of Atlanteans got wider and wider until all were dancing and singing their joy!

This would surely have put a triumphant smile on Padre José's face, realizing that the whole Atlantica had claimed full ownership of their own homeland! The multitude of people danced itself to exhaustion, and then, true to tradition, they spread blankets on the ground—loaded with food and drink to share and fuel friendly conversations until sunset.

Couples and small groups roamed from one blanket to another, sitting cross-legged on the grass or walking off to observe the imposing majesty of Pico Alto above or the fantastic panoramic views of the San Lucas Valley, all the way down to the checkerboard of black lava walls of the verdant vineyards along the coast.

Mário and Monica were totally exhausted as they walked off to the same little knoll at the edge of the crater where, nineteen years before, they had pledged their love to each other for the first time. They sat there, remembering and leaning on each other pleasurably, as they intended to do for the rest of their lives.

A tall man in blue jeans, a tight-fitting western riding jacket, and a cowboy hat—with his horse walking behind him—moved through the groups. A few feet from the small knoll, the man stopped, pulled out a gun, aimed it toward Mário's back, and shot twice.

Mário fell backward, stirred just a little, and then stopped moving. When Monica grabbed him, his eyes stared at her! Thank God, his heart was still beating strong!

Matos, with the gun still in his hand, and his eyes bulging like those of a madman, stared at the crowd as he mounted his horse and rode away fast down the trail to San Lucas. A large group of young men began to chase him, and others went looking for their horses, but they soon lost sight of him.

When Matos got down to San Lucas, he stopped at Batoldo's old tavern, put his gun on the table, and told the old man to bring him a bottle of whiskey. While he scrambled to obey his command, Matos looked at him with a madman's glare. "I had to do it; don't you agree? A man can't lose what he has spent a lifetime to get and do nothing about it, can he?"

He grabbed the bottle and mounted his horse again. He was unfamiliar with the roads, and he took a wrong turn. Instead of turning to the Burnt Ridge Road, which could have taken him to the airport and perhaps a plane back to the United States, he headed down toward Ponta Negra and the oceanfront. When he realized his mistake and turned back, he was confronted with the fastest downhill runners coming down the narrow road, which was sealed by five-foot stone walls through the verdant vineyards all the way to Ponta Negra.

When Matos met the insurmountable barricade of rage in front of him, he turned back down again toward the sea.

They pelted him with rocks.

When he reached the rough and bare hard lava beds, stretching a few hundred feet inland from Ponta Negra, the horseshoes drew sparks and slid on the lava surfaces, further spooking it.

Matos tried to steer it back toward the advancing crowd, but he lost control of the animal. Scared by the loud clatter of his own hooves, he panicked, turned back toward the ocean, and headed straight out to Ponta Negra.

When the horse saw a large wave approaching the black rocks and breaking into a white cloud of heavy sea spray, he suddenly stopped, slipped, and tumbled sideways down the steep cliff.

Matos was propelled over the edge and hit his head on the rocks on the way down. The approaching boys only saw a body with a cowboy hat still strapped to his back, being rolled up by the waves and repeatedly tossed against the rocks surrounding the bay.

One of the boys—about seventeen, round face, wavy air, tears running down his cheeks—looked toward St. John's Hill and prayed that his uncle was still alive.

Thank God his prayer was heard!

Dear reader, the last time you "saw" me as a protagonist in Mário's story, I was saying farewell to him as he left prison in Santa Cruz. That was more than thirty years ago, in 1975! After his departure from Santa Cruz, I remained in jail for almost another year.

I was happy to see him go home! It also gave me new hope that I would be released one day.

As you already know, Mário and Monica soon got very busy with the Homeland Coalition in Atlantica, and their frequent letters comforted me and gave me the strength to endure the following long months. I often joined them emotionally, and with every piece of Toro's brown paper I scribbled their continuing story on, I was proving to myself that their unrestrained optimism about Atlantica was justified.

But when I heard the news that Matos's bullets had knocked Mário to the ground and sent him to a hospital in mortal danger, my shaky emotions caved in. Whatever courage and calm I had managed to muster disappeared, and I felt wrapped in a dark cocoon of loneliness and despair.

My emotional breakdown led in short order to intellectual cynicism regarding the evil core of the economic and political powers of this world, from where I never had any good reason to expect much. Suddenly, I was overcome by the feeling that Mário's life had been in vain. I couldn't think straight, much less write, and I stopped writing.

When I was released from prison four months later, the good news from Atlantica was that Mário had survived and was recovering well. Everything got better!

Once free, I got busy taking control of my businesses with renewed enthusiasm. I rapidly regained my sense of commitment to the causes that Mário and I had worked on together, starting with Nossa Terra. As if to make up for lost time, I became a workaholic.

And for all these years, I have done nothing else. Two months ago, I decided that the conditions were finally right for me to slow down, retire, and plan a long overdue visit to Mário and Monica in Atlantica.

My first retirement project was to read Mário's and my own prison writings back in the 1970s. To my surprise, I find them as timely in 2005 as they were when we wrote them.

In the early 1970s, the Club of Rome scientists had already wrung their most serious warning about the earth's environmental limitations to take care of the nearly four billion human beings alive at the time.

Today, scientists are reissuing the same warning: if we don't change our habits, there is no way the nearly seven billion of us today can survive much longer on the planet we have been sucking dry. We must urgently learn to share our Mother Earth like brothers and sisters. We must stop our overconsumption guided by good politicians who are capable of changing our shortsighted for-profit-only capitalism into the cooperative economics of sustainable frugality.

Fortunately, many economists are beginning to see that their true mission is to discover a more "cooperative capitalism," redesigned to work for everyone's benefit and not the unearned profit of just a few.

So, my dear "earth-ship fellow traveler" of the twenty-first century—that's how some of us thought of each other back in the 1970s when our earth-ship was beginning to falter—I am now going to finish Mário Garcia's story for you because it is as relevant today as it was back then.

What follows includes my cousin Monica's story also. She is a determined woman without whom some of the changes in the life of modern Atlantica would not have happened. In modern Atlantica, she became as powerful a force for the good as our noble aunt, Countess Barbosa, had managed to be for the bad. Indeed, Monica's story is that of another rich landowner who understood well that it was in her hands to solve the problems of many poor Atlanteans. And she did!

As a result, Mário's and Monica's stories became intimately connected to the development of Atlantica's success in sustainable development, which is another story that I am here to tell.

However, before I finish, I promise to take you with me to visit the two of them in San Lucas, where it all began for Mário sixty-eight years ago. It was there that he learned, from his family and Padre José, to live as a true child of the earth and to become a brother to all his fellow human beings, in a God-souled universe, which he still sees as the outer skin of God Himself.

So, let me not spend any more time on background issues and start by telling you what happened to Mário after the near-fatal shooting at St. John's Hill celebration in 1976.

One of Matos's bullets missed its target, and it was found in the ground a few inches below where Mário was sitting. The other hit him on the lower part of the vertebral column, where it lodged.

The San Luis Hospital doctors removed the bullet and did what they could to clean out the wound, but the serious damage to the bone and the nerves was permanent. It nearly paralyzed his right leg and seriously weakened the left, but he was alive and would recover!

With the miracles of medicine, followed by physical and occupational therapy, Mário learned to efficiently use his damaged body. Though sometimes pain ridden, he did not lose any of his ability to appreciate life as a miracle to be thankful for and enjoyed. He eventually learned to be mobile with the help of a wheelchair until it became second nature to him and part of his identity. To many around him, he became affectionately known as the San Lucas Man on Wheels.

In some respects, Mário's physical impairment sharpened his insights regarding our human condition. It also helped him understand the urgency and the true dimension of Monica's and his own future mission in the building of the new Atlantica.

And so, Mário and Monica, utilizing all the favorable circumstances of regional autonomy in Atlantica, advanced together full of enthusiasm and love for their homeland, so much so that the story of the past thirty years of their lives cannot be told apart from the recent history of the new land they very significantly helped create.

After Mário's long recovery, mostly in San Lucas, he and Monica moved right into the Vila Miséria Slum. Due to their unique circumstances and extraordinary talent, they became the heart and soul of the Millennium Village project, which eventually combined the best of public and private efforts to transform the lives of thousands of Atlanteans from slum dwellers into the builders and owners of their own residences.

From Santa Cruz, I followed their progress with great excitement, mostly through long telephone conversations. We continued to discuss the details of our current projects and rely on each other's advice to overcome current difficulties.

One day, around the end of 1979, Mário was explaining the size of their current challenge. Monica's dream of building a new community in her old abandoned plantation turned into a slum at the heart of Vila Miséria required aligning a lot of political and technical skills and influences in the same direction. As politically unaligned citizens and with no government-related responsibility, Monica and Mário were at the mercy of the government to rezone, build accesses and infrastructures, develop approvable plans, and mobilize a host of other essential services from the public and private sector.

"But, André," Mario told me one day, "your cousin was made for this job! With her at the helm, the plan has begun to take shape—and the good news is that your cousin's Millennium Village dream project has been approved. It will be built gradually for the next twenty years. As you see, André, we have our work cut out for us for quite a while!"

As our conversation over the wires was getting entirely too long, I decided to challenge Mário, a bit jokingly, to become again the writer of dreams as once he was in prison. I said, "Now that Monica seems to be the busy one, use some of your free time to explain to me how the new Atlantica government has organized itself to achieve such heretofore impossible bureaucratic tasks in such a reasonable amount of time. I want to know how this efficient new Atlantean government built itself from the ground up!"

He accepted my challenge, and a couple of weeks later, I got the following long letter in the mail:

Hello, André,

You have convinced me to write to you again about dreams!

This time, I am going to write not about the "Land of Dreams," but about a possible "dreamland" slowly arising right here in Atlantica.

You want to know details of how our new Atlantica built itself from the ground up. I think it did it in three crucially important ways: it reinforced its millennial land-related cultural values; it formed a corruption-averse government, and it made room for all Atlanteans to contribute to and share Atlantica's bounties through a fully active labor force.

(1) The Love of the Land and Its Cultural Values

I think the key to Atlantica's current success is an uncompromising love for the land, though this is a value shared by all the nations of Europe. What we Atlanteans added here was intensifying and refining our understanding of unity with our land due to our unique circumstances.

As islanders in the middle of an unending ocean, we can never lose sight of our essential connection to the soil under our feet, as if it were a life raft.

Indeed, André, here in Atlantica, it seems that after we gained autonomy, we found something deeper that unites us: a sense of identity and a closer affinity to our land and to each other. An insightful sociologist might say that modern Atlanteans have refined their traditional Atlantean culture to include an even more altruistic and environmentally sound way of life. Just like the bees in a beehive find the intelligent resonance of their beehive spirit and gain capacity to do together things they could never do alone, modern Atlanteans working together have achieved a degree of wellness, satisfaction, and happiness that their ancestors could only dream with.

By now, André, you might want to ask, "Why did you wait for so long? Why didn't this happen in past Atlantean and European history?"

(2) A Corruption-Averse Cooperative Government

I think, that the answer to that fair question is that we have succeeded in forming a corruption-averse government.

The Carnation Revolution generated a crop of good politicians both in Portugal and in Atlantica. The Carnation Revolution had a strain of purity that found ideal circumstances to grow here in Atlantica, where good politicians made the good decisions that became the source of our current success.

First, our politicians understood that an autonomous region in Atlantica, organized within the "principle of subsidiarity," could contribute the most to the national whole. So, they negotiated a regional statute that allowed the key political and economic decisions to be made closest to the people who were going to execute and benefit from them. This way, ordinary Atlanteans can become the owners of their own lives and the builders of their own dreams.

Yet, obtaining this good and fair regional statute was just the first step.

The new regional Parliament leaders realized also that their only chance to bring success to the region today was for the elected MPs to clearly define how they were going to work efficiently together to ensure that all Atlanteans had an opportunity to share in the bounties of their homeland. In other words, Atlanteans needed to have a privilege-fighting, corruption-averse government!

The initial step in this direction was for the political parties to agree formally that their function was to help elect party affiliated members of Parliament (MPs,) but that once elected, their main responsibility was not so much to implement party-favored policies in their districts but to work specifically to further the interests of their constituents. This meant that MPs had to be free to negotiate the projects and form the alliances across party lines that best responded to the needs and desires of those Atlanteans living in the districts that elected them.

To be practical and true to this spirit, the Parliament's first collective action was to <u>develop specific process rules aimed at controlling the primitive political instinct of partidocracia</u>, which is the absolute control of the government's functions by the victorious ruling party, who then dictates how its MPs shall vote and act in their districts. It is widely known that partidocracia is what often opens the door to corruption.

These new political process rules have generally led to fairly negotiated win-win decisions where everyone has a chance to contribute, and then return to his district with a sense of having become a respectable "proportional winner."

As president of the new regional government, Antunes acted scrupulously within the spirit of these political process rules. He showed political humility and wisdom from the start.

First, he approached the Republicans, led by Dr. Figueiroa, knowing and admitting that they were better positioned to attract much-needed private investment and better access to international markets, essential to the development of the regional economy. Antunes even agreed that a Republican be appointed as the chair of the Trade and Investment Committee of the Parliament.

Antunes also recognized that the Communist Party had considerable support from the working class and the Atlanteans on the lower steps of the economic ladder. He assured them that their proposals would get a fair hearing and be taken seriously. They would be given equal opportunities to become proportional winners in the shaping of policies and programs in the areas of their special interest, such as employment, housing, social services, and others.

This decision to adopt "cooperative" process rules in the Parliament gave all the parties—including the Monarchists and the Greens—a rightfully respectable voice.

With rules favoring cooperation, as opposed to destructive opposition, the MPs were ready to tackle their all-important decisions on the immediate goals for regional development and its financing. Yet, unexperienced as many of them were, they also agreed, wisely, that their first step should be to seek the best available advice about the international best practices for regional development.

So, before they convened to decide on fundamental strategies and initiatives, the Parliament gathered a nonpolitical

*commission of the best available
domestic and foreign talent to
make recommendations for the
development of specific regional
development policies and programs.
     The commission's
recommendations were summarized
as follows:*

"The overall goal of the regional government is to create conditions and opportunities for all Atlanteans to share equitably the bounties of their homeland."

In order to achieve this vision in a sustainable way, Atlantica needs to increase first the productive capacity of all its human and natural resources. In other words, only when Atlantica's economy achieves a higher level of productivity can the resulting new wealth be distributed to all Atlanteans in a sufficient and sustainable manner.

Achieving a "sustainable higher level" of productivity in today's global environment economy requires that Atlantica must immediately identify its economic clusters of comparative advantage and concentrate most of its meager public investment funds in those areas that can produce sustainably the additional wealth needed.

Next, the commission recommends the immediate implementation of a skills training program aimed at the "full" employment of the regional labor force, including all the women who heretofore had not been given opportunities equal to those given to men, particularly in the economic clusters where Atlantica enjoys competitive advantages for growth.

The initial objectives for these clusters of "comparative advantage" in Atlantica include:

Dairy Industries. The transformation of the small-size operations of pasture-fed meat and dairy products into value-added, quality-product industries, still under local control, but aimed at both local consumption and export.

Fishing Industries. The development of the traditional fishing sector into state-of-the-art sea-related industries, with capacity to respond with value-added products to the growing international market demands, including new areas of activity such as whale-watching activities and sea-related sports.

Tourism. The development of sustainable nature tourism, within the strictest good practices of conservation.

These "expert" recommendations were taken seriously by the Parliament, who used them as the basis for the regional development policy of "slow but steady economic development without excessive borrowing from the outside, relying mainly on local savings and investment and the region's demonstrated capacity to pay."

Having defined this broad economic development strategy for Atlantica, the Parliament concentrated its efforts on the mobilization of the public and private resources necessary for its implementation.

The key instruments used to this effect were:

* The immediate formation of a Regional Bank of Foment where all the economic development public funds available to the region could be accumulated and managed.
* The legislation of incentives to private savings and investment in regional projects.
* The official support to the formation of credit unions and cooperatives in the areas of comparative advantage.
* The formation of the Regional School for Entrepreneurial Development.

Through the combination of these instruments, the region gained capacity to finance successfully the most important regional development projects, including:

* The completion of the regional power grid.
* The formation of municipal clean power producing cooperatives.
* The financing of new equipment for the enlarged dairy products and fisheries cooperatives.
* Loans for Cooperative Housing Development

This is all achieved without recourse to the usual transferal of public service responsibilities, through privatization, to commercial investment conglomerates. The region has also avoided economic development loans from economic development international institutions, such as the IMF or the World Bank, because these often, through their required free trade agreements, open the door through which greedy international investors siphon resources out of the poor regions they are supposedly trying to help.

(3) A Fully Active Labor Force

André, by now, you must be ready for a coffee break! I sure am, and I am

going to take one! I will come back
to tell you about the most important
instrument of our regional
development (in my opinion).

I hope you are rested and ready
to strain your attention a bit.
Atlantica's "full-employment policy"
is complicated stuff, and it steps on
a lot of toes! In the end, I trust
you will agree that the economic
justice revolution in Atlantica could
only be achieved through the full
understanding of its unique full-
employment policy.

From the start, the Atlantean
Parliament understood that the well-
being of all Atlanteans could best be
achieved through the contributions of
a fully employed labor force.

In order to achieve this
apparently impossible goal of
full employment, the Parliament
decided to transform its
traditional unemployment fund
into an employment security fund,
designed to guarantee the insertion
in the labor force of all those in
need of work for a minimum
acceptable living wage.

The <u>Gainful Employment Fair Distribution Program (GEFDP)</u> is Atlantica's vehicle designed to achieve full employment. It is aimed at three important objectives at the same time:

* It fulfills every Atlantean's constitutionally guaranteed fundamental right to employment.
* It contributes to the needed increase in the regional production of wealth.
* It becomes one of the most efficient ways to combat the chronic problems of poverty.

Being that full employment has foiled the efforts of most countries, it is not surprising that the early implementation of the GEFDP program in Atlantica faced initial resistance from all sides of the arena of labor negotiations. Indeed, putting the unemployed in the center of the labor negotiations arena as a matter of priority would have been a challenge to the status quo everywhere.

Up to this point, it appears that labor legislation in Portugal—and practically everywhere else in the modern world—deals primarily with the rights and benefits of those already employed, while the fundamental and constitutionally defined right to work of the unemployed is totally ignored. Indeed, the unemployed are not even given a seat around the official labor policy negotiation tables to demand their rightful share of gainful employment!

But luckily, in Atlantica, the initial resistance to a full-employment policy was overcome early on. Eventually, most of those involved in labor negotiations came to agree that the Parliament's full-employment policy was the right thing to do, and that when every Atlantean's constitutionally guaranteed right to work was respected, everyone came out winning.

<u>First, all workers in the now fully employed regional labor force "win" job security.</u> Even though the majority of workers already feel secure in their current jobs, they realize that if things go

wrong—and they often do nowadays—
the GEFDP will fulfill their
fundamental right to employment,
along with a living wage and
rights, enough to keep him or her
out of the poor house. Clandestine
employment is no longer legal or
desirable in Atlantica.

Second, the private employers
in the region also win. This new
regional policy is not blind to
the private employers' need for a
highly motivated and productive
workforce. Therefore, the new labor
legislation provides the employer
with real incentives to adopt profit-
sharing policies with their workers
as a motivating and productivity-
enhancing practice. Additionally,
and importantly, it gives the
employers the flexibility to contract
exactly and only the workforce they
need, be it part-time, full-time,
seasonal, in-training, temporary,
etc. This in exchange for a slightly
higher employment tax than the
one they used to pay in prior times
for unproductive government-paid
unemployment benefits to idle
workers.

With these new economically relevant incentives shared by workers and employers, the private-sector businesses in Atlantica have generally succeeded and also improved their productivity. They show no inclination to leave the region where they belong and play a leadership role in the sound economy they help create and lead. These employers are keenly and proudly aware that the government and Atlanteans respect them for providing security and well-being in the region.

Third, the regional government also wins. A more productive, fully occupied labor force makes more and more dependable tax payments into the regional employment security and social security funds. This adds stability to the region's finances because there is a stable tax revenue base. In exchange for these benefits, the regional government and its municipalities, like the private employers, had to rethink and restructure their personnel needs. At first, they had to reduce the size of their full-time—but often redundant and inefficient—labor forces in order to make room for the more flexible and productive part-time employees with benefits. Part-time or temporary employees are regularly and appropriately trained to respond efficiently to the specific public service needs of the region. They are contracted as needed for part-time, emergency, seasonal, in-training, and other positions. Often, they include those in need of emergency employment through the GEFDP program.

Fourth, the Parliament and its constituents, the Atlanteans, also win. The regional policy of incentives to economic cooperation between workers and employers has reduced traditional labor tensions, it has kept regional productivity high, and it has supported full employment. As a result, the Parliament has seldom had to implement the ultimate emergency measures, such as the temporary reduction of working hours or the temporary increase of "general" taxes, in order to ensure that all Atlanteans have their fundamental

288 ~ Manuel Januário

right to work for a living wage respected, as a constitutionally guaranteed priority.

Conclusion

In conclusion, André, the consistent application of these "cooperative capitalism" strategies has resulted in a significant slow but steady increase in the production of wealth in the region and a much fairer distribution of the wealth produced. The result is a significant improvement in the quality of life for all Atlanteans!

It is a fact that, after thirty years of autonomy, there are still social problems in Atlantean society. However, the regional government is pledged and prepared to resolve them as a matter of social and economic justice before it abandons them into the hands of private social welfare agencies or charitable organizations.

The per capita income of Atlanteans is still low compared to that of some EU countries, but income inequality is much lower in Atlantica than it is in the rest of Portugal and other richer countries. Poverty has also been averted, even in rural areas, where part-time or temporary-employment income many times enables small farmers to stay in business and meet their basic needs.

If there is one lesson to be learned from the Atlantica experience, it is that an unusually large group of social justice-minded politicians have established policies that go beyond the installed interests of "for-profit-only" market economies and have created a profit plus benefit economic system, ultimately benefiting all Atlanteans.

The Atlantica experience has shown that it is possible to put social and economic justice ahead of installed interests, enabling all to pursue together their rightful well-being.

In a nutshell, André, this is a snapshot of the new Atlantica.
Abraço,
Mário

~

Now that I have shared Mário's synthesis of how regional development evolved in Atlantica, we are ready to visit this dreamland in the making to see for ourselves how it is working today. Before we do, let me back up a little to briefly update you about what's been happening in Santa Cruz, where I have been. You will appreciate the contrast with Atlantica.

Let me start with my personal side. In 1980, I finally got married to Teresinha, our first teacher in Nossa Terra, and one year later, our son, Mário André, was born. Mário André, because Mário and Monica are his godparents, and we would like nothing more than for him to carry into the future our genes and our cousins' generous spirit.

After our marriage, Teresinha became even more passionate about our socially minded community-building projects, and she added to them a needed stability and steadfastness. As an educator and motivator, she knows how to draw the best from each person she works with, and she has brought success to many of our new ventures.

Not surprisingly, both of us became workaholics, and we embraced the challenges that constantly put our joint talents to the test.

Our communications with Mário and Monica remained very strong, but our visit to them was systematically postponed.

In the meantime, the state of Santa Cruz moved on, and Brazil became a strong player in the globalized world economy.

Unfortunately, while Atlanteans were learning to live well and within their means, utilizing their limited resources in a sustainable way, Brazil—and the globalized world in general—appeared unconcerned with the growing problems of overconsumption for some and continued extreme poverty for others.

In spite of the urgency to achieve the poverty-eliminating Millennium Goals, universally approved by the United Nations in 2000—and the equally important scientists' warnings about humankind's life-threatening actions to the environment—nothing was altered significantly.

In the past thirty years, if our best scientists had been heard, humankind could have become a human family living in sustainable, close-knit San-Lucas-like and Nossa-Terra-like communities and villages—across Brazil, across India, everywhere—feeling their direct links to our sustaining Mother Earth. Instead, the major part of the human race, with the G7 at the globalization controls, has chosen to become a single economic global village of financially overactive producers and consumers, and they have become mortally dangerous to the earth and to themselves.

And the sad and dangerous reality is that the "global village" lights up and opens its doors for business daily with even more innovative ways to motivate everyone to consume even more. In reality, this global village isn't global or inclusive as it claims to be. It is not equitable, and it is not fair! Each day, it resembles more and more a huge, international for-profit-only supermarket with a crowd of millions—or billions—of hungry or moneyless beggars still standing at the door as the disinherited bastard children of Mother Earth.

Enough of my anxieties and frustrations! Let's go visit Mário and Mónica in Atlantica!

I, for one, crave the sunshine that Mário and Monica were to me as we grew up and worked together. I hope to regain the steady courage to continue my small mission in the confusing globalized world where I live and recover the peace of mind I often shared with Mário—even in the midst of our many frustrations.

Mário André has finally graduated from college, and as we

promised him, his reward is going to be a visit to Atlantica. He is going to meet his godparents for the first time.

You, my dear reader, are invited to come along with us. I am certain that our visit will add a lot to what you already know about the effective action and pervading optimism that permeates Monica's and Mário's timely life stories. Let's go to Atlantica!

~

After our long trip to Lisbon with a stopover there, we are finally approaching Atlantica.

As we come in from the east, there it is. Pico Alto, in all its seven thousand feet of majestic beauty looks like it was born right out of the bowels of the Atlantic Ocean!

Circling it widely, we head toward the airport with an always clearer view of what has to be one of the most beautiful lands on earth. As we get closer, we begin to see the old city of San Luis spreading under the sun. It is just as enchanting as when I was a student there, years ago. It is now recognized as "Patrimony of Humanity," and it sits at the center of a much larger city, extending into where the Vila Miséria slum used to be.

The city of San Luis is not the focus of our interest. The Barbosa's Palace, where as a student I stayed with my aunt, the countess, is now a museum. Mário and Monica have permanently retired to San Lucas. Monica's father, my uncle Carlos, died, and my cousin Roseta lives in the tea country on the south side of the island. We intend to visit her there later.

So, having no one to see in the city, and having told Mário and Monica we would show up any day unannounced, we decide to hire a taxi and go straight to San Lucas.

Mr. Teles, the taxi driver, is a middle-aged man who obviously is a local native. With a broad smile, he calls each local person by name, bestowing on them a special importance. Atlantica is obviously Mr. Teles's world, and he is both showing it to us as well as welcoming us into his own home!

Because of his extroverted personality—and because we show great curiosity—Mr. Teles quickly transforms himself into a well-informed tourist guide churning out his well-organized information about to-day's Atlantica, needing only an occasional question to spur him on.

As we approached the city, soon after we left the airport, he says, "There it is! That's the New Millennium Village Community, though curiously, it was finished in 1998, two years before the new millennium arrived. That's where I live! That whole area was the Vila Miséria slum, where I also lived before.

"This community should be considered, and it probably is, the greatest achievement of the new Atlantica. The Eolic Park on top of that ridge, catching the westerly winds, pushed up the hillside by the sea breezes, produces our green energy, as do the sun-powered photovoltaic panels mounted on the roof of each new house.

"All the electricity generated is fed into the regional power grid. Today, we are 90 percent energy self-sufficient in Atlantica, using exclusively renewable resources in all our new power plants."

"That's fantastic, Mr. Teles! How did it all happen?"

"That's probably a bit more complicated than I can explain, but I will try. Initially, our politicians helped us understand that energy was essential to our future development, and for that reason, we should aim at becoming energy self-sufficient.

"Being that there was a lot of international talk about renewable and clean energy resources in the late seventies—and we were blessed here with practically all of them—the government was smart enough to seize the opportunity to develop agreements to work together with state-of-the-art equipment producers. Atlantica was just the right size for some of their early pioneer projects.

"Next, the government communicated to everyone that the central government would provide a new regional power grid, and each municipality would be given expert assistance to develop a local energy-generating plan adapted to local needs and energy-production potential.

"In the meantime, the regional government went to Lisbon, to Europe, and to the Central Banks to find sufficient capital to start the Regional Bank of Foment to loan investment capital to the qualified local user-investors, willing to become members of energy-generating cooperatives using 'appropriate' technology.

"The government's idea was to keep energy production in the hands of its users by extending to them, in fair and equal terms, the credit that had been preferentially available to profiteering investors only. The effort generally succeeded. Currently each municipality has a semiprivate energy program utilizing water, wind, sun, wave, biomass, hydraulic, or geothermal power.

"People like me are now able to respond to their energy needs as local investors and consumers, making a single monthly payment for both the electricity they consume and the energy cooperative shares they own.

"I am looking forward to the day when, about ten years from now, my cooperative fellow investors and I will own outright that farthest eolis over there and drastically reduce our monthly payments."

I said, "Eolis?"

"Oh! That's a new word we invented here. Having imported a lot of new technology from the first-generation inventors outside, we had to invent something here for ourselves, and the word was the easiest part! So, we called our wind generators *eolis* instead of wind turbines or such. But eolis or turbine, that's what's powering us all the way to San Lucas!"

"How so, Mr. Teles?"

"This is a plug-in hybrid taxi you are riding! It is still equipped with an internal combustion gasohol engine. But, right now, we are being propelled by an electric engine, turned on by a set of lithium batteries. If I keep it plugged in during all my rest periods and/or at night, I practically don't have to use the internal combustion engine in most of my short rides. The development of our alternative energy resources has been so successful that it is now cost-efficient to power the majority of our public transportation vehicles and most private cars with locally produced gasohol or lithium batteries.

"The batteries are loaded by night, while the island is asleep, and the strong sea breezes go on producing power in excess, which sells cheaper after hours. It makes a lot of economic sense these days to transform our garage outlets into power stations! Of course, when it comes to car travel, it also helps that our distances here in Atlantica are much shorter than yours are in Brazil."

Mr. Teles drives off the road for a short rest, at a high viewpoint with Burnt Ridge on one side and the ocean on the other. He wants us to have a look at the Wave Power Central on the distant seashore. Each incoming wave rotates the turbines that feed energy into the regional power grid, which is mounted on the mountainside and over our heads.

Mr. Teles walks us to the other side of the rest area, which overlooks a fantastically beautiful panorama, dominated by two mountain lakes. The larger one sits below our level, surrounded by green pastures and separated by blue and white hydrangea fences. The small one is inside a crater higher on the mountain.

Pointing at the high voltage lines overhead, Mr. Teles says, "If you follow these lines, you will see the pump houses at the upper end of the big lake. Right now, wave power is being used to pump water up the hill into the small lake, which works as our energy reservoir. From there, the water comes back down to the hydraulic turbines in the quantity needed to generate the extra power we will need when we all decide to go to work at the same time tomorrow morning. These lakes are particularly important when the sun is not yet hitting the photovoltaic panels on our roofs and the wind is not blowing."

While still in the parking lot, an eight-passenger van goes by full of men, followed by a slow-moving truck loaded with road-maintenance equipment.

"Too bad we didn't get on the road ahead of them! But, really, I shouldn't complain! Those are really the taxi driver's best friends."

"How so, Mr. Teles?"

"That's a '*fachina*' crew. Fachina is the work the farmers did together in the old days to maintain their rural roads. With the development of farmers' cooperatives, the roads had to be improved—and the farmers needed more cash for improvements in their own operations. That's where the government came into action and resolved the two problems at once by creating the modern fachina crews.

"These combine full-time drivers and road-maintenance equipment with farmers who need supplemental income and are willing to become part-time government employees, doing road maintenance as needed in their own territories, like in the old days. And they always do a great job because it is their own roads they are fixing and their own incomes they are supplementing!"

I say, "Mr. Teles, if the Atlantica government's president knew your true worth, he would make you his public relations secretary!"

"Oh no, Mr. …?"

"Castro. This here is my wife, Teresinha, and my son, Mário André."

"Mário André? Having two names like that is becoming fashionable here also. We must have imported it from Brazil along with the telenovelas!

"Now, about my capacities, Mr. Castro. Well, they really tried to make something out of me, but all they managed was to make me a cabdriver ... yet one who owns his cab ... and a happy one at that!"

In his extroverted style, he unfolded his whole life story to us, as if he were just trying to help us pass the time along a suddenly twisty small road.

"You see, Mr. Castro, when the Carnation Revolution of 1974 made its way across the Atlantic, it found here a dreamland for revolutionaries, where everything was still waiting to happen. The government started trying to educate everybody, which was the right move. They found me—young, unemployed, and homeless—in Vila Miséria. Eventually, they put me to school, taught me how to read and write, and put in me a desire to learn more. When the time came to get their investment out of me, knowing that I liked to be always on the move, they went to the Bank of Foment—where they stored what they called economic-development funds—and gave me a loan, which they called a small business loan. It was just big enough to buy my first cab. It came with all kinds of strings attached, but after I paid it off, they cut the strings and left me alone. I've been able to make a pretty good living ever since."

"Fascinating! I am not used to meeting people who have such positive things to say about their government!"

"It's true that the government helped us a lot, but it took much more than government action to accomplish all we have achieved in Atlantica. The whole area of the Millennium Village was the old Vila

Miséria slum. The heiress of that prime real estate on the edge of the city, instead of putting it up for sale to developers, donated it all to a residents' housing cooperative. She also moved into the community—with her husband in a wheelchair—and provided the necessary leadership to secure the financing and planning for such a huge project.

"History will show that what this courageous woman did for the people and her firm leadership in the community at large was more than enough to repair the historical wrongs of her noble ancestors.

"And that's before we account for what her husband did for people like me. Without his help and training, I—and many others like me—would have never been able to build our houses with our own hands and enjoy the lives we have lived.

"If it weren't for the respect I have for their privacy and their current way of life, there are no two other people in this world I would like better to introduce you to. And they live right in San Lucas, which is where we are going!"

I looked at Teresinha and Mário André in the back seat. Their smiling eyes were moist, like mine, and our emotions smothered any additional questions to Mr. Teles, while he concentrated on the winding road.

We finally arrived in the center of San Lucas square. We swung our light luggage around our backs, asked Mr. Teles to point us in the direction of Mário Garcia's residence, and started walking down the little road.

The man sitting in front of the house looked at us intensely as we walked faster and faster. Then he shaded his eyes with his hand to diffuse the sun's brightness and started yelling, "Monica! Monica! Your cousins are here! Your cousins are here!"

And all five of us huddled together, kneeling around the wheelchair in order to hug each other more lovingly and gather into a smaller circle our emotions, all wrapped up in tears, smiles, and caresses. This lasted for a long while before any words were spoken, and before any of us came out of the huddle to become an individual again, staring at each other through the cloud of haze provoked by the joy in our eyes.

In the following weeks, Monica and Teresinha teamed up like long-lost sisters, and they talked endlessly, as if trying to ask each other all the questions they had never had a chance to ask before and express all their thoughts and feelings in words they had been wanting to share with each other for years.

Mário André and his *padrinho*, Mário, also took to each other immediately. Mário André even began to get up at sunrise to go down to the seashore with Mário to watch the waves. Daily exercise kept Mário's back muscles tuned up and offered the best protection against his recurring backaches.

I often joined them later. I sometimes took a snack to them, and we would stretch the exercise into midmorning and come back the long way, involved in passionate conversation.

I was often stunned by their dialogue, which ranged from the most ordinary to the most challenging. Spurred on by Mário's curiosity, Mário André responded with excitement, and the words came out of them with the same cadence, as if they were two persons running together on the same track. Let me reproduce some of them, which reveal the Mário I knew very well long ago and the Mário André I knew less well than I thought.

"Mário André, tell me about your studies."

"When I entered the university, I was all enthused about economy.

I wanted to study economic development, much as my dad had studied initially, supposedly in order to trigger the economic growth needed to finally help our region overcome its underdevelopment and clean up its pools of poverty. However, mostly due to the voracious amounts of reading I was doing about the environment, climate change, and the limits to growth imposed by the planet itself, I soon came to the conclusion that the continuous economic growth proposed by the globalizers was not the solution to our underdevelopment problems. I finally reached the conclusion that my father used to tell me was also your own, Mário: 'The poor in their frugality have more relevant things to teach our overstressed and overpopulated planet today than do all the rich and their economists combined.'"

"You are not going to blame me for changing the focus of your studies, are you?"

"Not at all, Mário! But if you want to understand why I gave up on economics, you have to be willing to hear a fairly long, and perhaps hard to follow, classical economy-bashing speech."

"Economy-bashing is a sport I like myself! Lecture on!"

"Here it goes! You asked for it."

Mário André concluded his 'long lecture' by saying, "When I fully realized that the globalizers' schemes generally resulted on the control of the major resources of a poor country by a foreign investment conglomerate, often transforming those resources into value-added products with local cheap labor to be introduced later in their international markets for great profits, while leaving behind a more polluted environment and still very high levels of poverty, I was ready to quit economics forever!"

"In favor of what, Mário André?"

"Business management."

"And why business management?"

"PLORDICOCO! That's why! PLORDICOCO! As a manager I will have a better chance to plan, organize, direct, coordinate, and control our small efforts more efficiently and in a professionally sound way. This is what I hope to be able to do to ensure the continuation of what my father and you began in Nossa Terra and my father continued with our reforestation projects beyond Monte Queimado, much before I was born!"

"Bravo, Mário André! With that kind of eagerness, you have convinced me to volunteer to join your team ... if I meet minimum requirements, that is!"

"Don't worry about requirements, wise old man! We will figure out a way to bring you up to speed!"

They talked endlessly like that!

During the course of our conversations, I often caught myself pointing at the dark shadows hanging over the same modern world that my son, Mário André, saw bulging with bright challenges!

One day, we were rolling our way through the traditional verdant vineyards, now being rehabilitated as part of the "World Patrimony Site" project proposal for the area. The vines were strong with fresh green growth that contrasted with the black lava corral walls, built around them for wind protection and warmth.

Mário said, "Isn't this a paradisiacal place—where men and nature are cooperating to find sustainable harmony?"

Mário André said, "Yes, Mário! And in the hands of today's San Lucans, the ancient verdant vineyards, once lost to *filoxera*, can again become a sustainable cluster for local development!"

I said "That, Mário André, proves that there is still hope, even in rocky places like this! Yet, for the older generation of activists, like me, sometimes the current situation in our globalized world looks gloomy and our challenges unsurmountable."

"True, André," Mário said. "However, it is not all lost yet! Today, we benefit more fully from the solidary and incremental technical advances of the human mind, linking together the wisdom of Greek philosophers, Chinese early inventors, Arab scientists, and sages of many other times and cultures.

"Together they built for us along the centuries the foundations of a shared cultural, scientific, and technological patrimony that today is already able to catapult Russians and Americans together as members of one human race into space!

"And from their broader and more enlightened perspective up there, their insightful appeal to us down here is to appreciate and preserve this earthly paradise that is our one shared homeland.

"I, for one, think that our determined thinkers and scientists will continue to improve the human capacity to read more clearly the blueprints of the universe and discover more of the technical skills and the algorithms that our Mother Soul continuously uses to build and sustain her space-time outer body from the inside, including us. This is what sustains my hope today!"

Monica and Teresinha brought lunch and invited us to go down to Ponta Negra with them.

The five of us sat on the lava cliffs before the splendorous dark blue of the bay on a clear day. It was an ideal situation for small talk, a place and time to remember the moments of joyful pleasure intensely felt here in the past. It was also a time to share today's little pleasures.

Turning to Mário André, Monica said, " Godchild, this is the ideal place for you to tell us about your girlfriends, about a potential wife. After all, you are the guy charged with the task of carrying to the next generation the weight of the historically accumulated sagas of the Castros of Santa Cruz and the Barbosas of Atlantica, along with the less 'historical' but equally legitimate feats of your school teacher mother, married to nobility, and your plebeian godfather, Garcia of San Lucas."

"For just a godmother, you are surely becoming a bit pushy, Dona Monica, aren't you!"

"Might I ask why not? After all, we are in a closed circle of the friendliest kind. Godchild, is there any chance that any of us here could cause you any discomfort by talking about your girlfriends?"

"To be honest, you two ladies do! Both of you have raised the 'wife bar' so high that it becomes a nearly impossible task to find a damsel who is able to match your demonstrated capabilities. Take my mother here. She has such dedication and practical love for her child, her husband, and all those within her circles of friendship and influence that I am sure she cannot ever be matched by anyone. As for you, my dear godmother, do you really think it is possible to find a girl anywhere in this world who is capable of matching your beauty, the richness of your spirit, your capacity to give for so long to everyone in need, your sense of socioeconomic justice, and your immense capacity to achieve."

Mário and I were clapping louder than the ocean that joined in the applause.

Mário, perhaps deliberately, left our promised trip to Miradouro for the last day.

While Monica, Teresinha, and Mário André left early morning for one last climb up to St. John's Hill, Mário and I wheeled our way through the narrow road alongside fields of taro and corn and up toward the end of the San Lucas Valley.

There were practically no barriers to Mário on the narrow and winding roads. The wheelchair had been extensively adapted to

Mário's needs, until it reached the current multifunctional sturdy substitute for the legs it replaced. Behind the back, he had installed a rack with special holders for the elbow crutches, which he still managed to use for short distances. Below the rack, another sturdy platform had been welded to add space for an extralarge battery with enough power to propel him through longer trips, sometimes on fairly rough ground.

He also had attached to one side a small flap that could be raised into a platform where he could carry his gardening tools, vegetables, and fruit baskets. The front wheel frames had also been made longer to add stability, and the front wheels were larger and wider in order to move easier over uneven ground.

When our climb got steeper in the direction of Miradouro, the dairy cooperative driver showed up, as agreed, to take us up the rest of the way—wheelchair and all.

I helped the driver lower the heavy wheelchair from the van, and we both helped Mário on to it, but he didn't sit. Instead, he grabbed one elbow crutch from the rack behind the chair, and using me as the other, we walked very slowly toward the seat carved some centuries ago by the mystic Frei Matias[5] on the lava rock outside the cave that still bears his name.

We were alone. We could only hear the occasional distant moo of a cow and the loud singing of a thousand birds, expressing their joy and marking their position in the phenomenal panorama below our lookout point. They obviously did not have the feeling of tightness Mário and I had begun to feel in our throats, resulting from an elastic

---

[5] Frei Matias was a Portuguese mariner who, supposedly, participated in the armed conquest of strategic points along the spice route to India in the 1500s. Eventually he got so sickened with the violence upon the Native peoples that he abandoned ship in San Lucas, isolated himself in the mountains, and started living as a Franciscan monk, eventually settling in the cave behind this viewpoint.

band knit out of the goodbye thoughts that our brains had been weaving and were now wrapping tightly around our necks.

The black lava seats had been warmed by the late-morning sun.

"What a joy it is that you finally visited us, André! I want to thank you, but words aren't enough. In the past few years, I have thought about you a lot, and I have missed you, my brother."

"So have I! So have I!"

Mário grabbed my hand. I had a sensation of unity and closeness even deeper than the feelings of friendship, brotherhood, and solidarity that we always had for each other. It was a sensation that we were sitting together inside a reality that was bigger and stronger than us, and it felt as if we were entering a familiar ground, where we had our roots planted and felt at home.

We entered that comfortable, shared space and stayed there for hours that day—sometimes talking, sometimes listening to the silence, sometimes evoking our shared life experiences—but what I remember best now is the content of Mário's words and insights. Those built around us an aura inside which I felt there was a possibility of finding a deeper understanding of life, an open door to inner peace and joy, the peace and joy that I sometimes felt when Mário and I were trying to build a better world with space for the poor brothers and sisters who touched our lives in Nossa Terra.

I said, "What troubles me most these days is that life takes me on a frequently pleasant merry-go-round ride but then drops me off on the sidelines where I feel rootless and alone in a puzzling world I still don't understand!"

Mário said, "It is in those moments of loneliness and uncertainty, André, that it is important to come to a place like this viewpoint and go deeper inside our minds, like Frei Matias and Padre José did many years ago. Here, after their very active participations in their merry-go-round of life, they felt reattached to the inner intelligent harmony of their surroundings and the universe beyond. Here, they felt the soothing effects of that harmony even in the midst of the excitement and confusion of the moment. It's only when we become conscious that, in spite of our insignificance, we are linked to and dependent upon the total reality of the universe, that we truly know ourselves and feel 'complete,' as a tiny part of all that is! At that moment, we come to know ourselves better, we gain consciousness of how secure the roots of our existence are, and we can begin to find genuine peace and joy. André, the moment we come face-to-face with our complete selves could be here and now!

"Here, today, our shared and miraculously 'superintelligent' scientific minds locate us deep inside our cosmic reality, and we can comprehend that we are obviously engineered to be much more than just shortsighted food gatherers and survival-of-the-fittest predators. We are obviously here to be awed by our world and to contribute to its awesomeness. Otherwise, why should we be able to look from deep inside our modern minds and understand clearly that we are part of a much bigger sun than our day-creating lantern up in the sky? Why should we be able to observe today the awesome details of how we are part of the sun ourselves?

"Yet today we do! The sun's rays hit the ocean, which rises into those clouds and forms the wind that blows them overland ... where they are cooled into the water that falls on this accumulated stardust of the unending ages ... where that apple tree over there knows how to select the exact quantities of diluted minerals and vitamins calculated to produce those apples ... which we will have for our lunch, linking us to the earth ... the earth that is, like us, also warmed and made alive as an homeostatic Gaia whole inside the same sun, thereby becoming also sun, like us!"

"Yet, sometimes, Mário, my brain seems to have been conditioned to function only at the mere survival level in the Darwinian survival-of-the-fittest world. Today, in my country, many of my peer landowners still won't share an inch of their vast territories with their needy fellow citizens. Worse yet, greedy economic globalizers continue to manipulate the earth's resources—and its poor people—for profit while their government, and church leaders legalize and baptize their 'rich-always-get-richer' capitalist schemes? If our older mystic brothers were at this Miradouro today, Mário, what sense would they make of this?"

"André, I think they would look at it from the inside, like we did, with better-informed scientific minds but with the same mystic-to-the-atom's-core realism and awe. They would see the world as a work in progress. In spite all these abuses of economic justice and our 'moral' sluggishness, things *are* getting better! Many more of the children of the world are getting their education these days, and millions of our poor brothers and sisters are escaping death by hunger, malaria, et cetera. And fortunately for us, André, you and I know the better world can happen! We have Nossa Terra and the new Atlantica to prove it! Our own personal experiences should align us with the optimism of our older mystic brothers. They saw themselves as 'complete' men only when linked to others as brothers in the human family living in a shared earth.

"So, André, I agree with Padre José. From God's point of view, what we call 'evil' is probably the good we haven't managed to accomplish yet. And if we look at our remaining problems realistically, we will see that we have already diagnosed them correctly—and it is well within our reach to eliminate them. As intelligent humans, we know how to stop making weapons to kill each other with! We know how to stop digging oil out of the ground! We know how to start reducing the production of plastics 10 percent every year until we make none!

We know how to stop wasting so much of our food and making sure no one dies of hunger again!"

"I want to share your optimism, Mário, but it still seems like only an uncaring and distant God would tolerate the pain and suffering that free people very callously—and sometimes very *democratically*—continue to inflict on each other."

"I know what you mean, André! I also don't understand fully the why and the usefulness of our human pain and suffering. However, I can understand even less how God could possibly be uncaring and distant from any of us. Personally, I know Him, as my inner core. He is the real Owner, the Maker, and the Keeper of this body that He loans me each day. I quite erroneously call it mine when I know so little about it.

"Sometimes, André, I feel like I understand God better as my Mother. Somehow, I experience that I am umbilically connected to Her. I feel the continuity and the contiguity with Her! I don't honestly know where I end and where She begins! To live in time, I absorb Her life each moment through Her earthly placenta, which links me constantly to Her creative cosmic womb. I use the neurons that She invented, patented, and packed inside my amazing skull using quantic and nanotechnologies that we humans are barely beginning to understand.

"To shape a 'tiny life' of my own, I move and act with my fellow human beings within the limits of our shared ideas and dreams, using the energy She lovingly winds up within us to be partly controlled by the intelligent freedom that is built into our minds.

"I know I am not equipped to know and feel Her completely, but I know Her well enough to be certain that She is also the source of the love I am capable of, the love I can use to dwarf human suffering and pain around me, the love that generates the peace and joy I crave for and sometimes feel, and the peace and joy I have always wanted to share with you, my brother." Mário was smiling at me with deep emotions shining in his eyes.

I jumped up impulsively and gave him a big hug. And we sobbed on each other's shoulder for a long while, sharing our profound and seamless brotherhood, still shielded by the aura built by our words and emotions at the edge of Miradouro.

The band of goodbye thoughts around my neck was still strangling me, and abundant tears were still wetting my face, but deep inside, I felt the pleasurable swelling of new seeds of inner peace and joy.

I saw Monica, Teresinha, and Mário André coming down the hill toward us, and I saw them in an entirely new light. They really put a smile on my face!

Mário André, Teresinha, and Monica sat down, and we shared lunch together—enjoying the beauty and the meaning of this special moment.

It was three o'clock, and we knew Mr. Teles was waiting for us by the church.

Each few hundred feet we walked down the hill, we turned around and waved.

Higher above us, still at Miradouro, I could see Mário and Monica. Mário, in his wheelchair, was practically indistinguishable from the land around him. Monica stood taller behind him, but I "saw" them as "complete." They were one with their Mother Soul, inseparable from Her and from each other, forming a single silhouette against the blue sky alongside Pico Alto.

It has been two weeks since we returned to Santa Cruz.

The day after we arrived, Mário André disappeared into the city to conduct a training workshop for bank employees who are now assigned by one of our major banks to implement with us a "banking for benefit" project, applying some of the ideas of the "Banker of the Poor" in Bangladesh and elsewhere.

Mário André, as you recall, believes strongly that, in order to be practical and thrive economically, the poor must find a way to live better and do more with the few "money" crumbs that fall from the tables of the rich, "at least until the rich understand the earth is not their own and decide to share it with the poor, doing away with the injustices of their poverty."

The truth is that he is trying to grind pure selfishness out of current capitalism and help it redesign the more cooperative characteristics it needs today. I sure hope that he—and other young persons working with him—will bring significant change and improvements to the five favelas where they are concentrating their work. I am very proud of my son!

Days after we arrived from Atlantica, some of the seedlings at the Nossa Terra producers' cooperative were destroyed by some stronger than usual winds and excessive rain, apparently caused by climate change. In Mário André's absence, I rushed there anticipating that I might be needed to help resolve the problem, only to find that the problem was already resolved by the cooperative's manager.

"The wind-maker must have decided we needed to practice our rebuilding skills one more time! This time, we did it faster. In two days, we were back in business," he said confidently.

I appreciated in a new way his capacity to make the world a better place.

At home, Teresinha waited for me with the same smile she always has, and I noticed it this time! I have always loved her, but I didn't always see and appreciate her smile sufficiently before.

In my inbox, I had a fresh email from Mário and Monica. Before I say goodbye, I will share an excerpt of their email with you:

> Climate change is real. The UN secretary general has just given voice again to the pressing warnings of the scientists. As we noticed in the news recently, our planet is running into stronger winds than usual! It seems the hotter and smokier air we are putting inside our atmospheric air balloon is gaining speed and swirling into ever more destructive typhoons in Asia and causing killing floods and fires in America. Our decks get flooded under the constant rains, but our earth ship is still standing its course. Thankfully, most of us are still safely aboard, and able to continue our chores a little longer. The brothers and sisters we lost to the floods leave us with heavy hearts. Perhaps they would still be with us had we humans been smart enough to reduce the heat and smoke of our overconsumption. But it is not too late to take action! We are still learning.

> My dear earth ship fellow traveler,
> I hope this time we have spent together has strengthened the conviction and optimism that Mário shared with us in the beginning of our conversation. We were in jail, but we were still dreaming of a better world. He

uttered the following words: **"We are driven by our dreams! And there is no other reason for us to be capable of having such dreams if it weren't to make them real—as we humans surely can!"**

Até sempre, my earth ship fellow traveler! Traveling with you has been a privilege!

Be well!

André

About the Author

Manuel Januário is an American born in the Azores. He holds a master's degree in Adult and Continuing Education from Washington State University.

His professional experience is rich and diverse.

As the Executive Director of the Community Action Council of Spokane County, WA, he faced and experienced the many challenges of the poor, responsible as he was for the development and administration of many anti-poverty projects financed under the Economic Opportunity Act of 1964.

Years later, as the Executive Director of a Consortium of five Native American Governments, Manuel dedicated his professional endeavors to the creation of employment as well as, career development opportunities designed to empower and lift unemployed Native Americans out of chronic cycles of poverty.

He capped his more than twenty years of work in underserved communities by conducting training to 'service providers' in the Pacific Northwest and Alaska.

Manuel now lives in a small farm with his wife Paula Pincho.

About the Book

Andre is a rich landowner, while Mário is an immigrant college student. Although from different backgrounds, they both come to America to learn how to overcome economic underdevelopment in their own countries. Sadly, they discover that the American economic system perpetuates conditions of poverty for many while others become unreasonably rich, leaving behind a trail of environmental degradation.

It is Mário and Andre's solid friendship that shows them the way forward. Through many twists and turns in several countries, their shared experiences teach them that underdevelopment can be overcome through a new economics of frugality (as opposed to the current economics of over consumption), that respects the economic rights of all our fellow earth citizens and the planet's own sustainability.

Unfortunately, putting into practice their cooperative capitalism principles challenges installed interests and brings mortal danger into their sincerely committed lives.

CPSIA information can be obtained
at www.ICGtesting.com
Printed in the USA
FSHW012044030821
83803FS